BLACK OUT

HOT Heroes for Hire: Mercenaries: A Black's Bandits
Novel

LYNN RAYE HARRIS

The Hostile Operations Team® and Lynn Raye Harris® are
trademarks of H.O.T. Publishing, LLC.

Printed in the United States of America

First Printing, 2020

For rights inquires, visit www.LynnRayeHarris.com

Black Out
Copyright © 2020 by Lynn Raye Harris
Cover Design Copyright © 2020 Croco Designs

ISBN: 978-1-941002-52-0

Prologue

THEY WERE ONTO HIM. NOBODY HAD SAID SO, BUT HE knew it nonetheless. They were coming for him.

He rushed through his house, throwing clothes into a case, grabbing his laptop and passport.

Panicking.

"Think," he told himself through gritted teeth.

He flung himself down in his desk chair and logged onto his computer. He'd kept records. He'd been careful, but it didn't matter now. He opened up the accounting firm's secure login portal. Once he was in, he deposited the spreadsheet he'd been keeping. It was separate from the official records and *they* didn't know he had it.

Or hadn't known. Maybe they did now.

It had everything in it.

But if he got caught while trying to escape, he

wouldn't be caught with it. He could deny he knew anything.

Who was he kidding? *They* wouldn't believe him—but he could try.

If the worst happened, it was still there. Someone at Barton, Barnes and Blake would figure it out.

He hoped. God, he hoped.

He'd point them to it when it was safe to make contact. Until then, he planned to disappear. He had enough money.

Hopefully he had enough of a head start.

He heard the slamming of car doors. The neighbor's dog started to bark.

Time to disappear.

Chapter One

THE NUMBERS WEREN'T RIGHT. ANGELICA TURNER—
Angie to her friends—stared at the spreadsheet on the
screen in front of her. It wasn't syncing with the client
account's statements, and it annoyed her.

It shouldn't be her job to figure this one out. But
one day last week, Charles Martinelli didn't show up
to work. He quit, or so the official story said. She
wasn't entirely certain he hadn't been fired, especially
if all his accounts were this screwed up. Not that she'd
heard anything that suggested he'd been fired, and she
wasn't about to ask.

Whatever the case, the shit job of cleaning up this
particular mess fell to her. She almost didn't see the
spreadsheet in his files, because he'd labeled it oddly,
but once she'd opened it, it bore the Cardinal Group
name. They were a small venture capital firm,
investing in local businesses for a pool of anonymous

investors. It was a nice idea and good for the local economy. But if she couldn't figure out Charles's work, she was going to have to start over. Re-enter all the company's statements, redo all their deposits and expenses. She didn't relish that idea at all, especially since she had other accounts to take care of.

The life of an accountant began to get a little insane at the start of a new year. Corporate tax returns due March fifteenth and personal ones due April fifteenth. It was a lot of work. She'd been with Barton, Barnes, and Blake for almost two years now, and while she couldn't say she hated it, she didn't love it. With the exception of this particular account, the job wasn't as challenging as she might like.

She loved some of her coworkers though. Liam Wood was a great guy. They'd been hired on the same day, so she felt a certain affinity with him. He'd been the one who'd clued her in months ago when her best friend started seeing Jace Kaiser. Liam had seen them in a restaurant and told Angie all about it. Maddy had to confess after that.

Thoughts of Maddy and Jace inevitably led to the man she didn't want to think about. Colton Duchaine. Colt was one of Jace's coworkers, and he made her stupid heart want to give him a chance in spite of the fact she knew it wouldn't work out.

Colt lived a dangerous life. He and Jace were spies. At least that's what she thought they were. There was certainly no doubt they were involved in a high-risk profession. She'd gotten a firsthand look at that when Jace's sister had kidnapped her at gunpoint.

Angie shivered. She still had nightmares some-times, though mostly she was fine. Jace had saved her and Maddy both. When Angie'd found out that Colt had been shot, she'd been devastated. She knew it was her fault because she'd led Natasha straight to him.

No matter that he told her it wasn't, she couldn't help but think if she'd been a stronger person when Natasha abducted her, she might have thought of a way to escape instead of leading the assassin to Maddy and Colt.

That wasn't the only reason she couldn't get involved with Colt. She'd had more than enough experience with dynamic, handsome men, thank you very much.

Men who looked like Colt had far too many temp-tations in life. She'd been there, done that with her ex. She wasn't doing it again.

No matter how sexy the temptation.

Angie clicked one of the columns and sighed in frustration. She dashed off an email to the client, asking for any additional statements they might have before she started going through the columns and making note of everything that was off. If they didn't send anything additional that resolved it like magic, she'd have to make a list of individual transactions and ask for information on each one.

Her cell phone rang and she jumped. It was so

quiet in the office that the noise scared her. It was Maddy. Angie picked the phone up and leaned back in her chair. That's when she noticed it was dark outside. She hadn't realized she'd been working that long.

"Hey, babes," she said.

"Hi, Ang! You busy?"

Angie glared at the computer screen. "A little, but I'm about to call it a day anyway. What's up?"

"I fixed too much pot roast for dinner. I was hoping you'd join us."

Angie couldn't help but grin. Maddy knew she wasn't a cook. At all. And whether or not Mads had actually fixed too much pot roast or she was just thinking of her bestie, Angie wasn't going to turn down a home-cooked meal.

"That would be great. I didn't realize how late it was. I was just going to shut down and pick up something on the way home, but your cooking is even better."

"Awesome! I'll set a place for you."

"You sure Jace doesn't mind?"

"Why would he mind?"

"He's been out of town recently. And so have you. How'd the appraisal go?"

Maddy was an art appraiser for an insurance company and she often traveled to exotic locations in order to evaluate rich people's collections.

"Oh, it was great. I had to appraise some

Russian art in Japan—and Jace joined me when he finished with his assignment, so we haven't been apart as much as you'd think. Besides, I've missed you and I want to see you. Jace is perfectly happy with the idea, so please get here as soon as you can."

Angie laughed. "Okay, fine, I'll be there in twenty minutes. I have to shut down my computer and grab my coat."

"See you then, girlie! I can't wait to catch up!"

They hung up and Angie logged off her computer and put everything away. She was smiling to herself, happier than she'd been in days. Maddy did that. It was great having a best friend you could say anything to. And who could say anything to you.

Angie had worried just a little, if she was honest, about how much Maddy might need her now that Jace was in her life. But Maddy was the same person —only happier and with more excitement about the future.

Angie wished she had that same excitement. She didn't, and she didn't know how to get it. She'd thought the change from math teacher to accountant would do it, but it hadn't. Not yet anyway.

It didn't help that when she'd made the change, she'd also discovered her fiancé was a cheating douchebag. The life she'd thought she was working for imploded at that point.

Angie grabbed her coat and handbag and headed

for the exit. Liam's office door was open and his light was on. Angie peeked in.

"Hey," she said.

Liam looked up, his face fixed in a frown that melted when he saw her. "Hey. You leaving?"

"I am. I thought I was the only one working late. I didn't hear you at all."

Liam snorted. "I wish, but I'm here. Have to finish up the Garvin account tonight."

Guilt pricked her. She should probably be working on reconciling those statements, but she just couldn't face it tonight. Besides, corporate tax returns weren't due for another month and a half. There was time to get all her work done, even if she had to pop in and out of the Cardinal Group accounts for another week or two.

Damn that Charles Martinelli anyway.

"Did you get any of Martinelli's accounts?" she asked.

"A couple. You?"

"Oh yes. You find anything out of the ordinary with any of them?"

Liam's brows drew together. "Not yet. Will I?"

Angie shrugged. "Maybe. It's too early to tell, but I feel like he left a bit of a mess. Have you heard from him?"

"Nope. Talk about tanking your career, right?"

Sometimes Angie wished she could walk away like that. Just say *see ya, suckers* and not come back. But she'd already left one profession and this was the one that was supposed to fulfill her. So far, she wasn't feeling all that fulfilled.

"He was either very brave or very stupid. I'm not sure which."

"Yeah, I hear you. Some days I'd love to leave it all behind and retire to a beach somewhere."

"Sounds like a dream. Okay, I'm out of here."

Liam tapped some keys. "Have a good night. See you tomorrow."

"Yep, see you. Don't work too late."

"I won't. The girlfriend is bringing dinner over later, so I'll get home in time for that."

Angie said goodbye, then went and got into her car. She sat there for a long minute while the heated seat warmed her up. A man strode down the sidewalk in front of the office building and over to the door. He peered though the glass, and then rapped on it. Angie debated lowering her window and telling him the office was closed, but he continued down the street.

She put the car in reverse and dismissed it from her mind. Soon she'd be at Maddy and Jace's, eating dinner and having a glass of wine with two of the people she loved most.

She'd worry about how to fix the mess Charles had made tomorrow.

———

COLT KNEW the instant he pulled up on the street in front of Jace and Maddy's place why they'd invited him. He gripped the wheel with both hands and sighed. Maybe he should keep on driving, but then he'd have to explain why he hadn't shown up after all.

And Maddy would be hurt. He didn't think Angie would care, but Maddy would—and that was enough to make him put the Yukon in park and get out. He stood on the street and studied the Cape Cod-style house that Maddy had inherited from her grand-mother. Jace was helping her fix it up, and they'd started an addition on the rear of the house that would be a new master suite. Colt could see the vapor barrier covering the OSB from this angle. It was bigger than he'd realized from the plans Jace had shown him.

Jace and Maddy deserved it. Jace was one of his best friends, plus they worked together. And Maddy was so sweet she gave him a toothache—but in the best way possible. Not a pairing he'd have seen from a mile away, but it definitely worked. Humanized Jace, which was something he'd needed.

Maybe Colt would find that someday too.

Angie's older model BMW sat in the driveway. The metal still creaked from the engine compartment as it cooled, which meant she hadn't been there long. Colt drew in a breath and gripped the bottle of wine he'd brought before walking up to the front door and ringing the bell.

The door swung open and Jace stood there. "Hey, man, glad you could make it."

Colt arched an eyebrow. "You might have mentioned there was an ulterior motive," he said, low enough that Maddy and Angie wouldn't overhear.

Jace gave a small shake of his head. "Strict orders from my lady. No can do."

"Fine. Here's a bottle of wine, traitor."

Jace laughed and held the door open wider. "Come on in. You can handle it."

He could. He wasn't sure Angie could. He hadn't seen her since New Year's Eve in this very house when she'd kissed him at midnight. It hadn't been a particularly sexy kiss, but it had certainly rocked his brain and left him aching. Just a simple press of her luscious lips against his, and he'd dreamed of her for days.

He walked inside and shrugged out of his coat. Jace took it and hung it on the hall tree. They actually had a small entry hall now. It was one of the renovations they'd done to make the house more modern and livable for their lives together.

Colt followed Jace into the open living area. The kitchen had been expanded and opened up. There was a big island where a wall had once been and you could see all the way into the kitchen now. Maddy was busy taking something out of the oven. Angie perched on a chair by the island, twirling a glass of wine between her fingers, and talking to Maddy.

She looked up when he walked in with Jace. Colt

could see her entire body stiffen, and a wave of disappointment washed over him. Whatever the reason, she still wasn't comfortable around him. Wasn't ready to let anything happen between them.

"Hello, ladies," he said as Maddy came around the island all smiles, arms open.

"Hi," Angie said as Maddy enveloped him in a hug.

"Colt, I'm so glad you could make it! I know it was short notice but I didn't want all these leftovers and I thought, well, who else could help us eat this roast? So I came up with the two of you."

"I'm glad you called me. You know I love a home-cooked meal."

Maddy was all smiles as she went back to the stove to stir something. "Have a seat. It'll be ready in a few."

Angie's beautiful green eyes met his for a second and then she dropped them to her glass. Colt's gut twisted—and then he decided what the hell. She clearly didn't care for him, so he wasn't about to twist himself up in knots trying to be nice.

"Want some wine?" Jace asked.

"Sure."

"The one you brought, or the one Maddy opened?"

"Is it red?"

"It's a Napa Valley cab."

"Sounds good."

Jace poured a glass and handed it to him. Colt took a seat at the bar and looked around the room. "I still can't get over how much bigger this space is since you knocked out the wall and redid the kitchen."

"Right?" Maddy said brightly. "And the floors! Who knew we'd fine that gorgeous heart pine beneath the carpet?"

"Uh, just about any renovation show on HGTV. Which I know you love watching," Colt teased.

He hadn't even known who Chip and Joanna were until he'd met Maddy. Now he knew all about shiplap and farmhouses, though Maddy wasn't trying to turn this place into a farmhouse. She'd found another show apparently, one that was more about renovating older homes. Some couple in Mississippi named Ben and Erin. It pained him that he knew these things, but he did.

Maddy laughed. "Okay, you got me. I hoped we'd have hardwoods. I'm so glad we did—but I'd have gone shopping for antique flooring if they weren't there."

Jace rolled his eyes, but it was lovingly done. "Yeah, she would have. And she'd have dragged me with her. To every single architectural salvage store on the eastern seaboard."

"Come on, it would have been fun."

Jace dropped a kiss on her forehead. "Spending time with you is always fun. Even if it's in antique stores."

Maddy elbowed him and he laughed. Colt felt a pang of something sharp in his chest. Right in the middle, behind his ribcage. "Smells delicious in here, by the way," he said. "Thanks again for inviting me."

"Thank you. And you are always welcome. You know that."

"I do." And it meant more than she knew. Colt didn't talk much about his life or where he was really from, but he remembered family dinners around his *grand-mère's* table when he was a child. He'd felt such a sense of belonging back then. It'd all changed too soon, but that was life.

Maddy took a tray of rolls from the oven and began putting them in a basket she'd lined with a colorful cloth. "I think we're ready, if you want to go to the table. Jace, can you carry the roast over and put it on that trivet? Thank you, honey."

The round table with four chairs sat beneath a carefully aged chandelier. Angie looked up at him as they reached the table. This time her gaze didn't dart away. She seemed... shy?

He blinked. Was that her problem?

Before he could ponder it further, she started to tug her chair out. He stepped over and did it for her, pushed it in again when she was seated.

"Thank you," she said softly.

"You're welcome."

It was all he could do not to touch her. Not to skim his fingers down the column of her neck and

14

over her shoulder. He could see more of her cleavage than was safe from this vantage. She was wearing a white silky button-down shirt, and though it was modestly buttoned, standing behind her revealed just enough of the curve of her breasts to make his mouth water.

Colt moved away and took his seat.

Jace helped Maddy into her chair, and then the four of them were passing food and eating together like it was something they did every day. Maddy carried the conversation at first, but Angie warmed up after some wine. Her cheeks flushed and her eyes sparkled whenever she turned them on him.

She was so damned pretty to him, with her gorgeous deep red hair and her pale complexion. Yeah, her skin showed every blush, every emotion. He wondered how lovely she'd be lying beneath him as he slowly thrust into her slick heat, building them both to an explosive orgasm. How many tales would her skin tell him then?

Colt felt the tightening in his balls and knew he had to leave that line of thought or be stuck at the table for the rest of the evening. Somehow, he managed it. By the time the evening was over, he'd successfully kept all thoughts of a naked Angie at bay.

When she announced she needed to get home, he planned to wait for her to leave first. Then he'd slide out the door and head back to his rented house that wasn't too far from Jace and Maddy. He'd only settled in Maryland within the past few months. Before that he'd resided in hotels and the apartment he kept in Paris. Working for Ian Black meant you could live wherever you wanted, so long as you were able to travel at a moment's notice.

"I should go as well," Colt said as Angie said her goodbyes. "I'll walk you out."

Not what he'd intended to do, but it popped out of his mouth before he could stop himself.

She blinked, then nodded. "Thank you."

He helped her into her coat, then put on his own. After kisses and hugs at the door from Maddy, they stepped outside into the cold night air. His breath frosted in front of his face. Angie was quiet as they went over to her car. She touched the handle and it unlocked. Then she turned to him and raised her gaze to his again.

Those green eyes jolted him. They always jolted him.

"It was nice seeing you, Colt."

"Was it?" He'd meant to say *you too* but that wasn't what came out.

Her lashes dropped, then lifted again. Her gaze stayed with his. "Yes, it was. I know you must think I'm flaky as hell. I'm really not. I'm just… scared."

Of all the things she could have said to melt the distance he was trying to maintain. "You don't have to be scared of me, Angie. I won't hurt you. I'm not Tom Walls."

Her eyes clouded at the mention of the man who'd assaulted her. The man Colt and his buddies had threatened if he ever went near her again.

"I know you aren't."

"Then why do you always look like you're ready to bolt the instant I show up?"

"I'm not scared you'll hurt me like that. I'm scared I'll get hurt if I let myself like you too much. And then what? You're a part of Maddy and Jace's life, just like I am. I wouldn't want it to be awkward."

Colt snorted. "You mean it's not awkward now?"

She blinked. Then she laughed. He didn't expect that, so it was a surprise. It was also a lovely sound. He could get used to that laugh in his life. "Um, right. It is awkward, isn't it?"

"Bingo." He reached past her and pulled her car door open. "Get home, Angie. Stop worrying about life and just live it, okay? And when I text you tomorrow, answer. Texting never hurt a soul. We can at least be friendly. It'll be less awkward at times like this."

She smiled at him. Her hair smelled like flowers and fresh rain. He wanted to drop his nose into the silky mass and inhale, but he didn't. "I'll answer. Promise."

She sank into her seat and started the car. He pushed the door closed, then waited for her to back up and onto the road before he went over and got inside his own vehicle.

Maybe there was hope after all.

Chapter Two

Angie was going over the Cardinal Group account when her phone dinged the next afternoon. Martinelli's figures still didn't make a whole lot of sense to her and the client hadn't answered her email yet. She'd finally sent a preliminary list, asking for clarification on some of the transactions. She couldn't move forward until she got them. She glanced at where the phone lay on her desk. Her heart skipped a beat as fresh heat flooded her.

"Geez, Ang, it's just a text," she muttered.

Colt: *Hey. How are you today?*

How she'd survived sitting next to him at dinner last night when her body was on fire with longing and embarrassment she'd never know. She'd texted Maddy when she got home and told her it was a sneaky trick to pull, inviting her over for dinner but not telling her Colt would be there.

Maddy had texted back a sorry and a whole bunch of other stuff too. Angie was still thinking about the things Mads had said to her about seizing the day and living life to the max and taking chances, etc. So here was a chance. Pick up the phone and answer Colt. She'd promised she would.

Answering him didn't mean they were dating or anything. It was a text, nothing more. It was also a break from the monotony of a spreadsheet that wouldn't give up its secrets.

She stared at the phone's screen. She had to admit she liked him. Thought he was sexy as hell. Wanted to jump his bones and see if he looked as good out of clothes as he did in. She was pretty sure he did.

But he scared her, not because she thought he was the kind of man who wouldn't take no for an answer, but because he was the first man she'd felt a hint of interest in since she'd kicked her ex out of her life.

Maybe it was the fact they were always being thrown together because of their connection to Jace and Maddy, or maybe it was sitting beside him in the hospital when he'd been recovering from a gunshot wound, or the way his gaze smoldered whenever it met hers—but her fascination with him hadn't abated so much as grown bigger.

That was worrisome. The next time she fell for a guy, he needed to be a nice, stable guy who was more nerdy than athletic. More dad bod than *American Ninja Warrior* bod.

And someone who wasn't the prettiest person in the room. Those guys got too much attention—whether they wanted it or not.

She took a deep breath and typed. *Hi. I'm fine. Working. How about you?*

Colt: *Off right now. Just doing some housework.*

Angie blinked. Housework? Then again, why not? She'd just never pictured him pushing a vacuum or cleaning toilets. *Can I pay you to clean mine? Haha!*

Not that she had the money to pay anyone to clean for her, but he didn't know that. Plus it was a joke.

Colt: *Maybe. How much are you offering?*

Angie chuckled. *I somehow don't think you mean that.*

Colt: *Oh, I don't know. If it gets me an invitation to your house, I might just clean it for free.*

Her skin glowed even while she told herself not to fall for the charm. *I'm going to have to think seriously about your offer.*

Way to go, flirting with him. Angie rolled her eyes.

Colt: *I cook too, you know.*

Angie: *Wow, really? Because I don't. I can burn water.*

Colt: *Invite me over and I'll cook. I'll buy all the groceries and everything. You can invite Jace and Maddy too, if it makes you more comfortable.*

Angie nibbled her lip. Oh boy. *I'll think about it. It's a very tempting offer.*

And it was, because he *was* gorgeous and it'd been a long time since she'd gone out with anyone. Plus there were all those fireworks that constantly exploded inside her whenever he was around.

Colt: *Let me know what you decide. Okay, gotta get back to work. The oven won't clean itself.*

Angie: *Um, I think they do? Self-cleaning ovens, right? I know I'm not making that up.*

Colt: *Yeah, but I'd rather clean it myself. The self-clean feature takes 3 hours and it makes the house hot.*

She was impressed he knew that. She certainly didn't. *Well, have fun.*

Colt: *Thanks for answering me today.*

Angie: *I promised I would.*

Angie stared at her phone for a few moments, then turned her attention back to Martinelli's spreadsheet. But she couldn't stop thinking about Colt, and about how when she wasn't overthinking it, talking to him made her feel kinda good. Maddy kept telling her she had to get back on the horse sometime.

Why not now?

She snatched her phone up. Before she could change her mind, she sent a text: *How about dinner in a restaurant to start with?*

"Oh hell, what have you done?" she moaned after she pressed send. No way to call it back now.

Angie turned her attention back to her work. The longer her text went with no answer, the more disappointed she became. Even when she told herself it was for the best. Clearly, Colt knew it too.

Five minutes later, her phone pinged with a text.

Colt: *Sorry, just saw this. I was vacuuming. Sounds good. Tonight work for you?*

And there it was, that shot of nerves cascading through her. She had so many reasons not to do this. But she *wanted* to see him. See if the excitement he roused in her was real or a fluke.

Angie: *Yes.*

———

THEY'D AGREED to meet at a restaurant in Annapolis that wasn't on the popular waterfront, but on a quieter side street where the tourists didn't necessarily flock in huge numbers.

Colt arrived before Angie. He'd been shocked when she'd texted him back and mentioned dinner. He'd thought he'd pushed a little too far when he'd teased her about cooking at her house. He'd expected her to ghost him the next time he texted, but he'd been in for a shock when he'd switched off the vacuum and had a message from her.

Not at all what he'd expected.

That she'd agreed to tonight was even more surprising. But she wasn't here yet so he didn't need to get ahead of himself. She could still ghost him. He told himself that if she didn't show up, he was done trying to win her trust and attention. They'd see each other at Jace and Maddy's, and she'd have to learn to deal with his presence. End of story.

But she didn't ghost him. She walked into the restaurant five minutes past when she'd said she would, and she apologized for being late.

"A client called as I was parking. I had to take it."

"It's not a problem," he told her, letting his gaze slide over her for a brief moment before meeting her eyes again. She was dressed in a dark wine-colored wrap dress that showed all her curves, and she wore high-heeled suede boots that disappeared beneath the hemline. Which meant they probably went to her thigh.

Colt's mouth watered for a second. *Jesus.*

"You thought I wasn't coming," she said.

He gave a brief shake of his head. "Not yet I didn't. You still had twenty-five minutes before I thought that."

"Surprise," she said with a smile.

He put his hand against her back and ushered her toward the hostess stand. When he gave his name, the girl took them to the table he'd reserved and handed them menus and a wine list.

Angie's color was high, but she studied her menu and pretended all was normal.

"Do you want wine?" he asked.

She hesitated before responding. "That would be lovely."

"What are you planning to eat?"

"Um, steak, I think. It's been a long day and I haven't eaten since breakfast."

Colt nodded. "Do you have a wine in mind or do you want me to choose?"

"Red. I don't care what. Nothing too expensive though. The nuances would be wasted on me."

His eyebrows lifted. "*Chérie*, you have to care."

It was her turn to raise her brows. "That sounded French. Do you speak French?"

"*Mais oui*," he told her.

It wasn't a secret that he spoke French at Black Defense International. It wasn't a secret at all, but he didn't often tell people outside the company about his language skills. Or that French was his first language, not his second. Hell, he didn't think anyone but Ian Black knew that detail.

Ian knew all the details about everyone, whether you told him or not.

"How didn't I know that?"

He shrugged. "It probably never came up before. And you have to care about the wine because the wrong red won't taste right with your steak."

"All right. You pick then. I assume because you care, you *do* know."

"I do."

He'd been raised to know and appreciate wine. He'd been tasting it since he was a child, drinking small glasses with dinner when he was old enough. It was a part of life where he came from. Part of his heritage, though he'd never be a part of the family business now.

The waiter arrived to give them bread and tell them the specials. They already knew what they wanted so he took their order and disappeared. Angie took a slice of bread from the basket and tore off a corner.

"I haven't been here in a long time," she said. "Thank you for suggesting it."

"Where do you usually go?"

"These days I grab something fast on the way home, if I don't have a microwaved dinner. Sometimes I go down to the waterfront with coworkers, but that hasn't happened in a while. There've been some shake ups at work and people are on edge."

"What kind of shake ups?"

"It's just been a general change of direction. Management has a new focus, and there were some changes at the top that have been trickling down. Barton, Barnes and Blake used to be a small company, but they've grown and opened offices in other cities, so that's required new ways of looking at things. It's made it less, I don't know, homey. We're still in our original office building, which is a turn of the century brownstone they've had for thirty years at least, though I think it was in one of the partner's family's before that. I expect we'll move to a bigger, more modern space one of these days."

"Do you ever think of going somewhere else?"

"Somewhere else as in a new city or a new job?"

LYNN RAYE HARRIS

He hated to think of her going to a new city. "Either, I guess."

She sighed and ripped off another small piece of bread. "I'm not sure. The salary is good and I have bills to pay, like most people. Mortgage, car, student loans. Plus I help my parents out these days. They're in Florida, and their retirement doesn't go as far as they'd like." She paused as she chewed. "I've already switched careers once—I'm afraid to keep jumping around, you know? I'm almost thirty. It's time to be settled and working hard for the future if I ever hope to pay everything off and save for retirement."

He frowned. She talked like she planned to be single forever. Not that he was asking her about it.

"You can change jobs, Angie. Hell, you can change careers again if you want to. There's no rule that says you have to be settled at any age. Might be more comfortable to have a retirement plan when you're fifty, but it doesn't matter how you get there."

"I don't know what I want to do. How's that for an answer?" She gave a little laugh. "I used to be a math teacher—maybe Maddy told you that—but I didn't enjoy the headache of teaching. Not the kids. They were great. The focus on test scores, and one learning style for everyone, and all the administrative bull that kept coming down got to me after a while. I didn't feel like I could make a difference, so I got the accounting degree—more student loans—and went to work as an accountant. I enjoy the numbers. I love spreadsheets and complex calculations. But I hate dealing with some of the clients. I mean some are great, but others..." She shrugged.

He knew she meant Tom Walls. He hoped she didn't have more clients like that one. "Do you still handle the Walls account?"

"No. He asked for a man and got one. I told my boss what happened, and he believed me. They still kept his business. And I don't mind that really because I'd rather we took his money than let him take it somewhere else. But I'm glad I don't have to deal with him anymore."

Colt was glad too. If he had to confront that asshole again, he might not be so nice a second time.

Hell, he hadn't wanted to be nice the first time, but removing appendages was frowned upon by the authorities. And Ian wouldn't have been too pleased either.

The waiter returned with the wine then. He removed the cork and gave it to Colt. There was a whiff of mold about it, but Colt let him pour a taste anyway. He swirled and sipped.

"This wine is corked," he said.

The waiter looked surprised. "I'm sorry, sir. I'll get another bottle."

He disappeared with the bottle and glass.

"What's corked mean?" Angie looked puzzled.

"Basically, it's when the wine tastes like damp cardboard. It comes from natural fungi in the cork that interacts with products used in the sanitation process. It's not too common anymore, but anytime you have natural cork, there's a danger of it happening."

"Wow, you really know your wine."

"You've probably had wine that didn't taste quite right before. Or smell right. That's corked, though there are other issues that can cause problems. Basically, if it tastes funny, send it back."

She seemed impressed. "Where did you learn all this?"

He shrugged. "I like wine. Good wine."

The waiter returned with another bottle and the sommelier, who apologized profusely for the previous bottle. The new one was fine, so the waiter poured two glasses and disappeared again.

Angie sipped from her glass and smiled. "Well, I don't know much about wine, but I know I like this one."

"It'll be perfect with steak."

"You surprise me, Colt. I had no idea wine was your thing."

"It's one of my things. I like good food and wine."

"And you cook and clean house."

"I'd make a great house husband."

Angie laughed. "I guess you would. Except you'd be gone a lot with your job, so maybe not quite so great after all."

"Maybe I just need a woman who'll keep me in style so I can quit my job and take care of the house."

She blinked. "You're joking."

He grinned. "Yep, totally."

He could picture himself settling down with someone the way Jace had settled down with Maddy, and the way Brett was currently settling in with Tallie. But, like them, he wasn't leaving BDI and giving up his profession. It was too important. Doing his job meant that the world stayed safe so ordinary people could get married and have babies and live their lives without any idea about all the rotten shit going on behind the thin layer of civility they enjoyed.

Angie's cheeks were beginning to flush pink with the wine, and her eyes sparkled. He pictured a future in which he settled down with her, in which he kissed her goodbye in the morning and went off to battle the world's monsters.

But he knew it wouldn't work. He couldn't ask her to be a part of his world. It was too dangerous, too unpredictable. She was too fragile. He'd have thought the same thing about Maddy and Tallie, to be honest, but it turned out they had hidden strengths that Angie didn't have.

How do you know she doesn't have them?

He pushed that voice away. He knew. She'd had trouble bringing herself to the level of merely talking to him. How would she ever grow accustomed to his life when it was filled with the possibility of violence and danger?

She'd had a taste of it once, when Natasha Orlova, aka Calypso, abducted her and then used her to get to Maddy—shooting him in the process—and he didn't think she wanted more. He didn't think she particularly liked that Maddy was going to marry Jace, but she'd never actually said anything to the contrary.

"How did you and Maddy meet?" he asked, deciding to steer the conversation in a new direction.

"High school," Angie said. "We met in home-room, and that was that. We've been best friends since we were fifteen."

"You grew up in Annapolis then?"

"Yes. It's home, though my parents moved to Florida about eight years ago. They were older when they had me, so they've retired and headed for warmer weather." She took another sip of wine. "What about you?"

He'd known the question was coming but he didn't have a good answer for it. He opted for the truth. It wasn't a secret. It just wasn't something he talked much about. Too many minefields to navigate. "I grew up in France. My dad died in an accident when I was fourteen, and we moved to California."

Her eyes widened. "Oh no. I'm so sorry about your dad."

He felt like she meant those words. He still had

trouble talking about it. Everything changed when his dad was killed. The trajectory of his life, his mother's life. "Thank you. It was a long time ago now, but yeah, it was hard."

"So you're French then?"

"I am. But I'm an American too. My mother's from Napa. She met my dad through work. They married and she moved to France. When he died, we moved back."

There was more to it than that, but thinking about those particular minefields would piss him off. And he didn't want to be pissed off while on a date with Angie. Especially since it might be the only date they ever went on.

"I guess you grew up bilingual."

"I did, though I consider French my first language. It's what was spoken most when I was a child. My mother was the one who spoke English to me."

"How did you end up in Maryland?"

"Ian Black found me and recruited me."

Angie tilted her head as she studied him. "I have a feeling you left a lot out of that story."

He had, but there were things he didn't like to talk about. "It's not all that interesting."

"Okay," she said. He liked that she didn't push. "What about brothers and sisters?"

"No brothers or sisters. I have three first cousins though." Cousins he hadn't seen in fifteen years. Not since his uncle took control of the family estate and fortune.

"Do you see them often?"

"Not often, no."

Their steaks came then. After the waiter was gone, Angie ate a bite of steak and then sipped her wine. "Oh my god," she practically moaned. "That's perfect, isn't it?"

He grinned. "The right wine makes everything perfect."

"Seriously, how do you know so much about wine?"

"My father was a winemaker. My mother works in the business. It's in my blood, I guess." That was more than he'd told anyone in a long time. Because it still hurt, knowing he'd been cut from the family business when his uncle took control.

"Yet you didn't go into the business yourself."

"I didn't. It's not for me."

Angie didn't say anything else about the wine, thank God. They moved on to more superficial topics then. Ones that didn't make his insides tighten, or cause the dull light of old anger to flare bright. After they polished off the steaks, they shared a slice of cheesecake.

Angie sat back and smiled as she put her fork down. "That was really good. I ate too much."

"I'm impressed, actually. Most women pick at their food on a date. At least that's been my experi-

ence." He liked that she ate something besides salad.
She had last night too.

"I guess this is a date, isn't it? And as for picking at
dinner, no way in hell am I wasting an opportunity to
eat great food."

"Me neither."

She laughed. Then she dropped her gaze, her
cheeks turning pink again. Before he could puzzle it
out, she lifted her lashes. "Do you want to have coffee
at my place?" she asked softly.

His groin tightened. "I'd like that. Very much."

Chapter Three

ANGIE WASN'T SURE WHAT HAD MOTIVATED HER TO ASK Colt over, but she couldn't rescind the invitation now. They'd sat in the restaurant for another half an hour or so, and then Colt paid the check even though she'd objected. He told her she could pay the next time and she'd accepted.

He'd followed her home, and now she was buzzing around the kitchen and preparing coffee—the one thing she could manage in a kitchen, along with toast and the microwave—while Colt walked around her living room and looked at her pictures. There were photos of her and Maddy, her parents, and even Pugsy Malone, the Pug dog they'd had growing up. There were pictures with friends, travel photos, and one photo of her and Dan and Maddy that she should probably put away but that she liked —in spite of Dan's presence in it.

"Who's this guy?" Colt asked, pointing. Naturally he'd have honed in on that one.

"You aren't curious about the others?"

"Nope. This one."

Angie finished scooping coffee into the basket, slid it in place, and flipped the switch. "Can I ask why?"

He looked up as she approached, arms folded over her chest. She knew it made her seem defensive, but she didn't unfold them.

"It's the way he's looking at you. Possessively. None of the other pictures have that."

Angie gaped at him. Was Dan really looking at her that way? Maybe. He'd always been the jealous type. And no wonder, since he knew intimately how to persuade women to sleep with him. He must have expected that some other guy was out there, ready to do the same to her.

"That's really kind of uncanny, you know. Yes, you're right. Dan was my fiancé. We were together about three years. We'd planned to get married, but the time was never right. Which turned out to be code for Dan liked the ladies and didn't want to settle down."

"Yikes. Sorry."

"Yep. You're probably wondering why I keep the photo displayed. It's not because of him—honestly, it's in the past and I no longer care." Not about Dan anyway. She did care that she'd been hurt by his betrayal. It's what made dating again so damned difficult. "It's Maddy and me and the mountain in the background. That was the first time we went skiing together. It was fun and the picture reminds me of that day."

"Who took the photo?"

"Ah, well, that would be Maddy's boyfriend. He didn't last long, though I'm sure she's told Jace about him anyway."

"I'm sure she has."

Angie sat in the armchair across from the couch. Colt didn't comment on it as he sank onto the sofa. But he had to know she'd put a table between them on purpose. Geez, she was really messing up, wasn't she?

"Angie."

"Yes?"

"It's okay. If you're more comfortable over there, I'm not offended. I'm still shocked you asked me over, so the fact you're sitting opposite and not beside me isn't a dealbreaker."

She could feel her blush growing even hotter. Damn her pale complexion anyway. "It's a little scary how you know what I'm thinking."

He grinned. "It's not too hard to figure out. You're blushing, and it started when you sat. I could tell you were arguing with yourself about whether or not you'd been too obvious when you put a table between us. Truthfully, if you'd sat on the couch and patted the cushion beside you, I'd have wondered if you were drunk in spite of the fact you stopped drinking earlier in the evening."

"I'm not drunk. You know that."

"I do. Now relax. We're going to have coffee and keep talking. Then I'm going to leave. If you let me, I'll kiss your cheek. And if you don't, that's fine too."

Angie pulled in a breath. Her body sizzled with awareness of the man across from her. He was tall, handsome, blond as a surfer—she was still surprised that he'd been born and raised in France—and his body rippled with muscle when he moved. He had the kind of scruffy beard she could imagine scraping sensuously over her tender flesh, and piercing blue eyes that didn't miss a damned thing. He'd worn a navy henley and dark green khakis, and looking at him made her belly tighten.

"I swear I'm not mental," she said. "But I can't seem to go back to being the person I was before."

"You experienced a lot of trauma in a short amount of time. It's normal to be mistrustful of people."

He didn't have to ask before what. He knew. She loved that he knew. It wasn't just the thing with Tom Walls—it was also the abduction and being locked in a cage with a bomb. It was knowing she'd led a killer straight to her best friend. Knowing Colt had been shot because of her. Those things were far more traumatic than a cheating fiancé and a bad break up.

"I hate that she shot you," Angie said. "It wouldn't have happened if I hadn't led her straight to Maddy."

Colt frowned. "I told you before it's not your fault. It's the job. And she was finding Maddy one way or the other, so stop blaming yourself. I'm alive. I'm fine. You didn't cause it to happen."

Angie pulled in a breath. Her throat was tight. "I know you don't blame me. But I sometimes blame myself."

"Then stop. Holding onto the past is like swallowing poison. It eats you up inside. You have to let it go."

"You make it sound so easy."

"It's not. I know that. You just make a choice every day—every moment if you have to—to move past it and stop letting it control you. You're giving this thing too much of yourself, Angie. Is it worth the cost in hours of your life that you're giving it? Or could you be doing something else with your time?"

She could feel her jaw drop a little. "I never thought of it that way."

"You should. Think of your life like a bank account. Everything you give your time to requires you to make a withdrawal. When you have a choice, choose the things that make you happy and fulfill you, not the things that make you anxious or sad."

"Wow. Okay, so do you have a psychology degree or something? Because that is some heavy shit right there."

He laughed. "No psych degree. Just the school of life. A psychologist might be horrified by what I just said. I don't know. But it works for me."

The coffee pot dinged and Angie stood. "I'm going to start thinking of it like that too. I know it's not a quick cure or anything, but I'm an accountant. Anything that uses bank withdrawals kind of trips my trigger."

He laughed.

"Cream and sugar? Black?" she asked.

"Black. Can I help?"

"No, you just sit there. I'll get it."

She returned with the coffee. This time she sat on the couch. They weren't touching, weren't even close, but it felt like a victory anyway. He smiled, and her heart skipped a beat. She smiled back.

He gently tapped his coffee cup to hers. "To new beginnings."

"New beginnings," she echoed.

———

COLT'S PHONE dinged with a text the next morning at the range. He felt it go off but finished his shots before having a look.

Angie: *I had fun last night. Thanks for dinner.*

Colt: *Me too. Thanks for coffee after.*

Angie: *I like what you said. It made a lot of sense. I'm working on filling the bank account, not depleting it.*

Colt: *I'm glad. You deserve to be happy.*

Angie: *I think so too. I'm determined to get there. Think you might want to get dinner again sometime?*

Colt: *Just tell me when.*

Angie: *Okay, I will. Gotta get back to work right now.*

Colt: *I'll call you later.*

Angie: *Great!*

Jace wandered over, pocketing his phone. He arched an eyebrow.

"So you went out with Angie."

Colt knew better than to be surprised. Angie would have told Maddy. Maddy told Jace.

"Yep. Isn't that what you wanted?"

"Me? I don't care one way or the other. But Maddy does, and she's thrilled. She thinks Angie's been existing rather than living, and she wants to see her happy."

Colt frowned. "That's putting a lot on me, don't you think? I like her—a lot—but that doesn't mean I'm going to be the one to make her happy in the end."

"I hear you, man. Maddy knows that deep down, but I think right now she just wants to believe it's possible. I think, aside from all the stuff with Walls and Calypso, Angie hasn't really taken any chances since she broke up with Dan. Maddy said she's gone out with a couple of men, but nothing serious."

"What do you know about this Dan guy?"

"Not much. They were together three years, but

he turned out to be a serial cheater and Angie dumped him. That was around two years ago, right about the time she started working as an accountant. She'd worked her ass off to get her accounting degree and save money for their future together, but then it all fell apart. She hasn't had a relationship since. Or that's what Maddy tells me."

"Can you blame her?"

"Nope."

"How does Maddy know I'm not a serial cheater?" He wasn't, but he wanted to know why she had such faith in him.

Jace shrugged. "She doesn't. But she knows if you hurt her friend, I know how to dispose of the body when she murders you."

Colt snorted. "Point taken. But Jace, we had dinner together. We went to her place for coffee—actual coffee, nothing more. I'm not ordering wedding invitations or booking venues, okay? It was dinner and coffee. We may have dinner again. I'm not promising anything, other than I won't deliberately hurt her."

"I know." Jace smiled a wolfish smile. "Just be sure you stick to that promise. Disposing of bodies is messy business. Plus I'd have a lot of explaining to do when Ian never heard from you again."

Colt shook his head as he put his weapons back into his range bag. "I thought domesticity would mellow you. Wrong."

Jace's eyes glittered for a second. "Domesticity

doesn't mellow guys like us, Colt. It only makes us fiercer and more protective of the ones we love."

———

ANGIE FINISHED up the account she was working on, then went to the break room to get coffee. Liam was there, pouring a cup for himself. He looked up when she walked in.

"You're looking rather perky today. Did you have a hot date last night?"

Angie couldn't help but smile. "Actually, I did."

"Whoa, really? Tell Uncle Liam all about it."

Angie grabbed the coffee pot with a laugh. "There's not much to tell. It's someone I know and I finally asked him out." There was a lot more to it than that, but she didn't want to go into details about her push-pull with Colt over the past few months.

"Anybody I know?"

"You don't know him. He works with my best friend's fiancé."

"An FBI guy."

"Yes." Neither Jace nor Colt were FBI, but it was a convenient way to describe what they did. She'd taken to calling Jace an FBI guy in conversation because it was easier than the truth. Which she still didn't really know, but based on her experience he was more of a spy than a cop. A spy for hire, she thought, which made him a mercenary.

"How's it going with Martinelli's accounts?"

"It's going," she said. "What about you?"

"Same. He had his own way of doing things, but I'm figuring it out."

"Liam..."

"Yeah?"

She hesitated, but then decided to ask anyway. "Are you finding any anomalies? Figures that don't reconcile?"

Liam frowned. "Nothing like that. Are you?"

"One account. I can't figure out where he got the data. It's like there's another account or something. I'm waiting for more information from the client, but I'm stumped." She hated admitting that. It felt like failure, and she never failed at numbers. It was the one thing she was really good at.

Liam shrugged. "If anybody can figure it out, it's you. That's why you always get the hard stuff."

Angie rolled her eyes. "Flatterer. Hey, did anybody else get any of his accounts?"

"I think Jenny might have. The three of us are the least senior here. Maybe you should bring it to Barnes or Blake's attention if it keeps giving you trouble."

"Not yet. I want to see if I can figure it out. I don't want the partners thinking I can't take the initiative and do my job."

"Gotcha."

"Have you heard anything more about Charles? Or heard from him?"

Liam shook his head. "Nope. All I know is what you know. He didn't give notice. He called and said he quit. He hasn't picked up his stuff yet, though. Probably too embarrassed. I have to admit I wondered why he quit like that. He always struck me as the sort who'd volunteer for anything so long as he thought it might help him get ahead. And he seemed to be on the fast track." Liam shrugged. "But sometimes those types burn out. Spectacularly. It's hard to sustain that kind of work load."

She knew what Liam meant because she'd had her own problems with trying to do too much. She was an overachiever and she wanted to do it all. She also felt like she had to work hard because she hated having any debt and she wanted to pay things off sooner rather than later.

But she'd learned how working too much could ruin all your plans for the future. When she'd caught Dan cheating, he'd blamed her for ignoring him because she was working all the time. She'd been devastated. And angry because she'd been doing it for *them*. She'd wanted to pay off her student loans and save enough money for a downpayment on a house. Instead, she'd impulsively bought her condo when her relationship imploded. Yet another thing she had to pay for, but at least it was for her.

She *had* come to accept that she'd been working too much and maybe ignoring her fiancé more than she should, but she still didn't accept it as an excuse for what he'd done. That was on him. It had taken her a while to get to that point, but she'd gotten there with Maddy's help.

"Angie, he made a choice. He made a choice. Blaming you for his choice is like blaming your neighbor because you ran over their mailbox. Makes no sense."

Mads was right, of course.

"It is hard to sustain," Angie said. "And speaking of work, I'd better get back to mine and get this figured out."

"Let me know if I can help."

"Will do."

Angie returned to her desk with fresh coffee, woke up her computer, and sighed as the columns appeared. The numbers hadn't magically fixed themselves while she'd been talking to Liam and she had no emails from the client with more information.

She'd figure it out though. She had yet to meet a spreadsheet she couldn't wrangle. Today was not the day to admit defeat, either.

Colt wouldn't. She didn't know a lot about him, but she knew that much.

She thought of him last night on her couch, a cup of coffee cradled in one large hand, his blue gaze attentive and breathtaking all at once. He made nerves dance in her belly and sparks kindle in her center. It'd been a long time since she'd had sex with anyone, and the idea of sex with Colt made her hot and achy.

Not that she planned to let him know that.

When he'd left, he'd kissed her on the cheek and then walked away. She'd wanted, so badly, to turn her head and press her mouth to his—but she hadn't done it.

She still wasn't sure she should, no matter how he made her feel inside. The last time she'd let herself fall for a guy, she'd ended up with a shattered heart.

It was more than that with him, however. Colt was a dangerous man, and she wasn't sure she could handle that life even for a little bit. She'd had a taste of what could happen when Natasha abducted her, and she didn't want to go through that ever again.

But Colt was incredibly tempting. He didn't blame her for getting him shot, though Angie still felt as if she'd helped make it happen. Probably always would.

If he'd been shot once in the line of duty, he could be again. She didn't want to get close to him and then have something like that happen. It had been terrifying the first time, and she'd barely known him. If she let herself fall for him?

Angie closed her eyes. "Stop," she whispered. "You're depleting your mental bank account with this nonsense."

She slid her mouse over a column and clicked. Time to push Colt—and any theoretical relationships

—from her mind and get down to business. This is what paid the bills. This is what she could rely on.

Not blue-eyed men with gorgeous smiles and dangerous professions.

Chapter Four

COLT DIDN'T CALL ANGIE RIGHT AWAY. HE DIDN'T want to seem too eager, so he waited until about eight that night. And he texted to ask how her day had been instead of calling. She answered right away.

Angie: *It's been a long day at work. I just got home.*

Colt: *Wow. It's not even tax time yet.*

Angie: *It's always tax time in this business. But no, you're right. Except that corporate returns are due March 15 and I've got several to get done. Nobody has their crap together, either. When you ask for their 1099 info, half the time they don't know who gets one. It's a mess.*

Colt: *Sounds like hell. Want to talk about it?*

He waited while the three dots indicated she was typing. They stopped, started again. And then the reply came. One word. *Yes.*

Colt punched in the button with her name. She answered right away.

"You don't really want to hear about 1099s, do you?" she asked.

He laughed. "Not unless you want to tell me about them."

"I don't. They'll get done, but it's a pain in the ass while trying to get information from clients. Part of the job."

"You sound frustrated."

He heard ice clinking into a glass. Then the sound of what he assumed was water from the dispenser in her fridge. "I am. And it's not really the 1099s." She sighed. "One of the accountants quit last week. Just walked out and didn't come back. So I got some of his accounts. But there's one I can't sort out. The figures are all wrong."

Colt's senses prickled. Not that it meant a damned thing, but looking for shady shit was a part of his life. It's what he did, and when something didn't line up, his mind started traveling a well-worn path.

"Why would they be wrong? And what do you mean he didn't come back?"

"I don't know why they're wrong, but they are. The bank statements and his spreadsheet don't match up. It's a lot of money, too."

"And he quit."

"That's what we were told. He left work one day last week and didn't come in the next day. He could have been sick or taken a personal day. At first I didn't think anything of it. But when he wasn't there for three days, it started to seem a little strange. Then an email went around from the partners telling us he'd quit, though he didn't seem like the quitting kind to me. I've even wondered if maybe he was fired, but of course the partners won't say. We might all be thinking it, but none of us have discussed it. I sure don't want to be the one who starts that rumor, you know? Anyway, Liam and I were given his accounts. And maybe Jenny too, but I haven't asked her yet."

"Is it typical to divide up the accounts like that?"

"Yes. If there were any major accounts, then one of the partners would have taken them. And there might be, but I don't know every account Charles had. Anyway, we got the rest. It's just a hell of a lot of work on top of all the other work. God I sometimes hate this job."

"I'm sorry, baby."

He heard her breath hitch in. "Did you just call me baby?"

"Does that bother you?"

"Not really. I was just surprised."

Colt lay back on the couch and picked up the remote. He clicked on a news station, keeping it on mute.

"Tell me about this guy," he said. "What's his name?"

"Charles Martinelli. He worked there for five years, which was another reason it was a surprise. But I also get how it could happen. Hell, some days I want to walk out and not go back. But I like paying my mortgage. Eating. Wearing clothes. You know, all the usual stuff."

He chuckled. "Yeah, I get that. But I'm sure you could find something else if you had to."

"Probably. But I don't think walking out the way he did would help with recommendations for a new job."

"No, guess not. So what would you do if you could do anything?"

She sighed. "I don't know, Colt. I really don't. I've always been good at math, which is how I ended up majoring in it. I enjoy numbers. Love solving equations and stuff. I'm not artistic at all. I envy Maddy because she gets to travel and view art for her job, but I couldn't do something like that. I appreciate art, but I have no artistic skills."

"I think if Maddy weren't an art appraiser, she'd want to be an HGTV star," Colt said with a smile.

Angie laughed. "You aren't wrong. She loves those renovation shows. As you can tell when you walk into her house. It looks amazing, and I love it. But I couldn't do that either. I don't see those things the way she does. I could do the math for adding an addition onto the house—dimensions, costs, that kind of thing—but I couldn't do the decorating part of it."

"That's an important part of the process, don't you think?"

"Oh, definitely. Still, it doesn't feel all that creative."

"It sounds like you enjoy accounting, but not clients."

Angie made a sound. "Yeah, that's pretty accurate. And that's a bit of a problem in this job. I should probably be a data analyst at a government think tank or something."

Colt pictured her at BDI, analyzing data and providing projections, and he didn't hate the idea. But he didn't really know if she'd enjoy it. He also didn't know if Ian needed another analyst, so he kept the thought to himself.

"Start applying then. Keep doing this job, but apply elsewhere. When you get a better offer, leave."

"I really should. I need to update my resume, start job hunting, hope my employer doesn't get wind of it, and then hope I don't land an even worse job. Oh, hell, I sound like my dad," she added with a moan. "He spent thirty years working for the government and when my mom would tell him he should find something else if he was unhappy, he'd say *'but Lisa, what if the next job is worse?'*"

"Then you get another one," Colt said. "You can do that. Maybe he couldn't because he was invested by then, but you can."

Colt knew all about taking risks and finding your way when the path you'd always thought was yours was suddenly blocked. It wasn't easy, but it was possible. Sometimes the only way out was to plow through the wall.

"You're right." She blew out a breath. "You know, we've been talking about me this whole time. Let's talk about you for a while."

"What do you want to know?"

"Do you like your job?"

"Yes."

"Well that was easy. Never want to quit? Never have a bad day?"

"I didn't say I didn't have bad days." Getting shot at wasn't exactly a good time when it happened. He also didn't enjoy killing, but sometimes it had to be done. "But no, I don't want to quit."

"I know what you do is dangerous. That doesn't bother you?"

"Not usually, no."

"When you got shot… you didn't want to quit?"

"Not really. I mean yeah, there's a little bit of apprehension that goes with getting shot, but I've never doubted I'm where I need to be."

He didn't remember the precise moment because that's what trauma often did—it wiped your memory of the details. But he remembered the alarm going off, shouting at Maddy. And the bang. He remembered the sound of it. He didn't remember falling, and he didn't remember the moment he realized he'd been shot.

What he remembered was waking up in the

hospital with tubes running out of him and feeling like he'd been run over by a train. He also remembered a lot of painful physical therapy as he got the use of his muscles back again.

"I'm really sorry that happened," Angie said softly.

His gut tightened. "It's not your fault, babe. We've been over this."

"I know. You don't blame me, and I didn't actually lead her to you or pull the trigger. But she wouldn't have found Maddy without me—which means she wouldn't have shot you."

"Yeah, but she might have shot you if you hadn't cooperated. You wouldn't be on the other end of the phone, and I wouldn't be wondering what you're wearing right now."

Angie made a choking sound, and he realized she'd been drinking something. "Oh my god," she said when she could talk again. "You nearly killed me. Water went down the wrong tube."

He couldn't help but grin. "Sorry." But he really wasn't because it had gotten her off the subject of him getting shot and her being at fault for it.

"I can't believe you said that."

"Why not? You have to know I'm attracted to you. I'm pretty sure you're attracted to me. Don't tell me you haven't pictured me naked."

"Oh lord, I am not having this conversation with you."

"You have, haven't you?" His dick started to respond to the thought.

"Colt," she said firmly. "Don't make me hang up on you."

He laughed. "Okay, fine. We won't talk about nakedness anymore. Unless you want to."

"I don't want to."

"You sound uptight. Know what's good for releasing tension?"

"Colt."

Colt laughed again. "Kidding, Ang. Sorta."

"You're terrible."

"I'm male."

"Same thing."

He laughed. "Look, you sound tired and it's getting late. Why don't you have a glass of wine and get some sleep. We can talk tomorrow."

He heard her yawn. "I am tired, you're right. Think I'll skip the wine and head straight for bed."

"Night, Angie."

"Night, Colt."

The line went dead and Colt dropped his phone onto the coffee table. But he didn't pick up the remote and unmute the television. Instead, he grabbed his phone again and dialed the man who knew everything.

"What's up?" Ian Black said by way of greeting.

"Probably nothing," Colt replied. "But I'm curious about something."

He told Ian about Charles Martinelli and how he'd quit work without notice. About how Angie was having trouble with one of his client accounts.

Ian listened without comment. When Colt finished, Ian said, "Run his name through the database and see what pops up. Can't hurt. Do you know the name of the client?"

"Not yet."

"But you can get it."

"Probably." If Angie wouldn't tell him—though he suspected she would—he'd get Maddy to find out.

"If nothing pops up on Martinelli, we'll plug the client in and see what happens."

"Thanks, boss."

"Sure thing. So she's speaking to you now, huh?"

"For the time being," Colt replied.

Ian chuckled. "Then don't fuck it up."

"Not planning on it, boss."

Ian was still laughing when they ended the call. Colt rubbed a finger over his temple, thinking. He could keep flirting, keep gently pushing Angie forward. Or he could back off entirely and let her find a guy who was more her speed. Another accountant. A scientist. Someone whose life wasn't ruled by volatility and violence.

Someone who wasn't living a lie.

ANGIE COULDN'T SLEEP. She was tired, but she couldn't stop thinking. She groaned as she sat up in bed after tossing and turning for a couple of hours.

She needed to sleep, but it just wasn't happening. She checked her phone for the time. *1:00 a.m.*

Crap.

She could lie there and toss and turn some more, or she could get up and do some work on her computer. She opted for work, so she threw the covers back and slipped on her robe. She padded out to the kitchen, poured a glass of Chardonnay from the box she had in the fridge—Colt would no doubt be horrified—and sat at the island to open her laptop. She pulled up the Cardinal Group spreadsheet and scrolled through the columns.

She clicked the tabs. There were several blanks, sheet after sheet, but she kept clicking them because she'd never done that before. Going relentlessly sideways until she ran out of tabs.

On the final tab, there was a number. Angie blinked. She'd only found it because she scrolled down instead of closing what appeared to be another blank tab. It was too long to be a bank account number, but she highlighted it and copied it over to her notepad. The number of empty tabs was ridiculous. What the hell was Charles doing anyway?

She counted the spaces. There were twenty-three numbers. She had no idea what those twenty-three numbers meant. They could be anything. Maybe it was an IBAN—an international routing number—but she didn't recognize a country code so that was probably out too. Could just be Martinelli's internal notations that made sense only to him, though why he'd put it onto a tab at the end of a bunch of blanks, she had no idea. She'd have to ask Liam if he'd encountered anything like it on the accounts he had.

Angie logged onto the company website to pull up the Cardinal Group's bank statements. Maybe she'd find that number somewhere in the information she already had.

NO FILE EXISTS

Maybe she'd clicked the wrong thing. She tried again. She was into the Barton, Barnes and Blake server, but there were no Cardinal Group statements anywhere. She sat back and blinked at the screen.

The Cardinal Group's account was closed, and it appeared that everything had been wiped from the server. Maybe they didn't trust anyone but Charles. Maybe he'd already gotten a job elsewhere and they'd moved everything to that company. Or maybe they'd hired him on as a full-time accountant.

She'd been into their account just a few hours ago. No one had told her the company was leaving Barton, Barnes and Blake. Hell, no one at the Cardinal Group had ever answered her emails either.

Angie took a swallow of wine. Worried the inside of her lip. Thought about texting Liam.

Instead, she picked up her phone and texted the

one person she knew would give her good advice. She didn't think he was awake right now, but he'd answer in the morning.

Angie: *Remember that account I was telling you about with the odd figures? It's gone. Everything wiped from the server. All I have is Martinelli's spreadsheet. I guess I should be thankful I don't have to work on it anymore, but still. It's weird. First he doesn't come back to work, then an account that wouldn't reconcile is gone too—and they never answered my emails. I don't know what to make of it, but it's late and I can't sleep and I'm babbling. Finger-babbling. Hope you're happily asleep right now. Wish I was.*

Angie put her phone down, finished her wine, and returned to the fridge to get a little more. Just for giggles, she sat at the island and repeated the process of looking for the Cardinal Group's files.

Nothing. A buzzing started at the back of her brain. She went looking for Charles's spreadsheet. She'd made a copy to work on because she didn't want to fudge anything up in the one he'd made. She wanted to be able to prove to her bosses just how jacked it was if she failed to resolve it.

NO FILE EXISTS

A chill shot down her spine. The spreadsheet was gone? Someone had closed the Cardinal Group's account, wiped their records, and wiped Charles's record of the work he'd done.

"No, no, no," she muttered as her heart kicked up. "I don't want any trouble. Not again. Fuck you,

Martinelli. Why'd you have to run away like a big chicken anyway?"

Her phone pinged with a text and she squeaked at the sound of it. "Calm down, Angelica," she said. "You're way too jumpy lately."

Colt: *What usually happens when an accountant quits?*

Angie: *They give notice. And there's a lot of discussion about the accounts they leave behind before they're gone. We contact the clients to introduce ourselves and let them know we'll be the new person handling everything and they can count on a smooth transition.*

Colt: *You said they didn't answer your emails.*

Angie: *No. I sent one to introduce myself, and two asking for more information on the account. No reply to any of them.*

Her phone rang. It was Colt.

"Hi," she said. "Sorry if I woke you."

"You didn't. I was awake."

Did he have trouble sleeping too? "You didn't have to call."

"Angie." He said her name with such calm authority. "You found something that scared you. I'm not going to ignore that."

She thought back to her text. "I didn't say I was scared."

"You didn't have to. It's a weird situation and it has you on edge. I can tell."

She didn't bother to ask him how he knew because it was true. "I am on edge. I wish I'd never gotten this account. The others were fine. This one makes me think Martinelli was up to something—or the company was. Which makes his quitting that much more suspect, especially since nobody at work has heard from him since."

"You said you still have his spreadsheet."

"Yes. I made a copy because I didn't want to do anything to his since it wasn't right. I thought if I couldn't reconcile the numbers and needed to alert my boss, it would be there as proof."

"So the original is gone?"

"Yes."

"What's the name of the company?"

"The Cardinal Group. They're a venture capital firm."

"No opportunities for mischief there," Colt said. She could hear the sarcasm in his voice. It made her laugh, in spite of how serious this whole thing felt. "Maybe don't tell anyone you have that spreadsheet, Ang. Keep it to yourself."

"I should delete it. Forget the whole thing." As if she could. This whole situation had her on edge and that wasn't likely to change. Deleting the spreadsheet didn't make the problem go away.

"Don't delete it."

Angie sighed in frustration. "I won't. I know it won't help."

"You never found any actual evidence of criminal misconduct?"

"No. The figures are wrong, but you can't prove

anything with that. It just means we don't have all the information yet. People sometimes forget to send all the statements, or they incorrectly categorize transactions. It happens. It's our jobs to sort it out and make everything neat and tidy."

"You could send it to me. We've got people at BDI who can analyze it. Maybe they'll find something."

She thought about it for half a second before she rejected the idea. It was tempting, but it was also against the rules. "I can't give it to you. It's confidential client information. I probably shouldn't keep it either—but I will for now."

"All right then. If you change your mind, my company will be discreet about it. I promise you that."

"I'll keep it in mind. Thanks for talking me off a ledge, Colt. I'm sorry I freaked."

"It's understandable. And you can talk to me anytime, babe."

She yawned again. "I'm finally starting to feel like I might get some sleep tonight. I really appreciate you listening."

"Go to sleep, Ang. I'll talk to you soon."

"Okay. Goodnight, Colt."

He said goodnight and they hung up. Angie checked the door locks again out of habit, checked the alarm to make sure it was set, then headed for bed. She was just settling under the covers when her phone rang again. It was Liam. "Have you heard?" he blurted when she answered.

Her eyes were gritty from lack of sleep. She rubbed one. "Heard what?"

"The building is on fire."

That made her sit straight up. "What? Triple B?"

"Yes! Murphy just called—it's burning to the ground."

Chapter Five

THERE WAS NOTHING BUT A BURNED OUT SHELL AND smoking remains as Angie pulled into the parking lot the next morning. Even the firemen were gone, though the area was surrounded with barricade tape to keep people from venturing too close. She didn't know why she'd come since there wouldn't be any work today, but she'd had to see it in person and not just on the news.

Apparently she wasn't the only one.

Liam stood in front of his car, hands in pockets, looking at what was left of the building. Jenny Clark was there and so was Jack Murphy. Last night when Liam called, he'd been passing on the information from Jack.

Angie got out of the car and went over to join them. "Hey," she said.

"Hey," they said back.

Liam put an arm around her. "Guess you had to see it too, huh?"

"It's unbelievable."

The air smelled like smoke and water, and the building shell was a sad sight on a street filled with old brownstones and neat landscaping. Barton, Barnes and Blake had occupied the building for thirty years of its long life. It'd been a mercantile at one time. And a haberdashery. Now it was gone. Other people stopped to stare too, but none of them were coworkers. Most continued on their way after they'd gawked a bit.

"It sure is," Jack said. "I could hardly believe it when I got the call. Mr. Barnes found out when the alarm company called him to report a fire on the premises. The fire department was here within minutes, but it was too late to save it. There was an explosion at some point, but I don't know whether the fire started before that, or if that's what caused it. It's lucky none of the surrounding buildings caught."

"It was an old building," Liam said. "Maybe the wiring sparked. Or somebody left a space heater running in their office. It's been cold lately."

They stared morosely at what remained of their workplace. Angie thought of the space heater in her office. She hadn't used it this week because she'd worn sweaters. Didn't mean someone else hadn't used theirs. But this on top of Charles quitting and the Cardinal Group files disappearing?

Too convenient. Though why would anyone want to burn down the office? The files were already gone before the fire started, and that could have been done remotely.

"I'm starving," Liam said after a moment. "IHOP anyone?"

Angie nodded. "Sounds good."

"I could eat," Jack added.

"How about you, Jen?" Angie asked when Jenny didn't say anything.

Jenny's eyes were red-rimmed and puffy. She'd been crying. She jumped when Angie touched her arm. "Jen? Breakfast?"

Jenny nodded. "I can come. Thanks."

"You okay?" Angie asked.

"I'm fine. I just—I had pictures of my kids in there. I can print them again, of course. I don't know why I'm emotional about this."

Angie hugged her. Poor Jenny had been through an ugly divorce recently and she was still recovering from the emotional trauma of it. "I'm sorry, Jen."

"I'll be okay. It's fine. I'm fine."

"Have you seen anyone else?" Angie asked the group at large.

"Mr. Barnes was by a few minutes ago. He said Blake's working on a solution," Jack said.

As if on cue, everyone's phones pinged with a text. "It's Blake," Liam said.

"Can you tell me what it says?" Angie asked. "I left mine in the car."

"Nothing much." Liam scrolled. "Basically, we're to work from home for now. Everything's in the cloud so he hopes it won't impact us too much. We can send forms that need printed to the Falls Church office. They'll mail them to clients. Blah, blah. No news on what caused the fire." Liam sighed. "That's it. Work from home. Contact your clients and reassure them, though Triple B's sending out an official email as well."

"I can't imagine how long it's going to take to get a new office up and running," Angie said. It hit her forcefully that this was a huge change in her life. She hadn't lost her job—not yet—but nothing was the same as it had been yesterday. It wasn't going to magically go back to normal in a day or two either. She'd thought getting the jacked up Cardinal Group account was the worst thing to happen to her lately. Apparently not.

"We'll be out of our jobs if they decide not to rebuild," Jenny practically wailed. "And maybe they won't with all the new branches they've been opening in other cities."

"Don't think that way, Jen. This is still the original BB&B. Tradition means something to those old boys," Jack replied.

"Come on, ladies," Liam interjected, looping an

arm around each of them. "Let's go drown our sorrows with pancakes and maple syrup."

"Sounds good to me," Angie replied. She didn't want to imagine the worst that could happen, or listen to Jenny have a meltdown over it. She made a note to ask Jenny if she'd gotten any of Charles's accounts before they parted ways for the day.

As she got into her car and stared at the smoking remains of the building, a cold shiver rolled through her and she started to tremble. Her first instinct was to call Colt. She'd called him last night after Liam's text about the fire. He'd helped her calm down considerably. He was good at that. Probably because he was used to chaos and uncertainty.

Now that she was sitting there in the cold light of day and seeing what was left of the building—well, it was unnerving as hell. The urge to call him and have him make sense of it was strong—but she didn't. She couldn't call him every time she felt uneasy about something. Besides, there was nothing he could do to fix it.

She put the car in reverse and headed for IHOP. Jack, Liam, and Jenny were already there. They had a table near the back and Angie pasted on a smile as she joined them. She shook her hair out and picked up her menu, determined to be as positive as possible.

Jenny was beside her, and when Jack and Liam started talking about the Super Bowl and who they thought would win, Angie turned to the other woman.

Jenny had always been sort of unassuming, but lately she'd started wearing makeup and coming to work in something other than a basic black suit.

Today she was wearing leggings with riding boots and a loose sweater. Her hair was in a ponytail, and there were worry lines at the corners of her eyes and mouth. No doubt she had a lot on her mind with that rotten ex-husband of hers.

Dan had been bad, but at least they hadn't gotten married and had children before Angie discovered his affairs.

"Hey, Jen—I wanted to ask you. Did you get any of Martinelli's accounts?"

Jenny blinked as her gaze snapped to Angie's. "A couple. Why?"

"I was just wondering if you'd encountered any problems with any of them."

Jenny frowned. "Um, no. Nothing out of the ordinary. Why?"

"I had one that wasn't quite right. But it's gone now, so it doesn't matter."

She thought Jenny might have stiffened. "Gone?"

"The company closed their account and the files are gone. They were deleted last night, apparently."

Jenny's mouth tightened. "I don't know anything about that."

"Doesn't matter since it's over. Just keep an eye out for wonky accounting in the files you have."

Jenny was frowning. Hard. "Wonky accounting?"

Angie cursed. Why had she brought it up when it was a moot point anyway? Charles was gone and the Cardinal Group accounts had been deleted. She didn't know who'd done it, but it didn't matter. Her involvement was finished. If there were other messed up accounts, then let someone else find them.

"It's nothing. I think Charles was just distracted. It's not a big deal."

"Who was the client?"

Angie hesitated. But it wouldn't be difficult to discover which account had been closed recently. "The Cardinal Group."

Jenny turned away quickly. "I don't know anything about that. I never worked on that one."

"I know," Angie said. "I did, but I'm not now so it's cool."

Their pancakes arrived and the conversation turned to other things. They spent an hour eating and drinking coffee, and then went their separate ways. Angie drove home, thinking about everything that had happened in the past couple of days.

People quit their jobs. Files disappeared. Fires happened.

It didn't *have* to be sinister. But it damned sure felt like it.

———

COLT DROVE to Black Defense International's

building and made his way through security. Hand-prints, eye scans, cipher locks. Ian Black wasn't letting anyone in who didn't belong. Which was good because BDI was a lot more than it seemed.

Officially, they were mercenaries. Unofficially, they operated like a cross between James Bond and Jason Bourne with a dash of Navy SEAL thrown in. It was a hell of a ride most of the time.

Colt stalked through the secret area of the building and into Ian Black's office. Ian had just returned from Africa and he looked up when Colt gave a cursory knock on the open door and strode in.

"You're looking a bit tense today. Did Angie Turner ghost you again?"

Colt gave Ian a look. Ian grinned, and Colt knew the boss was yanking his chain.

"No, she didn't. Her office building burned down this morning. And the account she was working on evaporated from their servers last night."

Ian's gaze sparked with interest. "You don't say?"

"It belonged to the Cardinal Group. They're venture capitalists. They have an office in Annapolis, and they invest in local startups, among other things."

Ian leaned back in his chair. "We have a missing accountant, disappearing financial records, and a burned out office building. Seems as if something's shady, doesn't it?"

"Looks that way from where I'm sitting."

"Did you find anything on Martinelli in the database?" Ian asked. "I'm assuming not since you didn't lead with that."

"Not yet. I want to surveil his house, see if he's there. Maybe he'll have some answers if we can find him."

"Go for it. Take Ty with you. I'll tell Dax to keep searching the records. I'll also see what I can find out about the fire."

Ian studied him with flinty blue eyes. Colt had stopped wondering what Ian's true eye color was. Tomorrow they might be brown. Or green.

"Don't let this situation distract you," Ian said. "If there's anything wrong, we'll find it. But don't get twisted around the axle. Angie Turner is a grown woman, and a pretty smart one too. She doesn't appear to be in any immediate danger, and you can't be with her twenty-four hours a day. Our missions take priority. I need your head in the game, Colt."

"Am I going on assignment?" Colt asked as coolly as possible.

Ian shrugged. "You never know, do you? Might have an asset in Paris who needs persuading."

Colt didn't like it but there was nothing he could say. That was the job. "Then I'd better get moving on finding Martinelli."

Ian waved him off and Colt went to find Ty. If Colt found Martinelli at his home, then this whole thing could be over soon. Tyler Scott was at his desk, pouring over intel reports. He looked up when Colt approached.

"Hey, man. What's happening?"

"Off to find a missing accountant. Want to help?"

Ty shrugged. "Sure." He shuffled the papers on his desk and slipped them back into a folder marked TOP SECRET before returning them to the safe and twisting the lock. Then he grabbed his coat and the two of them headed for the parking garage while Colt gave him the information about Charles Martinelli and everything that'd happened.

Ty whistled. "Somebody burned down the office, huh?"

"Could be a coincidence. It was an older building —turn of the century. Wiring can be dodgy in those."

"True. So hey, are you seeing the angelic Angie or what?"

Colt's belly tightened. Was he? "Kinda."

"Kinda. What does that mean?"

Colt unlocked the SUV and slipped into the driver's side.

"It means," he said, as Ty climbed into the opposite seat, "that we went on a date. It remains to be seen if we'll go on another one."

Ty's brows lifted. "You're kidding, right? That woman is hot. If you don't want her, maybe I can take a stab at it."

"No," Colt growled. He didn't bother to correct Ty that he wasn't the one who planned to decide whether or not they went out again. That was up to Angie. Though maybe it was best for her if they didn't, considering what Jace had told him about the guy who'd broken her heart. Maybe she just wasn't ready. If she ghosted him, he wasn't going to push.

Ty held up both hands in surrender. "Okay, man. Never mind. She's yours. Or not if you don't do anything about it. But whatever. Not my problem."

"Sorry," Colt said. "It's complicated."

"Always is with men like us, isn't it?"

Colt knew what he meant. His jaw tightened. "The job."

"It's not easy to be with men who do what we do. But she's Maddy Cole's best friend, right?"

"Right."

"And she survived being kidnapped by Calypso and then visited you in the hospital after you were shot."

"Yeah."

"I think she knows what she's getting into, Colt."

He wasn't so sure.

———

ANGIE SPENT the day at home, working on accounts. She put on Pandora and listened to the Britney Spears channel. She didn't care what anyone said, Britney was far more talented than people gave her credit for. The proof of that was how the hours slipped by while

Angie sang along to *Toxic* and *Oops I Did It Again,* among others.

"I'm Britney, bitch," Angie muttered while summing a column.

When the doorbell rang, she didn't hear it at first. She finally realized the buzzing sound wasn't coming from the song and she grabbed her phone to turn down the music. Then she hurried over to look out the peephole.

Colt.

Heat rushed from her belly to her cheeks and down into her toes. *Whoa.*

"Just a sec," she yelled as she sprinted over to the hall mirror to check how she looked. Her hair was piled on her head in a messy bun, but at least she'd put on makeup this morning. She'd changed into yoga pants and a silky button-down top when she got home, but it was presentable.

Angie yanked open the door with a smile. "Hi."

Colt looked a little gruff, a little intense—and a whole lot delicious. He was tall, with summer sky eyes and tightly cropped blond hair, and her insides melted just a little.

"Hey, babe. Mind if I come in?"

She stood back and held the door wider. "Not at all." And she really didn't mind. She'd talked to Colt so much over the past couple of days—in person, in text, and on the phone—that she felt comfortable with him. Being with him felt right somehow.

He strode in, then shrugged out of the black leather bomber jacket he wore.

She took it and put it over the back of a chair. "Is everything okay?"

He had on a black knit henley that clung to hard muscle, and faded jeans that accentuated things she didn't need to stare at. She very deliberately kept her eyes on his face.

"Yeah, everything's fine. I was nearby and thought I'd stop in and check on you. I hope you don't mind that I didn't call first."

She glowed inside. What the heck was that all about? "I don't mind. I was working anyway."

Britney sang *My Prerogative* in the background and Colt arched an eyebrow. "Working music?"

Angie folded her arms beneath her breasts. "Britney makes time fly. And she keeps me tapping my toes."

"Hey, it's cool. I like Britney. I was on her security detail a few years ago."

Angie's jaw dropped. "You were? Wow."

He shrugged. "It was just once. In Vegas when she was doing her show."

"That's so awesome. Did you talk to her?"

"Not individually. But she was nice to everyone."

"I'm glad to hear it. I hate when you find out someone like that is a jerk and then you can't buy more of their music." She went over to the island where she snapped her laptop closed and turned down the music. "We're all working at home for the foreseeable future. I drove by the building this morning. It's awful."

Colt followed. There were lines on his forehead from the frown he wore. "I saw it earlier. I'm sorry."

"Do you think there's something more to it?"

She kept thinking there must be, but what proof did she have? None.

He seemed to hesitate. Or maybe she only thought he did. "I don't really know. It's probably not related to Martinelli and the Cardinal Group, but we won't know until the fire investigators file their report. That could take weeks."

"So long?"

"It's not like on TV. The investigators have a lot to analyze, not to mention the destructive power of fire on evidence."

Angie frowned. She'd hoped there'd be answers a lot sooner. She wanted them so she could stop feeling this gnawing sense of unease in the pit of her stomach. "What about your people? The place you work seems, I don't know, able to get things done a lot faster."

"Often we can. But fire investigation really isn't our thing. We're more likely to be blowing things up than searching for evidence of arson."

Angie sighed. Her stomach chose that moment to rumble. She pressed a hand against it. "Sorry. I guess it's been a while since breakfast."

"You haven't eaten since breakfast?"

"No, but it was a big breakfast." She'd had pancakes though she probably shouldn't have. But they were so good and she'd been too upset about everything to deny herself.

Comfort pancakes. That's what they were.

"It's nearly five. Why don't you let me take you to dinner?"

Her heart thumped. Not because she was afraid, but because she wanted to spend time with this man. He made her feel safe. "Okay. But I have to change."

He seemed puzzled. "Why? You look terrific."

"I'm wearing yoga pants and an old shirt."

"You still look terrific."

Driven by impulse, she went over and put her hand against his chest. Stood on tiptoe to press her lips to his cheek. She hadn't kissed him since New Year's Eve when she'd worked up the courage to give him a quick kiss on the mouth. This kiss wasn't as daring as that one, but it made lightning blaze beneath her skin.

Colt didn't move. Didn't catch her to him or try to turn his head and meet her lips. He let her kiss him on the cheek and stood utterly still until she backed away. He frowned at her. A baffled frown, not an upset one.

"What was that for?"

Angie felt herself turning red. Naturally. "For being you. For saying nice things when you don't have to. For coming to check on me and not thinking I'm a nut for, well, anything. Thanks."

"I like you, Angie. I have a lot of thoughts about you, but that's the most important one you need to know. If nothing else, we're friends. You can count on me to be here for you."

She trembled in a good way. "I know I can."

"Good. Now go change so we can eat."

Angie headed for the bedroom, feeling buoyant. Maybe she should be more cautious, but her brain wasn't in control right now. She'd already let it have far too much input where Colt was concerned.

It was time to let go—and pray she didn't regret a second of it.

Chapter Six

COLT TOOK ANGIE ACROSS THE BRIDGE TO A restaurant on the eastern shore. It was a smaller place, out of the way, unlikely to be frequented by anyone they knew. Not that he cared about being seen with her. He didn't mind that. But he wanted her out of her usual haunts and somewhere different where he could observe those around them.

See if anyone stood out or seemed to be following them. A professional wouldn't be obvious, but Colt wasn't sure whoever was out there was a professional. Not with the clumsy way they'd deleted the Cardinal Group files and torched the building.

He was sure that fire had been arson. But why? There was no need to do it since they'd hacked the server and deleted the files. Unless they were covering up something else.

Colt had gone to Charles Martinelli's place with

Ty. The house was unlocked and it'd been ransacked. There was no sign of Martinelli. His car was gone, his wallet and keys, and it looked like someone had gone through his closet and taken out some clothes, which seemed to indicate that Martinelli had been in a rush to get the hell out of town.

They'd searched for a passport, but hadn't found one. The mail had been piled up on the floor beneath the slot and they'd gone through it. Nothing but bills and junk mail.

They'd taken his desktop computer back to BDI for analysis. Ty and Jace were running searches on passenger manifests for flights out of the country. Ian was mining his contacts for information on the Cardinal Group's partners and staff. Brett was currently in Germany with Tallie, shopping for furniture or something, so he was out.

Colt had taken point on Angie's safety. He'd thought Jace was going to argue with him over it, but Jace merely arched an eyebrow and said, "I trust you to take care of Maddy's dearest friend in the world."

Not that they knew Angie was in danger. It was an abundance of caution due to her having worked on the Cardinal Group account before it disappeared. Add in the fact Martinelli had done a runner, and they weren't taking any chances.

"This is really good," Angie said around bites of parmesan-crusted chicken. "How did you find this place?"

"Yelp."

She laughed. "Got me there. I use Yelp, but only when I'm traveling and need to know what's around. Or when I need the opening hours to a place I like because I've forgotten what they are."

"I like to search for new-to-me places with high ratings."

"You're a foodie."

"Nah, just half French."

"Why didn't you go into the wine business? You clearly like wine and food, and you said your father was a winemaker."

An invisible band tightened around his chest. "It wasn't an option for me. The business passed to my uncle, and my mother and I moved to America."

Uncle Guillaume had never approved of his brother's marriage to Colt's American mother. Though his father had entrusted Guillaume with the estate and believed he would honor his wishes, Guillaume had not. His sons were older because he'd married younger, and he'd brought them in to help run the company. There was no need for Colt or his mother in that scenario. They'd been cut out.

"Do you ever think about going back?" She was innocently asking questions, but each one twisted the knife a little deeper in an old wound.

"No. Besides, I like what I'm doing now. It's far more exciting."

"And dangerous. Unless winemakers have to worry about falling into a vat of wine or something."

He laughed in spite of himself. "Not typically, no."

"So you decided to become a spy instead."

"I'm not a spy."

"You work for Ian Black. I don't know what he does, but you can't tell me that man is not a spy. I've been around him just enough to know he's not ordinary."

Colt snorted. "No, he's definitely not ordinary. But we're a security firm, Angie. We provide services around the globe, which is why language skills are important. We aren't spies."

Not technically. On the surface, they worked for whoever could pay them. But that wasn't the real story. The real story was the mission. To protect and defend the innocent, and to put a stop to evil wherever and however they could. It was a never-ending mission.

"Okay, you aren't spies. Whenever Maddy and Jace speak Russian to each other, I feel like I'm in a Bond movie. It's cool though. I wish I spoke another language."

"Don't you?"

She blinked. "No. English is it."

"I was thinking about math. That's a language that scares a lot of people."

"Oh, cute. I guess it's kind of like a foreign

language to people who are terrified by it." She shrugged. "Equations have always made sense me."

"That's kinda how language is."

"You speak English and French. Anything else?"

"Italian and Spanish. A little German." And Farsi, though he wasn't telling her that one since it would give away that he often traveled to Iran. Those missions were highly classified and particularly dangerous these days. Not something she needed to know.

"Well damn, that's pretty impressive. I'm feeling a little under accomplished here."

"I'm pretty sure you aren't. Equations, remember?"

She laughed. He liked the way her laugh sounded. Liked the way her auburn hair escaped her messy bun and framed her face. She was pretty, and though he'd seen her in smoking hot dresses and high heels, he liked her just as much in the jeans and sweater she'd put on. It was a deep mustardy-gold sweater in a chunky knit with a loose neck and a shoulder that kept slipping down to reveal her bra strap. The bra was gray, and he wished he could see more of it.

"Yes, all right, you win. I can do math without fear, and I can balance a mean spreadsheet. I can also do your taxes—and that's magic, I swear. Nobody likes taxes."

She made him laugh.

"Only accountants and tax attorneys. And the IRS," he added.

"Right."

"Did anybody from the Cardinal Group ever contact you?"

"No. I sent three emails. They never answered any of them. That's not unusual with some of these clients. I've been bugging one of my accounts for 1099 information for almost a month now. The deadline to send them out is in two days, so they'd better get a move on it."

"The Cardinal Group knows you had a problem with the account then."

"I didn't phrase it like that. I said I needed to verify some things in order to complete their tax return. We never tell a client we're having a problem. We don't want to give them any reason to doubt our competence. Barnes and Blake would be horrified."

"But not Barton?"

"Barton unofficially retired last year. He was eighty if he was a day, and his wife finally put her foot down. He still comes in every once in a while, but he's not involved in the day to day anymore."

Regardless of how she'd phrased her emails, he didn't like that anyone at the Cardinal Group knew she'd been having trouble with their account. The research so far indicated the firm was run by two men who represented a group of venture capitalists with money to burn.

It gave them a prime opportunity to skim a little bit off the top and pad their own pockets, which is what Colt suspected was going on. But what made Charles Martinelli run and why did someone burn down the building after the records were erased?

"Colt?" she asked when he didn't say anything.

He jerked his attention back to her. "Yeah, baby?"

She smiled. "I really shouldn't like it when you call me baby, but I do. I don't know why. Anyway, you seemed distracted there for a second."

"Sorry. Just thinking."

"About my situation, right?"

"Yes."

She sighed. "You're thinking it's not good they know I had trouble, because if they *are* up to something illegal, then they know I've seen something wrong with their finances."

He hated to admit it to her, but Angie was smart and she wasn't going to accept any half-truths. "Pretty much. Could just be that Martinelli fucked up a spreadsheet and quit work because he reached a breaking point."

Not that he believed it after seeing Martinelli's place. But he wasn't about to panic Angie with that knowledge. She already knew enough to be worried.

Angie nodded. "It could happen. Charles always seemed like he had his shit together—but as Liam reminded me, Type A personalities can flame out when they overload."

"Was Liam close to him?"

"No, definitely not."

"Anyone else?"

Her face scrunched adorably as she contemplated the question. "Honestly, I thought Jenny Clark was talking to him a lot lately. Jenny went through a terrible divorce last year. She has two kids and she shares custody with her ex, which has been hard on her since he left her for another woman. Charles is a horn dog, so he was probably just trying to get into her pants—or maybe he did get into them. I don't know, but I saw her in his office quite a bit over the past month."

"Do you think she's talked to him since he quit?"

"She's never said so. She seemed as puzzled as the rest of us when he didn't come back to work." She pulled in a breath. "I should tell you that Charles tried to get me to go out with him. He was pretty obnoxious about it for a while, but I thought he'd finally taken no for an answer because he stopped trying. Like I said, horn dog."

Colt didn't like how that made him feel. Yeah, he told himself it'd be better for her to find a normal guy to settle down with—but when he pictured it, it made him want to flip tables and roar.

"How long did he persist?"

"Pretty much the entire time I've worked there, which has been almost two years. There was an ebb and flow to it. He dated plenty, but he didn't stop asking me out. I never went for a lot of reasons, but mostly because there was something off-putting about him. To me, anyway. He was arrogant and too full of himself. He was a lot like my ex in that he liked to play the field."

"Any man who couldn't see that you deserved the best he had to give was a fool."

She blushed and dropped her gaze, and they moved on to other things, talking about everything from travel to cooking to football teams. She was a Baltimore fan. He was a San Francisco fan.

Angie paid the check—Colt tried to get it but she insisted it was her turn—before they walked out into the cold, late January night. The restaurant sat near the waterfront in a quaint little town and sailboats bobbed on the water. There were street lamps lining a walkway that followed the curve of the bay. The air was fresh and cool with the briny scent of the bay.

"Can we walk a little way?" Angie asked.

Colt looked down at her. She had on a scarf and a rust-colored wool coat with her hands thrust deep in the pockets, but she shivered. "Will you be warm enough?"

"I'm fine."

They walked toward the water, then meandered down the path. There wasn't anyone out there but Colt kept a wary eye on their surroundings anyway. It was ingrained in him to look for trouble. He didn't question the impulse since it'd saved his life more than once.

It struck him that he was walking with a beautiful woman by his side, yet he couldn't stop doing the job long enough to just enjoy himself. He was positive she wasn't in danger at that moment, but it didn't matter to the part of him that was always on alert.

They stopped when they cleared the trees and stared at the fat white moon as it perched above the horizon. Angie's teeth chattered and Colt put his arm around her to offer some warmth. She didn't pull away. Instead, she leaned into him and he rubbed her arm.

"You're freezing."

"I'm cold, yes," she said. "But that's not the only reason I'm shaking."

He glanced down at her, puzzled. "What's wrong?"

"Nothing's *wrong*. It's you, Colt. I'm nervous."

———

"SHIT, SORRY," Colt said, dropping his arm from around her. "I wasn't thinking."

Angie blinked. And then she realized he thought she was upset because he'd had his arm around her. That it unnerved her because of Tom Walls and the way he'd tried to force himself on her in his garage.

But Tom Walls was the farthest thing from her mind.

"You've got it wrong, Colt. I like your arm around me."

He frowned. "You do?"

"I do."

He put his arm around her shoulders again. Only this time she turned to face him instead of staying where she was. He looked down at her, his expression wary. She smiled even though the adrenaline rushing through her made the corners of her mouth tremble. And her teeth wanted very desperately to chatter. Part of it was cold, that's for sure.

But the biggest part was Colt. His nearness. His rugged masculinity. The fact she wanted to kiss him for real and see what it felt like. She'd spent the entire dinner thinking more and more about what it would be like to have sex with this man.

And she didn't hate the idea. At all.

No, it excited her. Made her shiver and shake with anticipation. She hadn't been with anyone since Dan. She was ready. Not that she intended to take him home and get naked with him tonight, but she could see a future in which it happened.

But first she had to kiss him. Or get him to kiss her.

Best way to do that was ask even though it terrified her. What if he said no?

"Would you kiss me, Colt?" she blurted.

His eyes widened. And then they blazed with heat as his gaze dropped to her mouth. "You want me to kiss you? Now?"

She burrowed into his side. "I definitely do."

He drew her against him. He was solid. Big and hard and lean and beautiful. She'd never seen anyone so beautiful as him.

He put his fingers beneath her chin. They were cold, but she didn't mind. The sharpness of the cold against her heated skin felt good. Maybe it would cool this flame inside her body.

"You tell me if you want to stop," he said, looking at her very seriously.

She couldn't help but grin. "How am I going to do that with your tongue in my mouth?"

He snorted. "Ang, you know what I mean."

"I do. I'm just trying to cover the nerves here."

"There's nothing to be nervous about, baby."

A shiver rocked her. "There you go calling me baby again. Making me tremble."

"Hush, baby," he murmured before dropping his mouth to hers.

Angie gasped at the wave of sheer pleasure cascading through her. Colt slipped his tongue inside her mouth and she thought her knees might buckle. Her heart raced and she clutched his jacket with both hands as her spine turned to jelly.

It was cold outside, but inside she was as hot as if she'd walked into a sauna. Colt stroked his tongue against hers carefully, as if he worried about going too far too fast. She'd never been kissed with such care in her life. Not even by Dan, and she'd been planning to marry him once upon a time.

Colt was gentle and cautious—and he made her utterly crazy by being so sweet. She wrapped her arms around his neck, pushed up on tiptoe, and kissed him back with everything she had. His grip on her tightened—and then he groaned and kissed her a little harder, and with a little less control.

When she pressed herself tighter to him, the bulge of his crotch was unmistakable. He didn't thrust it against her though. He was very careful not to.

The bitch of it was that she wanted him to do it. She wanted to feel the pressure of his cock against her mound, wanted to feel the tingles of excitement race through her, feel the anticipation of an orgasm.

It wasn't fair to him though. She couldn't ask for that and not want the rest of it. She *did* want the rest of it, but she was also worried about going too fast. Spending the night together and then watching him walk away because he'd gotten what he wanted.

He's not like that, Angelica.

She told herself he wasn't, but it didn't matter. She was scared of doing too much too soon. It'd been *so long* since she'd orgasmed with someone else instead of herself, but she was still wary about rushing into it.

Colt's hands ran down her back, then up to her shoulders. Gently, he gripped her and pushed her away. Her eyes snapped open to stare up at him. That kiss had been *everything.* It had rocked her to her foundations. She didn't ever recall a man kissing her like that.

Like what exactly?

She couldn't name it, but she knew it was special. One corner of his mouth turned up in a grin. "Sorry, Angie, but I have to stop. It's getting uncomfortable if you know what I mean."

She could only nod.

He skimmed his fingers over her cheek, into her hair, then he leaned down and kissed her forehead. "You're beautiful, Angelica Turner. I want to make love to you so badly, but I know it's too soon. And I'm willing to wait until the moment is right. Because you're worth it."

He stepped back and took her hand in his. They walked toward the restaurant and the parking lot where he'd left the car. Angie couldn't think of a single thing to say. Colt didn't say anything either. When they reached the car, he unlocked it and opened her door for her. Instead of climbing inside, she turned to him and fiddled with the zipper of his jacket. When she could finally look at him, she bit the inside of her lip for a second to keep from babbling about how great she thought he was.

"I want to make love to you too," she whispered. "Soon."

His gaze sparked. "When you're ready, let me

know. I'll get on a plane if I'm out of the country. I'll drive all night to reach you if I have to"

She believed he would. And for the first time in months, she felt beautiful again. Powerful. In control of her body and her sexuality.

Because of him.

Chapter Seven

Colt drove them back to Angie's building. His plan was to walk her up to her condo, stay for a while if she let him, then make sure she was in for the night with her doors locked and her alarm on. He'd received no calls from anyone at BDI telling him to stick with her for now, though he would set up surveillance on her building if a call didn't come. Ian would approve that much.

Angie had her head turned, looking at the moon. It wasn't full yet, but it was almost there. When she turned in his direction, there was a smile on her face. "I love the moon. Especially in winter. There's just something so hopeful about it."

"How's that?" he asked, intrigued. Everything about her intrigued him.

"Well, everything is dormant. The grass is brown, the trees have lost their leaves, and it's cold. But the moon cycles around and illuminates everything, and you know the season is turning. Sooner than you think, there will be Easter flowers coming up and warmer temperatures." She shrugged. "I guess that sounds silly, but when I would stay with my grandmother as a kid, she used to tell me things about the moon and the seasons. It makes me think of her."

"Where does she live?"

"She died thirteen years ago. But she lived in Virginia, in the mountains. She was an Appalachia girl her whole life."

"I'm sorry she's gone."

"I am too. I miss her."

He understood. "My *grand-mère* died when I was eleven, and I still miss her. I'm not sure you ever really get over it."

"It's the price of love," she said.

He glanced at her, struck by that thought. "I suppose so. You don't always have a choice who you love, do you?"

She didn't take her eyes off him. "Not always, no."

He had to turn back to the road or he would have probably pulled over and kissed her at that moment. Just because. Not that he thought he was in love, or that she was—hell, they barely knew each other—but for the first time he could see it happening.

Colt gripped the wheel and told himself to forget it. Angie needed more. She needed a man who had a regular job, a man who could be there nights and weekends and build a life with her. Not a man who traveled the globe getting into dangerous situations on purpose. Or one who couldn't be who he was supposed to be.

When they pulled up to her building, he switched off the engine.

"I'll walk you up." What he really wanted to do was go up and stay all night, even if staying with her meant sleeping on the couch.

"Thank you. Do you want to stay for coffee?" she added a touch shyly.

His chest tightened. "Do you want me to?"

"I'd like to spend more time with you, but I understand if you need to get home."

"I have nowhere I have to be right now."

Her smile was soft. "Good. I'll fix coffee, or I think I have some port. Maybe you'll even approve of the brand."

He grinned. "I might."

They walked toward the entrance together. Colt held the door for her and then followed her into the building. It was a beautiful brick building, with a central foyer that contained a front desk—staffed with an attendant but no security—couches, and a bank of elevators. He knew there was a gym and spa on the main floor because he'd scoped it out earlier. The building was similar to a hotel, except people weren't checking in and out.

"What made you choose this place?" he asked as they stepped into an elevator. He punched in the button for the fourth floor as Angie leaned against the wall, looking sexy as hell.

Damn, he'd never made love in an elevator before. His balls ached with longing at the thought of thrusting into Angie's sweet body while holding her up against that wall.

"Honestly, it was an impulse buy. I'd been saving money to buy a house when I got married. When we broke up, I was so mad I bought this place instead. It's not quite within walking distance of downtown, but it's not a long car ride. I can drive, or catch an Uber if I'm going to be drinking or don't want to fight for parking."

"Those are good reasons."

She shrugged. "Well, except for the impulse part. What about you? You rented a house not too far from Jace and Maddy. What made you choose that neighborhood?"

"I didn't want to spend a lot of time looking, and it was there. Maddy knows the owners. She made the whole thing happen."

"Where did you live before that?"

"Hotels."

She blinked. "Really?"

"Really."

"But where did you put your stuff? Furniture, clothes, CD collections—that kind of thing."

"I have a place in Paris."

She seemed surprised. "I didn't know that. I don't think Maddy knows it either because she would have told me."

"Maddy doesn't know everything about me," he said with a smile. Few did. They'd probably be shocked if they knew. Some might even be a little hurt. He hoped not, but it wasn't impossible. Not if they thought he was only playing at his job.

The elevator stopped and Colt automatically stepped forward to position himself between Angie and the doors out of habit.

The doors slid open onto a quiet hallway. Colt went first, leading the way toward Angie's condo. Farther down the hall, a man in a hoodie stepped out from the alcove in front of Angie's door. He stopped when he saw them.

The hair on Colt's neck prickled. The man turned and headed toward the stairwell with the red EXIT sign illuminated above the door.

Colt reached for Angie, tugged her close behind him and went for his gun while she gasped in surprise. Something about this situation wasn't right. The man's haste. The flash of recognition when he'd seen them coming. The fact he'd been at Angie's door.

Colt made a split-second decision. He pushed Angie into an alcove in front of a different door. "Stay here, Ang. I need to follow that guy."

He could tell she wanted to argue but instead she nodded. "Do what you have to do. I'll be right here."

"Do you know this neighbor?"

"Yes. It's the Coopers."

"See if they'll let you in. I'll be back as soon as I can."

"I could just go to my—"

"No," he ordered. "Here. Understood?"

Her skin reddened and he wondered if they were about to have an argument that he didn't have time for. But she nodded. "Yes."

"Thank you, babe."

He didn't wait for a reply before he took off at a run.

———

ANGIE WAS SITTING at the kitchen island with Mary Cooper when her phone dinged with a text.

Colt: *Are you at the neighbor's place?*

Angie: *Yes. Is everything okay?*

Colt: *For now. Come to the hallway. I'm waiting for you.*

They needed to talk about his bossiness if it continued, but for now she understood where it was coming from. She'd seen Jace do the same thing with Maddy from time to time. It was all that alpha protectiveness coming out. Could be infuriating, but also sexy as hell.

Mary was chatting about something that

happened at work today when Angie cut her off mid-story. "I'm so sorry, Mary. That's my, uh, boyfriend. I need to meet him. He has my key."

It was a white lie, but she didn't think Mary needed to know the truth.

"Oh? Great! I'm so sorry you got locked out. You know you can leave a key here if you like."

"I may do that. Thank you."

They said their goodbyes and Mary walked her to the door. Angie stepped into the hallway. Colt was waiting for her, leaning against the opposite wall. Mary made a noise that Angie thought was approval.

Angie introduced them, and Colt turned on the charm. Angie was ready to smack him by the time they were done. Not because she was jealous, but because she wanted to know what happened. He was prolonging the moment when they'd be alone and she could find out.

After Mary closed the door, Colt pressed a finger to her mouth to stop the question. He led her to her door. Angie's stomach dropped when he twisted the knob and the door opened. She hadn't given him a key.

"Did he break in—?"

"He tried," Colt said. "He didn't succeed."

Angie didn't realize she'd walked inside until Colt shut the door behind them with an audible click.

"How did you get in?" Her brain was trying to catch up to everything that'd happened.

"I picked the lock."

"But the alarm——"

"I disabled it."

"How in the hell did you do that?"

"I used your code."

Heat flashed through her. "How do you know my code?"

"Because I guessed. You're like so many people, Angie. You used your birthdate because it's easy to remember."

"And if I hadn't?"

"I'd have jammed the system."

"You know how to do that?"

"It's my job."

If she didn't trust him, she'd be terrified. Instead, she was happy he was on her side. She swallowed. "That's scary as hell. And it's not right either."

He gripped her shoulders, rubbed her arms lightly. "Sorry, Ang. I'm not trying to scare you. But it's possible, and I know how to do it. The guy who tried to break in might have known too."

"You should have asked me before you broke into my home," she said, stung.

"I couldn't. I wasn't sure he hadn't gotten inside before we saw him. I had to find out, and that meant entering and searching for signs he'd been in here."

She sniffed. It made sense, even if she didn't like it. "You didn't catch him. Obviously."

"No. He had too much of a head start."

"Oh my god. Please tell me it was just a random burglary attempt."

"I could tell you that, but I think we both know it'd be a lie."

"Dammit," she growled. "I knew this wasn't going to be easy. There's something up with that Cardinal Group account. Charles found something wrong and now he's gone. They know I've seen his work because I basically told them I had when I asked for more information. Crap on a cracker."

"Do you suppose you can let me have that spreadsheet now?"

Somebody had just tried to break into her home. What were the chances it wasn't related to Charles and the Cardinal Group? Zero, that's what. Client confidentiality was definitely out the window.

"Yes, but I want to be involved in the analysis. I want to know what's in it that made Charles leave so abruptly. It's like he just dropped off the face of the earth..." Another thought occurred to her then. A horrifying thought. Once her mind started down the path of something being wrong, it was hard to contain it. "Is he still alive? Do you think maybe—?"

She couldn't finish the thought. Colt ushered her over to a chair and sat her down in it. Then he knelt in front of her. His blue eyes were fierce. She saw protectiveness in that gaze. It was comforting.

"Honestly, I don't know. He's not at home, and his passport's missing. It looks like he packed in a hurry.

We're searching for him, though. There's absolutely no indication he's dead."

Angie started bouncing her legs up and down nervously. She folded her arms over her chest to ward off a chill. "You didn't tell me that before."

"No. I didn't want to worry you."

"You should have told me, Colt. I deserved to know. I'm in the middle of this."

"Okay, yes. You are. And I should have. But honey, listen."

She looked into Colt's gaze. Those fierce, protective eyes. A small well of calm opened inside her.

"Here's what we're going to do. You're going to pack a bag and I'm going to take you to my place. I'll get a team together to analyze the spreadsheet. They'll come over and you can be involved in the analysis. We'll keep searching for Charles, but I'm going to make sure you're safe first."

Her heart throbbed. She wanted to go with him. She was also annoyed at him for keeping things from her. "I could stay with Maddy. You don't have to—"

"No, Angie. You have to stay with me. It's my job to protect you. If someone comes looking for you at Maddy's, they won't care what happens to her. Jace will have his hands full with both of you to protect."

Guilt flared. "You're right. I know you are. But don't keep anything else from me, Colt. It's not fair. It's my life and I have a right to know."

"Yes, you do. I'm sorry. I was trying not to upset you."

"I'm already upset. I didn't do anything wrong but I'm involved in this crap anyway." She sighed in frustration. "But if it wasn't me, it'd be someone else at work. And they don't have the advantage of knowing you and Jace."

"That's true. You're the one who's involved, and I'm here to help. Let's do what we have to do to keep you safe so we can find out what's going on."

Angie closed her eyes and dropped her chin. Frustration hammered at her, along with fear. Dammit, she wasn't going to let fear rule her. Not like she had when she and Maddy were captives. She wasn't going to cower in a corner and sob while someone else did the hard stuff.

This time, she was rescuing herself. She opened her eyes and met Colt's gaze. Her tummy flipped at the look in his eyes. Okay, so maybe she didn't have to rescue herself when she had him in her corner. But she would do everything she could to help him.

"All right, I'll pack a bag. But you at least have to let me buy groceries if I'm staying with you. I can't have you paying for everything."

"I didn't pay for dinner tonight, did I?"

"Only because I had to threaten you to let me get it this time, even though you'd promised."

He grinned. "What can I say? I'm a Frenchman at heart. Chivalry and all that."

"I'll give you money for groceries if I'm going to be there for a while."

"You can do that if it makes you feel better."

Angie drew in a deep breath, feeling like she had a little bit of control over the situation. She knew she didn't, but at least the illusion was there. "Thank you." She got to her feet. "I'll pack. How long do you think I'll be away?"

"Better plan for a week at minimum. I have a washer and dryer, so you can take that into account."

"Okay, thanks."

"Need help with anything?" Colt asked as she moved toward the bedroom.

"No, I've got it."

He took out his phone. "I'm going to make some calls. Let me know if you change your mind."

Chapter Eight

It didn't take Angie more than twenty minutes to pack some things and grab her computer. Colt drove the few miles to his place and waited for her to pull into the single-car garage so he could park in the driveway behind her. He'd wanted to leave her car at her building, but she'd insisted. He'd checked it for a tracking device. There was none.

He knew she wanted her car so she didn't feel trapped, but he wasn't going to let her go anywhere in it. There'd be hell to pay when that conversation happened, but it was non-negotiable. He hoped it didn't happen soon.

He'd called Ian and told him what was going on. Ian was sending Tyler over to Angie's place to position some cameras—one in the hall outside her door, and a couple inside. Ty didn't have a key, but he didn't need one to get the work done. If someone came back and tried to break in again, they'd know about it. And hopefully have a good visual.

Angie pulled into the garage and got out of her car as Colt parked and shut off his engine. He grabbed her suitcase from the backseat of his Yukon and locked up before walking into the garage and over to the door that led into the kitchen.

Angie joined him as he unlocked the door and disabled the alarm. It was a cheap system put in by the owner, which meant it didn't have any teeth, but it would stand up to petty burglars. Professionals, however, were another matter.

Colt flipped on the light switch and walked inside. Angie took in the 1960s kitchen decor and her jaw dropped. "Whoa."

"Groovy, right?"

"The appliances are green."

"I believe it's called avocado."

She blinked. "How do you know that?"

"How do you think? Maddy."

"Oh, right." Angie laughed. "Well, it's certainly memorable."

"The whole house is caught up in the 1960s. I think it was built in '64, so there you go. But the appliances work, the heating and cooling are good, and it's close to everything."

"I'm surprised the owner hasn't renovated and flipped. So many people are flipping houses in this neighborhood."

"It's owned by three siblings who grew up in the house and inherited it after their dad died last year. They can't agree on selling, so they rent it instead. Come on, I'll show you to your room."

Colt led her through the small living room and down the central hallway. There were three bedrooms and two full baths, and he took her to the one with the full-sized bed that sported a frilly pink canopy and a *My Little Pony* comforter.

"It's not mine," he said as her eyes widened. "The house came mostly furnished, and this was the room reserved for the granddaughters."

Angie laughed. "Thank goodness. I was starting to wonder if I'd discovered your main flaw—bad taste in decorating."

"I'd let you have the master, but I don't fit in this bed. It's too short. The third bedroom doesn't have a bed, unfortunately."

Angie waved a hand. "No, I get it. It's fine. And thank you. I appreciate everything." She sucked in a breath. "This is not how I thought the night would end when you took me to dinner. I kind of thought I'd be in bed by now, texting with you about tonight and reading a book before falling asleep."

"You can still do those things, Ang. The bath in the hall is yours. I have the master. There are clean towels and soap, toothpaste, everything you need. Feel free to think of this place as yours. You don't have to ask me if you can use anything or eat anything. Just do it. We'll sort out groceries and anything else later."

"Thank you." She glanced at the bed again. "It's very pink, isn't it?"

"Yep. Like Pepto Bismal."

She snickered. "That's the shade. It's very unflattering to a redhead."

He could only frown. "Nothing could make you look bad, Angie. You could be wearing a garbage bag and you'd still be gorgeous."

"Oh my," she breathed before turning a much prettier shade of pink than the bed's linens. "You do know how to say the right things."

"I only speak the truth, babe."

She pushed her hair over her shoulder and lifted her chin. She was still pink, but she was trying not to let it get to her. "Do you have any wine? I could use a glass. I'm a bit keyed up."

He could think of something else to release all that tension, but decided it wasn't a good idea to mention it. "What kind of Frenchman doesn't have wine? Of course I do."

She tilted her head. "It's hard to think of you as French when you're so blond."

"Really? What do Frenchmen look like?"

She shrugged. "Like Kevin Kline in *French Kiss?*"

Colt laughed. "I saw that movie. Kevin Kline isn't French. The other two actors though, the cop and the thief—they're French."

"And they both have dark hair. I rest my case."

He laughed again. "Come on, Ang. Let's get some wine. And bring your laptop so I can see that spreadsheet."

———

ANGIE TOOK a seat at the kitchen table with her laptop while Colt opened a bottle of red. He poured two glasses and handed her one while she pulled her laptop open and navigated to the spreadsheet.

It was a little strange being here with him.

Okay, it was a lot strange.

And awkward. What was all that babbling about French men and blond hair anyway? Nerves.

She took a deep breath. She was in his house—this timewarp house with the avocado appliances—drinking wine with him like she did it every day of her life.

This after barely speaking to him for months and making him think she was a basket case with her hot and cold reactions to him.

He didn't seem to hold it against her though. If anything, he was amazingly understanding. Colt pulled out the chair beside her and sank down on it. He was close enough she could feel his heat, smell the warm, spicy scent of his deodorant. She liked being next to him.

"To finding out the truth," he said, lifting his glass.

Angie clinked glasses with him and tried not to get jittery at his proximity. She took a sip of wine to cover her awkwardness. Cherry and raspberry burst onto her tastebuds, followed by jam and oak and tobacco. She forgot being awkward.

"This is good. You really do know wine."

To think last night she'd had Chardonnay from a box.

He pushed the chair back on two legs and grinned. "One of these days, when things are a little more settled, I'll give you a crash course on wine tasting. You'll be the envy of your friends at the next party."

"Or not," she said with a laugh. "I think you overestimate the people I know. We drink grocery store wine, sometimes out of the biggest bottle it comes in —or, horrors, a box."

He arched an eyebrow. "Believe it or not, there's some fine wine in grocery stores. And boxes aren't always bad."

"Not what I expected you'd say."

"Predictable is boring. Whatcha got there?" he asked, nodding at the screen.

Angie turned the laptop so he could get a better look. "This is the spreadsheet in question. I don't have the statements anymore because they've been deleted from the server, but trust me when I tell you this spreadsheet does not align with the information in the statements. It's off by hundreds of thousands. Possibly more."

He scrolled through the tabs and columns. "The only reason you know this is wrong is because you had access to the statements, right? But without them, you have no proof of wrongdoing."

"Pretty much." She took another sip of wine. "But if nothing's wrong, who was the guy trying to break into my condo? Why bother with me at all if I can't prove anything?"

"They know you've seen it. That seems to be enough."

It made sense, but the whole thing seemed like a crazy Hollywood movie. "How do they know I haven't shown it to everyone at BB&B by now?"

"They don't. But you're the one who had access. You asked to clarify information so they know you saw something puzzling."

"Ugh, I should have been lazier on this one. I should have finished my own accounts first. But I just had to go and look, didn't I?"

"Too late to change it now. All we can do is deal with the consequences."

"If I could get my hands on Charles, I'd wring his neck. Assuming he's still alive." She hated adding that last part. She hadn't wanted to go out with Charles Martinelli, thought he was a bit of a creep, but she wouldn't want anything bad to happen to him.

"I can't guarantee he is, but nothing indicates otherwise yet."

"Would you tell me if it did?"

"Would you want me to?"

Angie pulled in a breath. "I think so. Yes."

"Think. Or know?"

She had to think about that for a second. But she knew the answer. She was done with letting others take control of her life or make decisions that affected her without her input.

"I know I would. If Charles turns up floating in the Chesapeake, I want to know."

"Okay then. If it comes to that, I'll tell you."

It struck her that he meant it. He wasn't just saying it to make her feel better, or make her think he valued her choice. It *was* her choice and he would honor it.

"What do we do now?" she asked.

"We finish our wine and get some sleep. Tomorrow morning, my team will arrive to analyze this spreadsheet and war-game our options."

"War-game?"

"Sorry. It's a military thing. We run war-game scenarios."

"Got it. Were you in the military?"

"Eight years in the Marine Corps."

It made sense. He carried himself like a military person. So did Jace, and she knew Jace had been in. She didn't know which branch though.

"Why did you leave?"

She thought he tensed. Or maybe she imagined it.

"I was on assignment in Iraq. I was the only one left alive in my squad after we got ambushed by militants. I decided that was my sign and it was time to go."

"Oh, Colt."

"It was a long time ago. I made it out. A lot of good men didn't."

He'd lived through it and decided to work for Ian Black anyway. She didn't understand his thought process, but she didn't ask for more information. She felt like he'd shared more than he might have wanted to.

"My team will also report on anything else they've discovered, provided it's not classified," he said, getting back to the topic of her spreadsheet and the situation at BB&B.

Angie nodded. "Thank you. For everything. For helping me, believing in me, and involving me. I know we'll discover the truth with you and Jace involved. And maybe we'll find Charles and stop the Cardinal Group from committing fraud. Though why he didn't report it to the authorities, I don't know."

Colt looked thoughtful. "Maybe he couldn't. Somebody must have known he'd found something or he wouldn't have run the way he did. He probably didn't have time to report anything."

She frowned. "Charles brought the Cardinal Group

to the firm in the first place. They were *his* clients. Maybe he knew the owners before. I never asked. But if he knew them personally and felt responsible, maybe he tried to talk to them about the problem before he reported it."

"Not a wise move then."

"No, I guess not."

Colt finished his wine. Angie followed suit. "Another glass?" he asked.

She only hesitated a moment. "I'd love one."

He poured them both more wine. "Why don't we sit on the couch and catch some news? Or maybe there's something you'd like to watch?"

She thought about it. She could actually picture herself curled up beside him on the couch, sipping wine and watching television.

Why was she comfortable with him now? It wasn't that long ago that being near him tied her up in knots, and now she felt like they were old friends. Oh, he *still* tied her up in knots, but they weren't uncomfortable knots.

Being with him was like putting on a comfy pair of sweats you couldn't get rid of because nothing made you feel as relaxed as they did.

He shot her a puzzled frown. "What's making you grin like that, babe?"

Angie tried to wipe the look from her face. She didn't think she was successful. "Sorry. I was thinking about comfy clothes."

"Do I want to know?"

She waved a hand. "Nah, it wouldn't make sense. And watching the news is fine."

They headed to the living room. There was only the couch—not a terrible 1960s couch, thankfully—and they sat on opposite ends. Colt put his feet on the coffee table and turned on the television. Angie sipped her wine and watched the news, but her thoughts were on Colt.

She watched him out of the corner of her eye, the way he handled the remote whenever he picked it up to mute commercials. The way his muscles rippled beneath his shirt when he lifted his glass and took a drink. The glide of his throat as he swallowed. She thought about him in a Marine uniform, his hair cut super short in a high-and-tight.

Shock jolted her as she realized she was getting turned on by watching him. Her nipples tightened, and she grew wet. Her body started to ache.

They'd shared exactly two kisses, and only one of those had been the kind of kiss that curled toes, but her body reacted like they were kissing right this minute. Excitement built inside her until she couldn't stand another second. She put the wine glass down and shot to her feet.

Colt looked up at her with a lazy expression. She could see the moment he realized something was going on, but she was too embarrassed to stand there while he scrutinized her. While he puzzled out all her secrets.

"I'm really tired," she blurted. "I think I'd better get ready for bed."

"See you in the morning. Let me know if you need anything. Doesn't matter what time it is."

"I will. Thanks." She hurried down the hallway and into the pink room.

Angie leaned against the door and gulped in air, willing herself to calm the fuck down.

Unfortunately, it didn't alleviate the problem.

He said to let him know if you need anything. You need something all right....

"No," Angie muttered. She got ready for bed and crawled beneath the covers.

Sleep was a long time coming.

Chapter Nine

THE NEXT MORNING, COLT WAS UP EARLY AS USUAL. IT wasn't seven yet and Angie's door was still closed. He hadn't heard her moving around at all, so he figured she wasn't awake. He'd had a hell of a time going to sleep with her so near, but he'd finally managed it. He could still see the way she'd looked at him when she'd jumped off the couch and announced she was tired.

Her face had been flushed, and her nipples stood out very clearly against her sweater. If he'd been a betting man, he'd have bet she was aroused. He wasn't quite certain why though.

Now he wondered if he'd imagined that part. Maybe she was just tired, like she'd said. He knew her well enough to know that she blushed easily. Could have been because she was embarrassed about being tired.

He couldn't explain the nipples. It was possible she'd been cold since it was still late January.

Colt made coffee and sat down to log onto his computer. His email contained nothing exciting, so he closed it and shut the lid. The guys would arrive in another hour. He decided to make breakfast before they got there. If the smell didn't wake Angie, he'd knock on the door. He knew she'd want to get dressed before anyone showed up.

He pulled eggs and cheese and mushrooms from the fridge, then grabbed a pan and threw in a pat of butter. He was just starting to beat the eggs when Angie's door opened. He heard her go into the bathroom. The shower started.

"Fuck," he said as his brain immediately turned to thoughts of Angie standing beneath the spray, stark naked, water dripping down her body, caressing her ivory skin the way he wanted to caress it.

Thoroughly. Completely. *Everywhere.*

"Stop, dude. Your balls are gonna turn blue if you keep thinking like this," he muttered beneath his breath.

Colt forced himself to think about other things— the old lady across the street who always frowned at him. She'd flipped him off the first time he waved to her. It still cracked him up. The neighbor next door told him not to worry when he'd asked if he'd done something to piss the old woman off—park in front of her house, walk on her grass, block her driveway.

"She's always been that way," Mrs. Williamson had said. "Been angry since the day she moved in forty years ago and not likely to change. Don't you pay her any attention, sugar."

He hadn't. Though at Christmas he'd noticed nobody came to visit her, so he'd left a fluffy new bathrobe in a gift bag on her doorstep a couple of nights later. Since she always got her morning paper in a robe that had seen better days, he figured she might need a new one. He didn't leave a card.

Sure enough, she'd started retrieving her paper in the new robe. God only knew who she thought it was from. He wasn't about to tell her. He'd paid less than thirty bucks at Walmart and it wasn't about being thanked anyway. It was about making an old lady a little happier, if that was possible, for a few minutes or hours. Or, hell, maybe days. He'd never know.

Colt put the mushrooms in the pan and sautéed them, then poured in the eggs and whisked them around until they started to set. He added cheese at the last, then folded the whole thing over and slipped it onto a plate. After he polished it off, he prepared to make another for Angie whenever she came out of the bathroom.

A short while later, she emerged dressed in brown leggings with brown suede ankle boots and a loose top that clung to the curve of her breasts. Her hair was freshly blow-dried and she'd put on a little makeup.

"Good morning," she said with a sunny smile. "Do I smell coffee?"

"Sure do. Want a cup?"

"Oh yes please. I can get it though."

"Sugar's in the bowl and there's cream in the fridge. Want a mushroom and cheese omelet?"

"Is that what smells so heavenly? I'd love one, thank you."

She poured coffee, added a healthy dollop of cream, then came over to lean against the counter and watch him. He could smell her shampoo—something clean and flowery—and he liked it.

"So you cook the mushrooms first?" she asked, a puzzled frown on her face as she concentrated on what he was doing.

He remembered that she'd said she couldn't cook. "Yeah, you sauté them in butter until they're soft, then you pour in the egg and mix it around. Almost like scrambling, but not quite. Then you let it start to firm up."

"I tried to make an omelet once. I burned the pan."

He stirred and shook and flipped. Angie never left his side. He liked having her there. He imagined this is what it would be like to cook for her after they spent the night in each other's arms. He hoped that would happen soon.

"I could teach you. It's not hard."

"Oh, I don't think you quite understand my

ability to fuck up anything on the stove. I will happily chop and slice ingredients, fetch and carry from the fridge, and wash the dishes. I can even kill my own spiders, lest you think I'm useless. But you really don't want me cooking."

He glanced at her as he turned off the heat and then plated the omelet. It was fluffy and yellow. He knew from recent experience it was delicious too.

"First, I would never think you useless. And second—that bad, huh?"

"Oh yeah. That bad."

He put the plate on the table and she sat down to eat. He joined her, bringing the coffee carafe over for easy refills. Angie cut into the omelet, slipped a bite in her mouth, and closed her eyes.

"Oh, you *are* a catch, Colt. Cooks, cleans, and knows wine."

He snorted. "You don't even know the best part yet, Ang."

She blinked. "What's that?"

He arched an eyebrow. It took her a second. She nearly choked on her coffee. When she recovered, she glared at him—but it was a good-natured glare. "You nearly killed me!"

He held up both hands. "Hey, I didn't say a word."

"You didn't have to." She speared more omelet. "You implied, and I know exactly what you're talking about."

"Just say the word, and I'll demonstrate that skill for you."

She grinned at him. "I'm sure you would."

He decided to leave it there since she was smiling and not running away. They'd made a lot of progress in a short time. Hard to believe it wasn't that long ago, at New Year's, when he thought she might never be ready to give him a chance.

"So how is it you never learned to cook? Nobody ever taught you, or you were a disaster from the beginning?"

She shook her head. "I think I could have learned, but by the time I came along, my mom was older. I was a surprise on her forty-second birthday—meaning she found out she was pregnant—and neither she or my dad really knew what to do with a kid. I don't think they ever wanted any—or they'd given up. I'm not quite sure. Anyway, she was a school principal by then and she worked a lot. I feel like I was... not neglected, but just sort of ignored. I had everything I needed, don't get me wrong—but I didn't have the kind of childhood where my mom made costumes and cookies and took her turn as room mother at school. She couldn't have done it because she was in charge. My dad worked at the GAO—the government accounting office—and he was also too busy to do those things."

"I'm sorry."

She shrugged. "It is what it is. I think that's why

Maddy and I bonded. Her mother was a disaster. Mine was distracted and tired. So who taught you to cook?"

"I learned from my dad and my *grand-mère*. They were very big into food. My mother taught me some things as well, but it was mostly dad and *Mémé.*"

Angie smiled. "I love it when you say things in French. It's so pretty."

"I'll say everything in French if it makes you happy," he told her.

"That would be lovely—except I wouldn't understand a thing you say."

"Oh, I imagine I could make some things understood."

She stared at him. Then she shook her head. "There you go again, saying things you think will make me blush."

"I didn't say it to make you blush."

"Maybe not, but it did."

He reached over and skimmed his fingers over the back of her hand, up her arm. Her pupils dilated. "I like it when you blush, *mon ange.*"

"What did you call me?" she asked, her voice little more than a whisper.

"I called you *my angel.*"

"I like that. It's very sexy when you say it."

"That's what I was going for. Sexy." He winked, then sat back.

She gaped at him before returning her attention to the omelet. "You like teasing me."

"I like *you.*"

She didn't say anything. Then she lifted her gaze, and he felt a jolt at the touch of her eyes on his. When she smiled, his chest tightened. Jesus, he had it bad for this girl.

"I like you, too, Colt."

"I'm glad. I was afraid you didn't for a while."

"I know. And I'm sorry. I told you why. I still feel like it was my fault—but I'm working on it. I mean I'll probably always feel some kind of guilt over the whole thing, but it wasn't me who did those things. It was her. Natasha."

"That's right."

Colt thought of the last time he'd seen Natasha Orlova. It'd been on a mountain in Spain, and she'd had Tallie Grant with her. Not to hurt her, but to rescue her. Once she'd turned Tallie over to Brett, she'd disappeared. Colt hadn't seen her since. He wondered if Ian had. There were undercurrents between those two, but Colt didn't know what it meant. Or what Jace thought about the whole thing since Natasha was his sister. Still hard to believe that bit, actually.

Colt for sure didn't care for Natasha, aka Calypso, since she'd shot him and left him for dead—though it'd been a hell of a shot that managed to miss anything vital and give him a fighting chance. He'd never know if she'd done it on purpose or if she'd just fucked up that day. He'd prefer if he never had to see her again, but it wasn't likely in this line of work. One day, she'd turn up. Like a bad penny, as the saying went.

"I know she's still out there," Angie said. "I used to imagine her coming for me, imagine waking up and finding her standing over my bed. But Maddy said that wouldn't happen."

"It won't." And if it did, Colt would hunt her down and blow her away. "But Ang, you shouldn't talk about Natasha. Don't say her name to anyone who isn't us."

She nodded. "I know. Mads told me."

"Good."

She polished off the last bite of omelet and placed her napkin on the table. "That was delicious."

He grinned. "Glad you think so."

He loved that she wasn't embarrassed to eat. He'd been around Angie during meals several times over the past few months, and with the exception of the first few when she was still tangled up over everything that'd happened to her with Tom Walls and Calypso, she'd always had a healthy appetite.

It was refreshing. He'd gone out with more than enough women who ordered salads and then pushed the lettuce around the plate while he ate steak. There was nothing wrong with eating a salad, even eating it as your main course—but for god's sake, *eat it.*

There was a difference between being on a sensible diet and starving yourself into someone else's idea of beauty. Angie wasn't too thin, but she wasn't overly plump either. She ate what she liked and she did yoga to stay trim. He knew because Maddy talked about going to classes together.

"What happens now?" Angie asked.

"We wait for my team to arrive. Then we'll go over what we know and have a look at your spreadsheet."

There was a knock on the door. Colt went to look out the peephole. It was Jace, so he opened up.

"Hey, man. You're early."

Jace frowned. "Sorry, dude, but the boss says we gotta bring her into HQ for this one."

Colt shot into alert mode. He scanned the surroundings outside the house, looking for trouble. "Something happen?"

"Don't know. He called ten minutes ago, said to come over here and fetch you both. Said he'd explain everything and hung up."

———

ANGIE FELT the tension rolling off Colt in waves. They were in his Yukon, following behind Jace's truck as they headed toward Black Defense International's headquarters.

"Why are we going there?" she'd asked when he said there'd been a change of plans.

"I don't know, but when the boss says we go, we go. It'll be okay, Angie. I won't leave your side."

She hadn't argued with him, though she'd thought about it for a split second. He'd told her they could look at Charles's spreadsheet at his house, but now they were headed to his workplace where somebody would no doubt try to take her computer and disappear with it.

She wasn't letting that happen.

But what did it matter if they took the spreadsheet and got to work on solving the mystery of what it contained? Did she really care? Clearly, there was something wrong or Charles wouldn't have split and a man wouldn't have tried to break into her condo. The more distance she could put between herself and the Cardinal Group, the better.

Except handing it over wouldn't automatically absolve her of responsibility. The Cardinal Group— or someone there—knew she was in possession of information that didn't line up with the official figures. She didn't think they were likely to forget it.

Colt pulled into an underground parking garage. He came around and opened her door for her. She smiled at him as she stepped onto the pavement with her handbag on her arm.

"Thank you."

"You're welcome, baby."

She shivered deep inside whenever he called her baby. There was no denying it. No matter how liberated and independent she thought she was—and she was—hearing this particular man call her baby sent little shivers of delight dancing up and down her spine.

When anybody else called her baby, it infuriated her. Not Colt.

Mon ange. He'd said those words to her this morning and she'd nearly melted. French was so sexy. Or maybe it was just sexy coming from him. What would those words sound like murmured in her ear while he was inside her?

Oh my...

Jace was waiting for them at the freight elevator. They stepped on and he pressed the button to take them to the fourth floor.

Angie tried not to gawk as the doors opened, but considering she'd just ridden in a freight elevator, she'd been expecting something a little less sleek.

They emerged into a hallway that led between offices and conference rooms. There was glass everywhere—glass walls, tinted windows that still managed to spill lots of light into the space, and a glass sculpture of an eagle perched on a pedestal at the end of the hall. Everything was high end, unlike her office at what used to be Barton, Barnes and Blake.

Things there had been a little timeworn, but in a good way. The building was—*had been*—old. The furnishings had been modern, because Triple B wasn't broke or poor, but also kind of artfully shabby.

They didn't have high-tech equipment with iPads that controlled all the electronics, or televisions that flared to life behind what appeared to be mirrors. That happened when Jace led them into a conference room with a huge oval table lined with leather chairs. He picked up an iPad, tapped it, and a mirror turned into a television screen.

He didn't turn the sound on, but it was an international news station with a crawl at the bottom. There were explosions on the screen and people looking both weary and terrified as they talked to the reporter.

Angie turned at the sound of voices. Four men entered the room. She recognized two of them, but the other two were a mystery. Ian Black stopped speaking to the men and gave her a big smile. He was a handsome man, tall and dark-haired with dark eyes. Though she swore he had blue eyes the last time she met him. Maybe she was confusing him with someone else.

"Hello, Miss Turner. How are you doing today?"

"I'm all right, thanks. Just wondering why I'm here."

"Of course." Ian gestured to a chair and Angie went to sit down.

Colt pulled out the chair for her and she sank down on it, murmuring her thanks. She was glad when he sat beside her. His presence was comforting in the company of all these seriously alpha men. Nobody had to tell her that's what they were. She could feel it in the air. The strength and determination, the will to do good. The absolute unwillingness to sit back and let things happen.

These were men who acted. They did not wait to be acted upon.

"I think you know Tyler," Ian said. "This is Jared Fraser."

"Ma'am," Jared said, nodding politely.

"And this is Dax Freed."

Dax winked. "Howdy."

Howdy? Was he putting her on? She took in his faded jeans and worn cowboy boots and thought, nope, he wasn't putting her on. This man hailed from somewhere in the south. Or maybe the southwest.

Beside her, Colt shifted in his seat. "I'm going to assume you found something, or we wouldn't be here."

"Nothing definitive," Ian said. "But not the kind of thing I wanted you talking about outside of these walls."

Angie darted her gaze between Colt and Ian. Jace was frowning, which wasn't good.

"Do you have the spreadsheet, Miss Turner?" Ian asked.

"Yes."

"And yours is the only copy you know of?"

Angie nodded. "We keep everything in the cloud at work, but I made a copy of Martinelli's work because I didn't want to mess with the original. In case I needed it for proof later—proof that I wasn't the one who'd screwed everything up."

Ian nodded. "Makes sense. Is your copy in the cloud?"

"No. I emailed it to myself so I could work on it at home."

"Does anybody know you did that?"

Angie frowned. What was he getting at? "I don't see how."

"You didn't tell anyone?"

"Just Colt. And now everyone in this room."

He acknowledged the information with a smile. "You emailed someone at the Cardinal Group to tell them you were having an issue with the account. Correct?"

"Yes. I told them I needed to clarify the figures. I thought they'd send updated bank statements. I sent my queries to the company secretary. There was no need to involve anyone else at that point. This kind of thing is not all that unusual. I mean Martinelli's spreadsheet is a little suspect, sure. But things get entered wrong, statements don't line up, and it's usually some little mistake somewhere along the way. Accounting is mostly an unexciting job. It's logical. Things make sense. And when they don't make sense, you go back and look for where you went wrong. Or, in this case, where Charles went wrong. I didn't have any reason to believe there was anything criminal going on."

"Just clarifying things, Miss Turner." Ian turned to Dax Freed, who'd taken a seat across the table.

All the men were sitting. Waiting.

For what, she didn't know.

"It's all you, Freed," Ian said. "Let's see what you've got."

The television screen flickered and the presentation began.

Chapter Ten

JENNY CLARK DIDN'T HAVE THE KIDS THAT WEEK, which meant she was free when the phone rang. She knew who it was without looking. She'd given him his own ringtone.

"Jenny," he said, sounding masculine and commanding. He made her shiver with that voice. "I need you to do something for me."

Jenny gripped the phone tight and stared out the window at the building opposite. She hated this apartment she'd had to move to when Dwight successfully hid his assets—their joint assets—from the lawyers. He'd lied and cheated and what happened to him? Nothing. He moved into a great house near the waterfront, started seeing a woman ten years younger, and had the kids every other week.

Meanwhile, she'd had to downsize so she could afford to take care of their kids properly. He paid child support, but he'd gotten that argued down too since they shared custody. She hated him. Funny how you could love someone so much at one time and then hate them at another.

"What do you need?" she asked.

She tried not to let disappointment color her voice. Hadn't she done enough already? She'd risked a lot for the man on the other end of the line. She'd let him into the building after hours so they didn't have to meet at a hotel. And then she'd erased files for him. Or she'd logged in and let him do it while they slugged back bourbon and laughed.

All those Cardinal Group files. Bank statements, credit card statements, spreadsheets. It had felt wicked and empowering at the same time.

She shouldn't have let it happen, but he'd *paid* her when it was over. Ten thousand dollars in cash delivered to her apartment by courier this morning. The day after the fire. Jenny tried not to let it bother her, but it somehow did. She knew she wasn't responsible for the fire, and yet it must have started soon after they'd left the building.

Still, she needed the money. If she got enough, she could go back to court. Fight for majority custody. Her kids should *not* be raised by Dwight and his bimbo.

He'd said the money was for her, because she needed it. Not because she'd been drunk and logged into the server for him. Not because she'd set fire to the building, because she definitely had *not*. But what if they'd left the space heater on? Was that possible?

There was another cloud in her sky. Angie Turner knew something about the Cardinal Group's files. She'd been working on them. Jenny hadn't known when she'd let him delete them. It didn't really matter who had been working on them—but why had Angie asked *her* specifically if she knew about wonky accounting?

Jenny shivered. She would have to tell him about it. She started to clear her throat, but he spoke.

"I need you to meet me later," he said. "I want to see you."

A current of pleasure slipped into her veins, soothing her. He didn't only want her to do things for him. He wanted *her*. They hadn't had sex since the night he'd deleted the files. Before that, he'd bent her over the desk and—

She shuddered with the memory of it. The raw way he'd taken her, pounding into her from behind. Pinching her nipples and telling her she felt so fucking good.

"I want to see you too. I need you." She could tell him about Angie's question later. After they'd made love.

He chuckled. "I can't wait to fuck your hot little pussy tonight."

Jenny's throat tightened. *God.* "What time?"

"Meet me at nine. You know the place."

He'd found a new place for them. Not a hotel, of course. He didn't like hotels. "Yes. Okay. See you then."

"Don't wear any panties, Jenny."

"I won't. Promise."

He laughed. Then he hung up.

———

THE PRESENTATION WAS TYPICAL DAX. Thorough, organized, and to the point. It was also sanitized for Angie's viewing. Meaning there was nothing too sensitive contained in it.

Colt didn't like what Dax was showing them. He made a mental note to ask for the extended version later.

Charles Martinelli had bought a plane ticket to Brazil. He had not boarded the flight. There was no record of him checking in, nor did he appear on any airport cameras. He'd simply disappeared.

Beside Colt, Angie swallowed. He knew she was wondering if her ex-coworker was dead.

"Dax," he interrupted.

Dax turned. "Yeah?"

"Do we have a body?"

Dax shot a look at Angie. "No. We have no evidence that he's dead."

The tension in Angie's body seemed to relax a little. Colt wanted to reach for her hand. He refrained. He knew she hadn't been a big fan of Charles Martinelli, but that was a long way from wanting him dead.

Dax continued. "We've analyzed his desktop computer. He deleted his browser history recently, and he used a VPN to mask his IP address. Except for the last time he was on. He must have been in a hurry. He logged onto the Barton, Barnes and Blake server and transferred a file from his computer onto the server."

"Quite possibly that spreadsheet you have," Ian said to Angie. He nodded and Dax continued.

"He also had some saved tabs—porn sites, sports cars, shopping sites. Stuff like that. He had two bank accounts. One that his paycheck went into, and another savings account. He made small transfers from the savings account to another account. That one is much larger, and it's offshore. There's at least two million dollars in that account—and Charles Martinelli is the owner of it."

Angie's jaw dropped. "Wait—are you saying that Charles was taking kickbacks? Or stealing from clients?"

Ian spoke. "We don't know, but either of those options are possible."

"And he transferred the spreadsheet to the BB&B server from his desktop? When?"

"The night before he didn't show for work. I think it was a few days later you were all told he'd quit?"

"Yes," Angie said. "But if he was stealing, and that

spreadsheet is evidence, why would he put it *on* the office server where any of us could access it?"

"Because he was afraid," Ian said. "We don't know for certain that's what he transferred, but we're working on tracing it."

Angie frowned. Colt could almost see the wheels turning in her head. "You said he had an offshore account. Where?"

"The Cayman Islands," Dax replied after a glance at Ian, who nodded. "The deposits to that account came from another account that seems to be located in the Cayman Islands—but not the same bank. We haven't traced that one back to a source yet."

"The Cayman Islands," Angie said, half to herself. She reached into her handbag and pulled her laptop out. "I think I might have something."

She flipped open the lid and powered up the computer while they waited.

"Here," she said, turning the computer toward Ian and Dax. "This number right here. I copied it from the spreadsheet. It could be an account and routing number. And maybe a pin too."

They were looking at it with interest. Ian gave her an approving nod. "I think you might be right about that being an account number. Dax, copy it down. Let's try to sort it out and see what we come up with. Can I see the spreadsheet?" he asked Angie.

"Yes."

He took her computer and looked at the screen.

"If we can have this, we can compare it to the Cardinal Group's official bank statements, and any other records we can dig up."

"I don't have their statements anymore," Angie said. "They were erased from our server and the company closed their account with us."

Ian grinned. "That's okay. I can get them."

"Is that legal?" she asked.

Ian shrugged. "Depends on who you ask."

Angie shook her head and shot Colt a look. "I don't want to know. And yes, you can have it."

"Great," Ian replied. He tapped a few keys and Colt knew he was logging onto the wifi and airdropping the spreadsheet to Dax. Once that was done and he'd scrubbed the network from her computer, Ian pushed it back to her. He slapped his palms lightly on the table.

"All right, kids. That's it for the moment. We have a lot more to do, so let's get cracking."

Angie's gaze darted around the room as the men pushed their chairs back and stood. Colt could tell she was confused about why they'd had to appear for a briefing when it was short and mostly about Charles Martinelli.

He knew exactly why.

Ian had wanted Martinelli's spreadsheet quicker than it would have taken to dig up the deleted file, and he'd known he could get her to give it to him if he presented her with enough information. He might have had Dax put more into the briefing, but once they had the potential account number and the spreadsheet, they didn't need to show Angie anything else.

Colt didn't know whether to be amazed or annoyed. He hadn't wanted Angie involved in the first place, but when she'd stated that she wanted to participate in the analysis, he understood why. She'd found the anomaly and she deserved to know the solution. Unless the solution could get her killed, in which case he didn't care if she ever knew.

"Thank you for coming in today, Miss Turner. We really appreciate your help."

Angie's mouth was set in a suspicious frown. "You left a lot out. And now you intend to proceed without me."

Ian didn't do her the disservice of lying about it. "This is potentially dangerous information. Do you really want to know more than you already do?"

Angie's chin came up. Her eyes flashed. "In fact, yes. I damn well do." She flung a hand out, encompassed the room. The whole building, probably. "I know you've got more going on here than just a nice little protective services firm, and I know you think you're doing me a favor. But somebody tried to break into my condo, somebody burned down the office building where I work, and somebody erased files in the middle of the night when they shouldn't have had access. I think I'm already in possession of dangerous information, don't you?"

She stood toe to toe with Ian, and Colt felt a swell of pride in his chest. She was magnificently fiery and beautiful. He wanted to kiss her. Wanted to slip his tongue into her mouth and taste her anger before sliding her clothing from her body and turning that fire into passion.

Ian studied her for a long moment. Colt felt a growl start to form deep in his gut. *Hands off*, he wanted to say. *She's mine.*

But Ian never touched her, and he never let his study of her cross the line into male appreciation of female beauty. No, he sized her up like he was sizing up her potential.

"You don't want to go home and forget all about this? Get your life back to normal?"

Her color was high. "Of course I do—but I'm realistic enough to know that isn't going to happen because you say so. You don't know who tried to break into my house—or you aren't saying—but I doubt you intend to let me walk out of here and return home. I have to stay with Colt, right?"

Ian laughed suddenly. "It would be best, yes. Okay, Miss Turner, I'll make a deal with you. You stay with Colt for now, let him protect you. There are some things I can't tell you because it's sensitive information and you aren't cleared. But if those numbers lead to an account in the Cayman Islands, I will tell you that. I will tell you everything I can that isn't sensitive information."

"Which means you can decide it all is and tell me nothing."

Ian looked at Colt. Colt didn't say a word. "I like her," he said. "I think we could use her around here."

"I'm here right now," Angie growled. "And I'll make my own decisions, thanks."

"Redheads," Ian said, oblivious to the danger. Or maybe he wanted to provoke her. Colt wasn't sure.

Angie drew herself up like a queen. "If you want to offer me a job, we can discuss it. But you'd better discuss it with me, not Colt or Jace or—or the Easter Bunny." Angie turned on her heel and headed for the door, flicking her fingers behind her like she was shaking off dust. "I'm done here."

Jace, Tyler, Dax, Jared, and Colt watched her go with variously dropped jaws. Ian didn't seem surprised at all. Colt looked at the others. They looked at him. Jace started to laugh, but he knew Angie better than they did.

Colt was beginning to know her.

What he knew, he damn sure admired. Had he really thought she wasn't strong enough? Where the fuck had he gotten that idea?

"Whoa damn, Colt, I wouldn't want to be in the car with you on the way home," Jace said.

Colt shook his head. "Dude, I wouldn't be so

smug. You know she's gonna call Maddy. Your ass is in a sling as much as mine is."

Jace's laughter died. "Well, shit."

Ian had his fists on his hips. "I could order her not to talk about it. But I somehow think that wouldn't work."

"Only if you want to die a fiery death," Dax said. "I, for one, would rather live to tell the tale."

————

ANGIE FUMED. She'd stormed out of the conference room with those smug as hell men staring at her, but her grand exit was marred when Colt chased after her and told her he had to go to the fifth floor. She would have to wait for him.

A lovely black woman with long wavy hair and a beautifully tailored suit seemed to appear out of nowhere. She introduced herself as Melanie and then showed Angie to a waiting area with a Keurig, an espresso machine, and a fridge with water, sodas, and snacks.

Angie took out her phone to look at email. She had no signal so she stuffed it in her bag again. She picked up a magazine and flipped through the pages angrily.

It was half an hour before Colt reappeared. She took a moment to appreciate how gorgeous he was as he stalked down the hall toward her, but she reminded herself she was more than a little annoyed at every male who'd been inside that room.

"You ready to go?" he asked when he reached her.

She scowled. "What do you think?"

He stood back while she got to her feet. She marched beside him through the building and back to the freight elevator. It wasn't until they'd emerged from the parking garage into the rain—oh great, it had started raining now—that Colt said something.

"I'm sorry about that, Ang."

She folded her arms over her chest and looked out the window. "I'm not an idiot, Colt," she finally said.

"I know you aren't. Ian knows it too."

She turned to look at him. "I know you think I'm fragile. I know you think I'm one freakout away from a nervous breakdown. But I'm not. I don't ever want to be abducted and threatened again, but I don't spend all my waking hours worrying about it. And Tom Walls? Yes, I was shocked. I didn't feel safe and I didn't feel normal for a while, but if it happened today? Right now? I'd kick that motherfucker in the balls. And if I couldn't kick him? If he overpowered me and ground his body against me now, I'd spit on him. I'd scream bloody murder and I'd threaten to sue. I won't *ever* take that shit lying down again."

She'd had a lot of time to think in the past few months. Yes, she'd been stunned by everything that'd happened in so short a time. She'd needed to process it.

She'd been scared for a long time afterward. Afraid to live. But then she got mad. She wasn't sure precisely when that was, but she was madder than hell now. And nobody was going to live in her head for free anymore. Colt had clarified that particular bit of wisdom when he'd said to think of her life like a bank account. She was done making withdrawals on behalf of other people.

"Holy shit, Ang," Colt said softly. "Where did that come from?"

She sucked in a breath and squeezed herself tighter. "I'm not entirely sure, but it's about time, right? I'm done letting people walk all over me. For any reason."

"I'm proud of you, baby."

She should be furious with him too. She wasn't. And there went that little thrill of pleasure rushing through her when he called her baby. "I didn't do it to make you proud."

"I know. I'm proud anyway. The way you stood up to Ian? That was epic. I don't think he gets that very often."

"He's a jerk."

"He can be. But he has a lot on his shoulders, more than you know, and it takes a toll. He forgets how to be human sometimes."

"I know he did a lot for Jace and Maddy. I don't hate him. In fact, that alone makes me like him more than he deserves." She pulled in a breath. "Did you find out anything else?"

"Not really. We don't know who tried to break into your place. He kept his face covered in front of the building's cameras so they didn't get anything distinguishable. Average height and build, dressed in black. Nothing usable."

"Was that number an account number in the Caymans?"

"Still working on it. Dax Freed is one of the best computer guys I know. He'll figure it out."

Angie leaned her heated forehead against the cool window. "I spent days trying to find the error. There is no error. The spreadsheet Charles had is for a secret account, not the official account. That's why they don't match."

"That's what we think, too."

"He transferred it onto the BB&B server the night before he supposedly quit. That's terrifying. He must have thought he was in danger to do that. But where is he now? Or did they really get to him and you just don't know it yet?"

"It's possible. There are a lot of ways to dispose of a body when you don't want it found."

She was cold inside. And hot on the outside. What the hell? "I saw the evidence of his—or someone's—criminal activity. I wish I never had. I want them caught. Whoever they are. And Charles—I don't wish him dead, but where in the hell did he get two mil? He wasn't some kind of crazy frugal guy who'd been saving his whole life and then died in an apartment with sixty cats. He was in his thirties, and he didn't scrimp on the good stuff. He drove a Porsche GT3. Not a brand new one, but still. His suits were Brooks Brothers, and he wore a Rolex. He bought custom Italian loafers and bragged about how marvelous they were. Ugh."

Colt pulled up to a red light and stopped, his hand draping over the wheel as he turned to look at her. "I know, Ang. That's why I do this job. I don't want the bad guys to get away with anything. I want to stop them before they do any harm. I don't know if Charles is alive or not—but I intend to find out."

She thought of something else then. "Was Ian serious when he said you could use me at BDI? Or was he just taking a jab at me?"

Colt smiled. "Ian makes a lot of jokes, but you always know they're jokes. He never kids about anything serious. He wasn't kidding about you."

"I'm an accountant, not a spy—or whatever you guys are calling yourselves today."

He arched an eyebrow. "You're a mathematician. You analyze data. You look for patterns and you do statistical analysis. You're exactly the kind of employee BDI can use. Not everyone carries a gun and fights in the field. We have plenty of people who man the desks and make sure we have the information we need to do the job. You could be one of those people."

"When you say it like that, it sounds intriguing. Though I have to admit, being an accountant is turning out to be much crazier than I'd have ever thought. My dad was an accountant for forty years— pretty sure he never had bad guys after him."

Working at BDI, analyzing data, and knowing the danger that Colt and Jace and the others endured wouldn't be easy. And then there was Maddy. What if Angie learned something that could affect Jace and had to keep it from her? That would be awful. And then if something happened to him? She would never forgive herself if she'd known something she couldn't share with Maddy.

"Think about it," Colt said. When she didn't reply, he reached over and gave her hand a squeeze. "It's data analysis, Ang. You don't have to worry about making decisions that affect the field operatives. You'd work with a team and your conclusions would be thoroughly discussed before any actions were taken."

"How did you know that's what I was thinking?"

He smiled. Her heart flipped. "Because I know you."

She was beginning to believe he did.

It was a thrilling thought.

Chapter Eleven

COLT DROVE BACK TO HIS PLACE AND PARKED IN THE driveway. He powered up the garage door and they dashed for the opening as the rain pounded down on their heads. Angie shivered, her teeth chattering as he slid the key into the lock and opened the door.

"I need to check the house," he told her. "Wait here."

She nodded. He didn't expect to find anyone inside since the alarm hadn't been tripped, but in his line of work he'd learned never to underestimate a determined foe. No one had tried to break into her condo again, but that didn't mean they'd given up. If they'd somehow traced her here, they could be waiting.

Clearing the house took no time at all, and then he was back to the kitchen. Angie stood in the garage, still chattering.

"It's safe," he told her.

She stepped into the kitchen and he locked the door behind her. He pulled her into his arms and held her, transferring some of his warmth to her chilled body. It was a measure of how far they'd come that she slipped her arms around him and held on while he rubbed her back.

"You're cold, *minette.*"

She tilted her head back, smiling up at him with a question in her gaze. *"Minette?* What's that?"

"It means kitten."

"And why am I a kitten now?"

She didn't seem upset about it, but she arched an eyebrow.

"Because your claws came out today, Ang. You look beautiful and sweet—and you're definitely both of those things—but you're also fierce and willing to fight back."

"You thought I was delicate, didn't you?"

He nodded. No sense lying. "Can you blame me? You avoided me for months. According to your best friend you haven't entirely been yourself. I don't think anyone could be blamed for thinking you were in a delicate state of mind after everything that happened last year."

"I know. I guess I was feeling delicate."

"But not anymore."

"No, not anymore. Like I told you in the car—I'm done with letting people get the best of me. Not that

I'm thrilled about everything I just learned about Charles and his spreadsheet and hidden accounts, but I'm not going to freak out about it either."

She tugged her lip between her teeth and an arrow of lust shot straight to his groin.

"I know Ian told you more," she added.

"Yes, but none of it relates to the immediate problem just yet."

He could feel her stiffening slightly in his embrace. "Which means you aren't going to tell me."

"That's right, but you already know that. I'm sorry if it upsets you, but trust me when I tell you there are good reasons for it."

She didn't need to know more than she already did about the Cardinal Group, or about the fact someone had used the Barton, Barnes and Blake alarm code—there was only one for the entire office —on the night of the fire. The code had been used to enter the building twice that night. Someone had come in at 10:13 and left again at 11:53. Someone returned at 1:00 a.m. They'd punched in, but not out. And the fire alarm had triggered within half an hour of that entry.

Which meant whoever started the fire had the alarm code. An employee? Or someone who'd gotten the code by other means?

There was no doubt the fire had been started on purpose. Though Colt had told Angie BDI didn't do fire investigation, they had explosives experts. Ian had gotten permission for his people to liaise with the fire investigators as they searched the premises—and they'd found evidence of an accelerant in what was left of Charles Martinelli's office.

What they didn't know was why. Why had someone taken the risk of burning down the building? The files were already deleted by that time. They'd been removed during the first visit that evening. Dax didn't know whose login had been used to do it yet, but he'd find out.

The second visit seemed to have been for the purpose of setting a fire. Could have been two different people who'd entered, and with differing purposes. But it sure didn't make a lot of sense just yet.

"Okay," Angie finally said, surprising him. "I'm trusting you, Colt. I know Jace can't tell Maddy everything, so I'm going to believe you when you say you can't tell me more. But when you can, I want to know."

"You have my word, *minette.*"

"I assume I have to stay with you for the time being?"

"That's the plan." And he was glad of it. He didn't want her in her condo right now. Not only because something was going on and she might be in danger, but also because he liked having her here. He liked this moment right now, when she stood in his embrace and didn't shrink from him.

"So long as you cook for me, I think I can deal."

"I will cook for you. Whatever you want."

"Whatever I want?"

He loved the saucy expression on her face. "If I can, I will."

"Can you do *coq au vin*?"

He snorted. "What do you think?"

"I think that's a yes. To be clear, I've only had it once. But it was really good and I'd like to try it again."

"I'll fix it for you. I need to do some shopping. Probably not today though."

"That's okay. Soon?"

"Tomorrow. Is that soon enough?"

"Sure. What's for lunch today? I'm starved."

He loved that she had an appetite. "We can order something and have it delivered. Suggestions?"

"Indian?"

"Sounds good. You warm enough now?"

"I think so. It was the rain, and maybe some left-over adrenaline from the meeting."

Reluctantly, he let her go. He pulled up the menu from his favorite Indian restaurant. They looked it over and he placed an order. Angie disappeared into the bedroom. When she returned, she was wearing a sweatshirt and she'd taken her boots off and put on fuzzy socks that were as thick as boots. She grinned at him as she sat cross-legged on his couch and opened her laptop.

Colt thought he could spend every day for the rest of his life like this. Angie in his house, wearing her comfy clothes and working on her computer. The only thing that would make it more perfect was if he had the right to touch her. He'd kiss her, strip her naked, and carry her to his room where he'd make love to her for the rest of the afternoon.

He shook his head. What the hell was wrong with him? Yeah, he wanted her. More than he remembered wanting anyone. But there was more to it than that. He wanted to talk to her. Joke with her. Share things with her that he'd never shared with anyone.

It was crazy shit, to feel this way. Hanging around Jace and Brett had made him soft. He saw what they were like with their women and a part of him wanted it too. But why Angie? She'd never given him a reason to think she could feel the same way.

Until recently, she'd barely spoken to him. She'd always fled whenever he'd arrived in the vicinity. It was only this week they'd spent time alone together without her trying to run.

He liked it. He hoped it lasted.

Their food arrived about forty-five minutes later. Angie tucked her laptop into her handbag. They sat at the kitchen table, eating chicken tikka masala, saag paneer and naan, and laughing about nothing important.

YouTube videos. Movies. Television shows. Books.

It was comfortable. Fun.

They finished eating. They sat at the table a while longer, talking, when Angie's face turned red and she sat back in her chair.

"Wow. I feel a little hot."

"Might be the spice," he replied, though it'd be a little odd for it to kick in after they'd eaten and not during.

"Could be."

She drank deeply from her water glass and gave him a smile. They talked a while longer and then she pushed her hair from her face. She looked weary. Run down.

"You know, I didn't sleep all that well last night. I think I might lie down for a bit."

"Go ahead. I'll be here if you need anything."

Her smile was wan. "You're a good guy, Colt. I really appreciate it."

She pushed her chair back and stood. She wobbled, and Colt shot up to steady her. She smiled again.

"Sorry. Just tired. I haven't been sleeping well since this started, so I guess it's more than last night catching up with me."

He watched her make her way to the bedroom. The door opened and shut. Everything was silent. He started to clean up the dishes and put away any leftovers.

It wasn't until nearly two hours had gone by and

Angie still hadn't emerged that he went to check on her. He tapped the door lightly.

She didn't respond so he tapped harder. Still nothing.

He opened the door and peered in. She was huddled under the blankets, her body curled into a ball. He started to close the door and leave her, but on impulse he went over and laid a hand on her cheek.

Angie was burning up with fever.

———

"IT'S NOT THE FLU," someone said. "Probably a twenty-four hour bug."

Angie dragged her eyes open to peer up at the men. Colt and... Jared? She thought that was his name. She'd met him earlier today at BDI, and then again a little while ago when he'd swabbed her throat.

She hadn't enjoyed it, but she'd felt so miserable that she'd agreed if it would help her pounding head.

"What do we need to do?" Colt asked.

"I'll give her some IV fluids to help with dehydration. There'll be some anti-nausea meds, some vitamins, and an antacid to help with stomach acid. Tylenol for fever. It'll help, but she's still going to feel like hell for at least twenty-four hours. You'll need to be careful if you're staying with her."

"I am," Colt said.

"Wait," Angie said, though speaking made her feel like she might throw up.

The two men looked down at her.

"Are you a doctor?"

"No," Jared said. "I'm an EMT."

Colt made a noise. "He's being modest, *minette*. Jared was an Air Force para-rescueman. He's an EMT, but the best of the best. PJs are the guys the Navy SEALs call when *they* need rescued."

"Okay," she said. Because what else could she say? If Jared was an EMT and he said she had a virus, and he was going to give her IV meds, then whatever. She'd let Maddy's cat give her an IV if it'd help this nausea go away.

Jared left the room and Colt bent down to stroke her hair. "I'm sorry, baby," he whispered. "It sucks to be sick."

"I feel terrible," she moaned. She wanted to cry. "Everything hurts."

"I know, *mon ange*. Look, I'm going to pick you up, okay? I'm putting you in my bed. It's bigger and more comfortable—and the bathroom is right there if you need it."

"No, don't give up your bed."

"It's fine, Ang. I'd rather you have it." He scooped her into his arms and she clung to him, trying not to sob or throw up as he carried her into the bedroom next door. It was slightly bigger than the one she'd had, but the bed was a lot bigger. It was a king and he pulled the covers back and placed her on it.

She was wearing her leggings and the sweatshirt and thick socks she'd put on earlier, but she was still cold. He tugged the covers up and she gripped them in her fists. Her stomach heaved.

"I think—" she said. Then she threw the covers off and tried to dash for the bathroom. She didn't quite make it.

Colt was there, gently holding her and pushing her hair out of the way while she puked on his bedroom floor.

"Oh god," she groaned when it was over. "I'm so sorry."

"It's okay, *minette*. It's okay. I've got you."

Embarrassment would have eaten her alive if she'd had room for anything else. But she didn't. She ached, her stomach hurt, her head hurt, and she was so cold she wanted to climb under the covers again and not come out.

Colt cleaned her up, got her back to bed, gave her some water—she nearly gagged on it going down—and then Jared returned with the IV. He sat beside her on the bed and went to work finding a vein and inserting the needle. Angie turned her head so she didn't have to see. She hated needles.

She heard Colt leave the room and return. She couldn't see him but she knew he was cleaning up the mess she'd made. Later, she would care. A lot. She'd be mortified and she'd think there was no way he'd find her sexy anymore. The days of him wanting to kiss her were over, that's for sure.

Except none of that mattered at the moment. All that mattered was feeling better.

"There you go," Jared said soothingly. "We'll get this into you and things will improve soon."

Colt was at her side again, taking Jared's place and putting a cool cloth on her forehead. She'd thought she was too cold for that, but the coolness of the cloth felt good on her heated skin. So long as she could stay beneath the covers, it was nice.

"I'm sorry, Colt," she said, choking back tears of frustration and pain.

"Nothing to apologize for, baby."

"I never get sick."

"You've picked up a stomach bug," Jared said. "The worst will be over in about twenty-four hours. Best thing you can do is rest and hydrate."

"Thanks, Jared," Colt said. "I appreciate you coming over."

"She's one of us, man. Least I can do."

One of them? She didn't know what that meant, but she liked the way it sounded.

"You gonna be okay if I show Jared out?" Colt asked.

"I just want to sleep."

"Okay, baby. You do that. I'll be here if you need

me." He stroked her cheek and then he got up to go with Jared.

Angie never heard him return.

———

ANGIE SLEPT FOR HOURS. When she woke, Colt was there to give her water before she felt asleep again. He'd removed the IV and disposed of it after it finished dripping medicine into her.

Colt texted Jace, who told Maddy—who blew up Colt's phone with worried questions and advice. Colt stepped out of the room to call her, reassured her that he would give Angie the platinum treatment, and agreed to a delivery of homemade chicken soup tomorrow. He could have made it himself, but it would keep Maddy busy. She'd also feel like she was doing something important for her best friend.

Oh, and he endured a chewing out for what happened at BDI earlier. Because of course Angie told Maddy at some point.

Maddy finished with "BDI would be lucky to have her."

Colt couldn't hide his surprise. "You want her to work with us?"

"I want her to do whatever makes her happy. I don't think doing taxes is it. Anyway, take care of her, Colt. She's used to doing everything herself and she won't admit she needs help. I'll bring soup tomorrow."

"Thanks, Maddy. I'll take care of her, don't worry. She's not going to want for anything while I'm around."

Colt had thought about bedding down in the pink room for the night, but when he went to check on Angie, the way she shivered beneath the covers meant he was going to slip in beside her and hold her. She didn't wake when he climbed into bed—fully clothed in a T-shirt and workout shorts—or when he slid his arms around her and gathered her close.

She burrowed into him, sighing, and didn't bat an eyelash. He ended up flipping the covers off his body, except where she snuggled against him, and powered up the television so he could watch something on low while she slept.

He needn't have worried the noise would wake her. She opened her eyes once, looked up at him feverishly, mumbled something that sounded like "You won't want me now," and closed them again.

He stroked her hair, feeling protective and tender, and wished she felt better. She could have picked up a stomach bug anywhere. It had probably been dormant in her body for the past three or four days. According to Jared, the rapidity with which it hit her was common. One minute feeling fine, the next feeling sicker than crap.

Eventually, he fell asleep with Angie in his arms. It

wasn't a restful sleep since he was very aware of her beside him, and because she flailed in her feverish state. He'd been a special operator in the military and he'd learned to sleep in short snatches whenever necessary. He'd also learned to come awake instantly at the slightest disturbance.

It was that or die because you never knew when a tango was about to descend on you and kill your entire squad with a well-timed explosive device. Waking up quickly was a necessary skill in those days. Still was.

Sometimes, even that couldn't save your squad. Sometimes they all died anyway, and you didn't because somehow you were luckier that day than they were.

As Angie jerked and twitched in her sleep, Colt woke again and again. But he also dropped back into slumber pretty quickly too. His dreams were restless, but they didn't descend into nightmare territory. He didn't relive that day when everyone else died, thank God. He didn't dream of it too often anymore, but it still had the power to turn him into a shaking mess when he did.

It was sometime early that morning, before first light but not too long before, that he woke to Angie saying something. It took him a moment to realize she was talking in her sleep.

"Miss having man b'side me." He thought this must be what she sounded like drunk. Slightly slurred, words running together. "Long time, no ses."

No sex?

"Miss it."

Her hand roamed over him and he tensed. If she reached for his crotch, he wouldn't be able to stop an erection. Simple biology. But she didn't. She slid her hand over his abdomen, up his chest.

Then she flipped herself over and burrowed into the pillow, her sweet little ass right up against his hip. He resisted the temptation to shape that curve with his palm. Not without her permission. That's not the kind of guy he was.

Colt stayed on his back. God forbid he turned toward her and she wriggled her butt into his groin. The hard-on would be epic. He put a hand behind his head, tried like hell to sleep again. Angie moaned in her sleep from time to time, but it wasn't a sexy moan. She was hurting and he hated that for her.

Finally, he dropped off again. This time when he woke, light was streaming between the crack in the black-out curtains he'd put on the windows. Angie was facing him again, her body huddled up against him, her cheek on his chest. He carefully pressed his hand to her forehead. She was still hot, but not as hot as she'd been last night.

He eased himself from the bed, went to take a leak, then headed into the kitchen to fix coffee. When he'd downed a cup and poured another, he went back to the bedroom to check on Angie. It was time for some meds and he needed to make sure she got them before he let her keep sleeping.

"Ang," he said softly as he sat beside her and put a hand on her cheek. *"Minette."*

Her eyelids drifted up, her green eyes red and watery as she peered at him. "Colt?"

"Yes, baby. You need to take some medicine. Can you do that?"

She groaned. Then she pushed herself onto an elbow. He handed her the Tylenol and held a glass of water for her while she sipped. When she finished, she flopped back down again.

"I'm sorry I puked on your floor." She looked miserable.

"I told you it's no big deal." If she knew the kinds of things he'd had to deal with as a Marine and then a mercenary, she wouldn't be apologizing. Puke was nothing in the grand scheme of things.

"You're sweet."

"If you think so. I'm telling you the truth. Are you hungry?"

She shook her head back and forth on the pillow. "No. I couldn't eat a thing."

"You'll have to eat something later. Maddy's fixing chicken soup. You can sip the broth. It'll be good for you."

"I'll try." She pulled the covers up and rolled to her side. A few moments later, she was asleep again.

Colt showered and dressed and returned to the kitchen to fix something for breakfast when his phone rang.

"What's up? Don't tell me Maddy's already made the soup and wants to bring it over."

Jace didn't laugh. Always a bad sign. "She's working on it. That's not what I'm calling about."

"Did someone break into Angie's place?" Because if they had, then BDI would have footage of it. And audio. Might help find whoever was after her.

"Not that. Somebody found a body in a car this morning."

"Shit. Martinelli?"

"No. Another accountant who worked at Barton, Barnes and Blake. Jennifer Clark."

Chapter Twelve

ANGIE FELT LIKE HELL. SHE DIDN'T REMEMBER THE last time she'd had the stomach flu. And no wonder because she must have blocked the memory. She huddled beneath the covers in Colt's bed, feeling badly that she'd taken his bed but also perversely glad she was here with him. She'd hate to be dealing with this at home alone.

She wasn't certain, but she felt like he must have slept beside her last night. She recalled snuggling against a solid shape that had all the warmth she wanted for herself. It was possible she'd imagined the whole thing.

She drifted in and out of sleep, waking and bolting for the bathroom a few times. Colt brought her medicine and juice and plain toast. Eventually, her head stopped hurting and her fever broke. She stopped feeling like she was going to puke every time she moved.

More than anything, she wanted a shower. She sat up and pushed the covers back. Her things were in the other bathroom, and her clothes were in the guest room. She stumbled toward the door. It wasn't closed all the way and she pulled it open. Colt was coming down the hall. He stopped when he saw her.

For the first time since this had started, she worried about how awful she must look. She remembered that she'd puked on his floor and he'd cleaned it up. He must have since she hadn't. Mortification rolled through her. She gripped the door tightly and met his gaze.

"Hey, baby. How you feeling?" he asked in a soft voice.

"Not great, but better enough to want a shower. My things are in the other bathroom."

"You feel good enough to stand up that long?"

"I think so. But I can sit in the tub if I have to. I just need to get some clothes first."

"Tell me what you need. I'll get it."

She thought of him handling her underwear and felt a pinprick of embarrassment. But what was the big deal? He'd held her while she threw up all over his floor. What was underwear after that?

"I need panties and a bra. Socks. I have some black yoga pants, and a sweatshirt that says *Best Cat*

Auntie on it. Maddy gave it to me as a joke. I watch her cat when she's traveling."

"I didn't say anything."

"You were thinking it."

He grinned. "Possibly. But Kitty loves me too, remember? I've watched her for Maddy a few times."

"Then you'll be getting your own shirt one of these days." It was amusing to imagine him wearing a *Best Cat Uncle* shirt. And if she was capable of amusement, maybe she wasn't going to die.

"Hit the shower, Ang. I'll get your clothes. Leave the door unlocked and I'll set them on the toilet." Before she could say anything, he said, "I'll knock first, don't worry. If you aren't in the shower, I'll wait."

She trusted him. She went into the bathroom and turned on the shower before peeling out of her clothes. When she was standing under the spray, warm water running over her aching body, she heard a light knock. "I'm in the shower."

The hinges squeaked. "Setting everything on the toilet. I'll throw your other stuff into the wash."

It felt nice to be taken care of for a change. She'd lived alone for so long that she'd forgotten what it was like.

"Thank you, Colt."

"No problem. When you're done, Maddy brought the soup over. I can bring you some in bed."

She started to protest and say she'd go to the

kitchen, but the thought was exhausting. "That would be lovely."

The door closed again and Angie put her hand against the wall to brace herself. She felt a sob forming in her throat. He cared about her, and she'd spent months acting like a bitch to him. Hot and cold, ignoring him, pretending he didn't exist. But she knew why she'd done those things.

He scared her. He was big and beautiful and full of life, though she'd seen him when he wasn't. She'd seen him in that hospital bed, fighting to recover, and she'd felt so helpless. Something about him had gotten to her, even then, and it'd scared her so much.

She'd watched her best friend fall in love and she'd envied that. Wanted the same thing for herself. She thought she'd had it once, but she definitely hadn't. If she'd been wrong once before, what said she wouldn't be again?

Of all the men in the world, why did she have to want a tall, blond, muscled mercenary who was half French, cooked like a chef, knew wine, spoke several languages, and always lived with a shadow of danger in his eyes?

That was the thing that tripped her up most of all. The danger. He embraced it like it was a natural part of life. Jace did too. How Maddy accepted that, Angie didn't know.

Then again, maybe she had no choice. Angie was beginning to think she didn't either. Colt Duchaine was the one who made her want to risk her heart one more time. It was insane.

Or she was.

Angie scrubbed her hair and body as hot tears fell from her eyes. She rinsed herself off, shut off the shower, shivered as she grabbed a towel and dried off. It was all she could do to dry and dress, but when she was finally in her clothes with her damp hair hanging down her back—she thought about using the hair dryer but the effort was too much—she returned to the bedroom.

There was a pile of sheets on the floor and Colt was changing a pillowcase.

Angie blinked. "You changed the sheets?"

"I thought you might like fresh ones."

Oh god, he was too much. Dan had never changed the sheets. Not once. He'd also never slept beside her while she was sick, or took care of her the way Colt had. The lump in her throat grew again. "That's so sweet of you. You aren't feeling bad are you? I'd hate it if I made you sick."

"I'm fine." He flipped the covers back. "Here, get in. I'll bring soup and crackers. How about a ginger ale?"

"Please."

She leaned back against the headboard and Colt tucked the covers around her. She watched him scoop up the sheets and disappear. He was calm and competent. He didn't bitch about having to do all the work while she lay in bed. She'd heard nothing but complaining out of Dan the one time she'd had bronchitis. He'd been such a dick about it after the first day that she'd dragged herself out of bed and microwaved her own food from that moment on.

Whenever he had a minor cold, however, he'd moaned and groaned like he was dying. She'd had to do everything. She should have realized much quicker than she had what a self-absorbed asshat he was. But he'd had one of those personalities that dazzled, and she'd stayed dazzled far longer than she should have.

Colt was back in a few minutes with a tray containing hot soup, crackers, and a can of ginger ale in a drink koozie. The tray had legs and he set it over her lap.

"You doing okay, Ang?"

She sniffed, her emotions flying high and threatening to spill over. "Better, thanks. Just tired. And a little hungry." She picked up the spoon and sipped some broth. The soup warmed her from the inside as she ate. "Oh, that's good. Mads can cook like a house on fire. I sure don't know where I picked up this bug, but I wouldn't wish it on anyone."

"I might wish it on a few people. Not you," he added with a grin.

"You sure you aren't feeling sick?"

"I'm fine, Ang. I've had more vaccinations against more weird shit than you can imagine. Goes with the job. I don't think you have to worry about me."

"I hope not. I'd feel terrible if you got sick too. I already feel terrible that I've inconvenienced you this much."

"I'm not inconvenienced, babe. I don't mind taking care of you."

The lump in her throat tightened again. "Thanks," she whispered, then covered her emotions by spooning more soup into her mouth. When she felt more in control of herself, she asked, "Has there been any news?"

"Nothing yet."

"The account in the Caymans?"

"We're close to solving it."

"I really need to check email, see what news there's been from work."

"You're sick, Angie. Maybe wait until tomorrow to worry about work. You need to rest. Give yourself time to recover."

She knew he was right, but she hated not getting anything done. She was the kind of person who was always busy, not the kind who lounged around and flipped through television shows all day. Yet that's what she needed to do right now. Watch TV and forget about work because her body needed to recover.

"I should let someone know I'm sick."

"Maddy called Liam. He passed it on to management. He'll take care of anything that's time sensitive until you can work again."

She glowed inside, and not just from the soup. It was nice to have a tribe who took care of you when you needed them. She wasn't always good at accepting help, but it was comforting when people proved they were there for you. Of course she'd had Maddy for a long time. Now she had Jace too. And Colt, it seemed.

But for how long?

"You guys have thought of everything, haven't you?"

"Pretty much." He picked up the remote and turned on the big television sitting on the dresser at the foot of the bed. "What do you want to watch? A movie? One of Maddy's favorite renovation shows?"

She thought about it. She probably wouldn't be awake for the whole thing, but there was one movie she could think of. A movie that made her laugh and feel good too. "How about *Groundhog Day?* Do you have that?"

His brows drew together. He was smiling though. "I can find it. I wouldn't have guessed that about you, Ang."

"It's almost Groundhog Day for real. I always watch it this time of year. Do you hate it or something?"

She hoped he didn't, but she wouldn't hold it against him if he did. Her ex hadn't liked it either, but that was the least of his faults.

Colt laughed. "I don't hate it. I like it. But it's an

older movie so I wouldn't have thought it would be your first choice."

"How little you know about me. I love old movies. *Casablanca* is a particular favorite. *North by Northwest* with Cary Grant. *Lawrence of Arabia.* Oh, and *The Guns of Navarone.* I could keep going."

He was smiling. "I had no idea. Why do you like those?"

Happiness was a quiet presence inside her. "My grandfather was a movie buff. Some of my favorite memories are sitting on his lap and watching old black and whites. He loved epics and action movies, and the classics like *Casablanca.*"

"He sounds like a fun granddad."

"He was. Watching old movies makes me feel like he's still with me sometimes. That's not why I like *Groundhog Day* though. I like that one because it's a sweet, funny romance."

"Then let's watch it. I haven't seen it in years."

"You'll watch it with me?"

"If you want me to."

"I'd love that," she said softly.

———

COLT KNEW when she'd fallen asleep again. Angie lay with her arm across his belly and her face against his chest. He had his fingers in her hair, twisting a lock of it around and around his index finger. It was soft, silky, and only slightly damp now. Onscreen, Bill Murray and Andie McDowell traded banter. Bill was a dickish reporter and Andie was the sweet and naïve producer who'd been sent to Pennsylvania to get footage of weatherman Bill with the groundhog.

The movie was cute and sweet and poignant, and it didn't surprise him that Angie loved to watch it. In fact, she kind of reminded him of the Andie McDowell character in a way. Maybe not naïve, but definitely sweet and hopeful. He frowned hard as he thought of the news Jace delivered earlier.

Jennifer Clark, known at work as Jenny or Jen, had been found in her car that morning by a jogger who'd noticed her slumped over the wheel. He'd knocked on the window. When she didn't respond, he tried to open the door. It was locked and he called 911. The police and an ambulance arrived within minutes.

No report on what had killed her yet, but initial evidence indicated she'd been dead for about six hours at that point.

Colt continued to twist Angie's hair as she clung to him. He couldn't tell her yet. Not when she was sick. The last thing she needed was to get emotional about Jenny's death when she was still recovering from a stomach bug.

So he didn't tell her, and he felt guilty about it. He'd left her phone in the kitchen, turned off, so no one could blow up her messages with the news.

His phone buzzed and he picked it up. It was Ian

so he answered as quietly as he could. Angie didn't stir.

"Yeah, boss?"

"How's the patient?"

"Better, but still not feeling great."

"And you?"

"I feel fine."

"Glad to hear it. Preliminary report on Jenny Clark is that she committed suicide. Prescription anxiety meds combined with bourbon. There was an empty bottle in the car. They ran a rape kit on her and she'd had sex just a few hours before. There were finger marks on her throat, but they didn't kill her. The age of the marks is consistent with when she had sex—she also had light bruising on her buttocks. A little bit of vigorous spanking, possibly. And there were bite marks on her nipples. Whoever she had sex with, it wasn't strictly vanilla."

"You're telling me she had a few orgasms, and then she drove her car to a parking lot near the waterfront and downed pills with bourbon?"

"It could happen. I don't believe it did, but that doesn't mean it couldn't."

"Do you think it's connected to everything else?"

"The million dollar question. Yes, I do."

"But you aren't telling me over the phone."

"No. You'll have to come in."

He knew what Ian meant. It was sensitive information and it had to be discussed behind BDI's secure doors. "Can't do that right now, boss."

"I know."

"Is she in danger?" He wasn't saying her name because he didn't want to wake her.

"I think she's fine for the moment. They don't know where she is. I'm putting Tyler and Jared onto your security. They'll be watching."

Staking out his house, Ian meant. "Is that necessary?"

"Right now when she's sick and you're distracted by it? Yeah, it's necessary. I don't expect any trouble, but I didn't live to be this age by being careless and whimsical."

Colt would never describe Ian as whimsical. It was almost comical to think of that word associated with him. "You're the boss, boss."

"Need you here in the morning. Jared can stay with your girl while you come in."

His girl. She was his girl.

"I'll be there."

Chapter Thirteen

ANGIE WAS FEELING ALMOST LIKE HERSELF THE NEXT morning. She managed to sleep all night, waking up only once to pee—and no puking, thankfully. It was nice not to have to run to the bathroom several times a night, or feel like hell when her stomach cramped.

Colt had slept beside her last night. She remembered that clearly. He'd been wearing a shirt and shorts, but he was there with her. They'd slept together. Just slept. It was a strange thought, and a nice one too. Who would have ever thought it?

She searched for her phone on the nightstand. It wasn't there. She didn't know what time it was, though she knew it was light because there was a sliver coming between the drapes. She got out of bed, feeling a little shaky, and went into the bathroom to freshen up.

Colt had moved her toiletries to the master. Her

heart thumped at his thoughtfulness. She went back into the bedroom, found that he'd brought her suitcase in, and rummaged through for something to wear. Her clothes from yesterday were neatly folded on a chair. She grabbed clean underwear and a bra and socks, selected another pair of yoga pants and a sweater, then went to take a shower. She pinned her hair up because it didn't need to be washed this time.

Freshly dressed, she emerged into the hall and headed for the living areas. She heard voices and stopped. She hadn't realized Colt wasn't alone. She listened until his visitor spoke again.

Jared Fraser.

Both men turned their heads as Angie walked into the kitchen. Colt was leaning against the counter, one leg crossed over the other. Jared sat at the table with a cup of coffee.

Colt moved toward her. "Baby, how do you feel?"

Angie smiled. "Much better."

He put a hand under her elbow to steady her and led her to the table where he sat her down. "Are you hungry?"

She thought about it. Her belly didn't rebel at the thought of food, which was good. "Maybe something light?"

"Soup? Or toast and egg whites?"

"Toast and egg whites sounds good."

"You got it."

She turned her attention to Jared, who was

watching her. "Thank you for the medicine. I think it helped."

"I'm glad. We don't usually do too much for stomach flu, but you learn a trick or two in the field. Helps lessen the impact a little bit."

"I can't remember the last time I was that sick."

"Hopefully it'll be a long time before you are again."

"God I hope so."

Colt finished the toast and brought it to her on a plate. He didn't put anything on it, but he set out butter and jam for her. She knifed up some jam and spread it on a warm slice while he went back to the stove to scramble up a couple of egg whites. "Is there any news?" she asked when she'd eaten half of the toast.

Colt tipped the pan and slid scrambled egg whites on her plate. She didn't miss the look he and Jared exchanged.

Colt dragged out a chair and sat down beside her. His expression was more serious than she'd seen it these past couple of days. "There's a little bit of news, Ang. Eat first."

She thought about rebelling, but her stomach rumbled and she decided she needed the protein. She ate the eggs and finished the toast while Jared and Colt waited. When she was done, she pushed the plate away.

"Okay. You can tell me now."

"It's not good."

Her heart dropped. "Did they find Charles? Is he dead?"

Colt's blue eyes bored into hers. "Charles is still missing, baby. But a jogger found Jenny Clark yesterday. It looks like she committed suicide."

Angie went cold and then hot. Her throat closed. She pressed the heels of her hands to her eyes and willed herself not to cry before glaring at them both. "Oh my god. I just saw her. She was upset about the fire, but she didn't seem suicidal. We went to breakfast. Oh god." She looked at Colt. "It doesn't make sense. If she was ever going to kill herself it would have been last year when Dwight—that's her ex—left her for another woman. It was an ugly divorce. They share custody of the kids. Oh lord, her kids…"

Colt put a hand on her back and rubbed. "I know, *minette*. I didn't tell you yesterday because you weren't in any condition to deal with the news."

She shook her head as a hot tear fell down her cheek. "I wish you had." The kitchen was getting blurry. She tried to push her chair back, but Colt blocked it with his foot. "I need my phone."

"I'll get it for you. Here."

He shoved a box of tissue under her nose. She pulled some out and pressed them to her eyes.

Her phone appeared on the table in front of her. "Look at your messages, but don't send any just yet, okay?"

She frowned. "Okay."

She picked up her phone and unlocked it. There were text messages. Lots of them. Liam had texted her. Maddy. Jenny.

Oh god.

Jenny: *Hey, Angie. I need to talk to you. Can we meet somewhere? Call me.*

Angie swallowed. "She tried to get in touch with me. She had a couple of Charles's accounts. I asked her if she'd found anything wrong but she said no. Maybe she found something later…. I can't believe she's gone."

Colt put an arm around her and squeezed her shoulders. "I know, baby."

"I think I need to lie down again." She got to her feet, her phone clutched in her hand.

"Baby, you need to leave the phone here."

Annoyance pricked her. "I can lie in bed and look at my messages. I'll be fine."

"No, Ang." His tone told her he wasn't going to let her take the phone from the room. And that made her angry.

"It's my damned phone," she spat. "You can't tell me what to do."

"You're under my protection, and I *can* tell you what to do." His voice was harder than she'd ever heard it. Commanding and final. "You aren't going to answer any of those texts right now. Or your emails. It's best if you stay dark, don't let people know where you are. Until we know what's going on, you can't take any chances."

She bit her trembling lip as anger and grief assaulted her senses. Colt and Jared both looked at her calmly, like it was no big deal. To them it wasn't. Neither the anger nor the grief. They were used to death.

If she insisted on keeping her phone, they could overpower her, take it by force. There was nothing she could do to stop them.

She was powerless, and she hated it.

"Fine," she growled. Then she threw the phone onto the table and stormed out of the kitchen.

————

"I THINK THAT WENT WELL," Colt said to Jared as soon the bedroom door slammed.

Jared snorted. "Only if pissing her off was your intention."

He hated that he'd had to do it, but she didn't realize how lucky she was to still have access to her phone. He'd checked for spyware when she'd been sleeping. There was none. He'd also made sure tracking was disabled. If this was a different kind of mission, he'd have turned it off, put it in a metal box, and left it that way.

"Angie's smart and logical. She'll realize it's for the best once she thinks about it some more. She's emotional. It doesn't help that she's just gotten over being sick."

Jared nodded. "She seems to trust you. I'd heard you were hung up on her, but she wouldn't give you the time of day."

Jared had been out of the country on assignment for a good part of the past few months, so he'd missed the push and pull between Colt and Angie. Still, people thought he'd been hung up on her? Maybe he had.

Maybe he still was.

"She spent time in the hospital with me after I was shot. When I got better, she cooled off. Seems as if she blamed herself and thought I hated her for it, so she avoided me."

"She might start avoiding you again once this is over."

"Maybe. But at least she'll be alive." He didn't really intend to give her the chance though. Yeah, maybe he wasn't the right kind of guy for Miss Angie Turner, but he wasn't giving up without a fight. Even if part of what he had to fight was himself. He stood. "I guess I'd better tell her you'll be here with her so I can head out."

"Make sure you don't present yourself as too big a target. I fear she might throw something at you the next time."

Colt laughed. "Yeah, I got you. I'll use the door as a shield."

He didn't though. He walked back to his bedroom, knocked softly on the door, and entered the room. Angie was under the covers, smashing the channel button on the remote, her eyes glistening with tears. She glanced at him, then concentrated on the TV again.

"I'm sorry, *minette.*"

She sniffed. "For what? Jenny's death, or ordering me to leave my phone with you?"

"Both." He went over and perched on the side of the bed. She still didn't look at him. Her pretty face was pale and tear-streaked, her eyes puffy. His heart twisted. "I'd do anything to change what's happened, but I can't. All I can do is protect you and keep you safe."

She looked at him, pulled her lower lip between her teeth. Her eyes were wet, wounded. "I hate this, Colt. Hate that I got sick, hate not being in charge of my own life, hate everything that's happened since Charles left and I got that account."

"I know."

"It's connected. It has to be. Jenny, I mean. She was crying the morning of the fire. When I asked what was wrong, she said it was silly. She said she was crying over photos of her children that had burned though she could just print them again. But if she could reprint them, why cry about it?"

"Some people are strangely emotional about stuff like that."

187

"Maybe. But what if she wasn't? What if it was something else? Maybe she knew something about Charles and the Cardinal Group. Maybe she wanted to tell me about it and somebody killed her to stop her."

He hated the idea that Jenny might have known Angie'd found something suspect in Martinelli's files. "Anything is possible at this point." He paused. "Ang, I have to go out for a while. Jared will be here with you if you need anything."

"How long will you be away?"

"An hour or two." He bent and kissed her on the forehead. She didn't pull away from him. "I'll be back as soon as I can."

She caught his shirt in a fist before he could sit up again. Their gazes met. "Do you promise?"

"Yes, I promise."

Her fingers untwisted the fabric. He stood. She was so small in his bed. He wanted to see her there when she was completely better—and he wanted her naked.

"Be careful, Colt."

"I will, baby. Get some rest. We'll watch one of those old movies of yours later."

———

IAN WAS WAITING for him when he exited the elevator onto the fifth floor.

"I was beginning to wonder if you could pull yourself away for an hour."

Colt didn't rise to the bait. "I said I'd be here."

"Come on then." Ian turned and led the way to one of the conference rooms. Jace was waiting. Dax.

And Brett.

Colt stopped in surprise. "Brett. Didn't expect you back yet."

Brett extended a hand. They shook. "Man, after all you did for me and Tallie, you think I'd stay away when you needed me?"

"You could have finished your vacation. It's not that dire."

Brett shrugged. "Both of us were ready to go. Tallie found the pieces she needs for the new store, so she's eager to get back to it. Besides, when she heard Angie might be in trouble, she knew you'd be involved."

Colt frowned. "How did she hear about that?"

"Maddy. The three of them have become friends since Tallie moved up here. She also knows Angie had a stomach virus, and she wants me to tell you she'd be happy to help out. Do the shopping, fix a casserole— that kind of thing."

Colt was touched. He liked Tallie Grant a lot. She was perfect for Brett. She softened his rough edges, made him more human. Like Maddy did for Jace.

Did he have rough edges that Angie could soften?

"That's sweet of her. Angie's over the worst of it, but I'll let you know."

Ian pulled out a chair and sat. "All right, kids. We ready?"

They took their seats and Dax began the briefing. "We found the account in the Caymans. Angie was right about the number. I had to unscramble it, but it was all there. Account, routing, and pin. Charles Martinelli reversed every third number, then went back in and cut the number into thirds before swapping it again. Which made it into a whole lotta nothing until the program figured it out and made a match for the routing number. After we knew which bank, we could start trying to find the account."

Colt would've been impressed if he'd expected anything less than perfection. As it was, he wasn't surprised. The people who worked at BDI were good at figuring things out. They had to be or the world would be in a lot worse shape than it was.

Ian propped his elbows on the table and leaned forward. "The condensed version is this. The account belongs to Gorky Construction."

"Shit," Colt said. "Martinelli was stealing from the fucking Russian mafia?"

They all knew that Steve Gorky and his sons were connected to the mafia. Construction, gambling, sex trafficking, drugs, weapons—those were the Russian mafia's rackets, and the Gorkys were a major part of it. Steve was first generation American, but that didn't mean a damned thing. He was in it up to his dirty neck.

They'd had dealings with him before, though nothing so close to home.

"Our old friends," Ian confirmed. "The Cardinal Group was founded by Christopher Shaw and Paul Sobol. Shaw and Sobol went to college with Martinelli—and Sobol's sister is Gorky's fourth wife."

That explained a lot. "Sobol and Shaw are laundering money for Gorky then. And Martinelli was a part of it."

Ian cocked a finger gun at him. "Bingo. Sobol and Shaw set up a business as venture capitalists—one guess where most of the capital comes from—and they use the firm as a front to move money for Gorky. They get kickbacks, Martinelli gets kickbacks, everyone's happy. Except Martinelli wants more and figures nobody will miss it since he's cooking the books."

"Well somebody sure as hell found out," Jace said.

Colt shook his head. "Martinelli is probably at the bottom of a well somewhere. Or he's been poured into a foundation in a Gorky Construction project. *Shit.* How is this connected to Jenny Clark?"

"Ah, but there's more," Ian said. "That spreadsheet doesn't just contain snapshots of Gorky's and Martinelli's accounts. There are two more accounts. The biggest one, besides Gorky's, has Paul Sobol's name on it. Shaw got money too, but he doesn't seem to have gotten the kind of cash Martinelli and Sobol did. Sobol was stealing from his brother-in-law, with Martinelli's help, who was also stealing for himself and logging everything. Dax, tell them the rest."

"It took a bit of digging," Dax said. "But I finally managed to trace the deleted files from the Barton, Barnes and Blake server. The files were erased with Jenny's login. So either she did it at someone's instruction, or somebody stole her login and did it themselves. Either way, she's connected to the Cardinal Group account and its disappearance. Could be a motive for murder. I also confirmed that Martinelli sent his spreadsheet to the company server the night before he didn't show up for work. It wasn't there before that. He did it deliberately."

"So someone could find it," Colt said. "Fuck."

"Yes," Ian replied. "It seems that way."

"And Jenny?"

"There's still no proof Jenny was killed. I got the report earlier and her death is consistent with an overdose. She had enough alcohol and Xanax in her system to kill an elephant. She had a prescription for the meds. But if somebody didn't force her to take those pills, I'd be surprised. The marks on her neck are consistent with the rough sex she had—they're also consistent with someone holding her and forcing pills down her throat, which wouldn't've been too hard if she was already drunk enough."

Colt's gut tightened. "If Jenny's death is a coincidence, it's a pretty spectacular one."

"That's what I'm thinking." Ian leaned back in his chair, looking speculative. "Here's what we do. We keep Angie in protective custody. We keep looking for Martinelli on the off chance he's alive, and we watch Sobol and Shaw too. Most importantly, we keep an eye on Gorky. Keep digging into his finances. Martinelli recorded some big transactions in Gorky's account. What were they for? I'd love to find a way to take him down this time. He's eluded us before, particularly with that drug ring last year."

They all remembered it. Gorky's people had been importing synthetic opioids and selling them to human traffickers as a way to keep their victims in line. Gorky'd managed to keep himself out of the fray when that particular operation fell apart. If there was something dirty and a way to make money off it, then Gorky was one of those scumbags that was in the middle of it. But he was a lucky damned scumbag who kept coming up smelling like a rose even when everyone knew he was nothing but a pile of shit.

"If we're lucky," Jace said, "maybe they'll try Angie's place again. If we can get somebody to talk, we can connect it to Gorky that way."

"They won't talk," Ian replied. "They're more scared of him than they are us."

"What if Angie goes home again?" Dax asked.

"No," Colt and Jace said at once.

"Not Angie for real," Dax said. "Can't we find a hot redhead to impersonate her?"

Colt might have growled.

Ian arched an eyebrow in Colt's direction. Then he looked at Dax again. "Too bad Victoria Royal isn't still with us. She'd be perfect."

Colt knew who Victoria was. He'd come aboard right after she left. The lady had legendary sniper skills. She'd left BDI and married a military operator from the Hostile Operations Team. Now she did contract work for them.

"Jamie Hayes could do it," Jace said. "She just needs a wig—or she could dye her hair."

Jamie had impersonated Maddy when they'd sent her to a safe house and wanted Calypso to think Maddy was still home. It hadn't worked, but not because Jamie wasn't good.

"Jamie's in Afghanistan, infiltrating a terror cell disguised as a journalist," Ian said. "Even if I was inclined to send for her, it'd take at least twenty-four hours to get her here. Besides, I'm not convinced it'll make any difference. So Angie goes home and someone tries to break in. What then? If they're watching her place, we could wait until she's feeling better and have Colt take her home—" He held up a hand to stop Colt's protest. "Not to stay, just to be seen. Walk her in, disguise her, and walk her out through the side entrance. It's a thought."

Colt grumbled. "I don't like it. Angie's not an operative."

"No, she's not. But she can't stay with you forever, can she?"

"No," Colt bit out. Except what if he wanted her to? The thought shocked him about as much as it thrilled him.

Ian stood, ending the meeting. "Keep watching our suspects—and follow the money trail. It has to lead somewhere. Dismissed."

Chapter Fourteen

IAN STALKED TOWARD HIS OFFICE, TENSION SCREWING his muscles tight. He fucking hated the mafia. Russian, Italian, American. Didn't matter. He hated them all. Everywhere he'd ever been, anytime he'd encountered organized crime, he'd been disgusted by the lack of regard for humanity. People like that were cockroaches. Leeches on the ass of life.

Users and abusers, destroyers of innocents. They didn't care, so long as they got their money.

Steve Gorky was one of the worst. Ian had wanted Gorky's ass for years now, but the motherfucker always managed to slip the net. He was dirty as fuck, but he had enough legit businesses that he somehow conned politicians and judges to do his bidding whether they thought they were or not. Hence, he always got away with it, whatever it was.

Ian shoved open the glass door to his office and

went to sit at his desk. He had shit to do and no time to dwell on his encounters with the mafia. He pulled up his secure email and checked for the message he kept hoping would come.

The message that would let him know Natasha Orlova was alive. He hadn't seen or heard from her since that moment on the mountain in Spain when she'd flown away in a stolen helicopter. Nothing about her silence was unusual, except that he usually had some rumor of her out there. She was a gun for hire, an assassin of the highest order. She commanded a high price, and she left no trail.

There were always rumors of her, a trail of destruction that followed in her wake like sparks from a match. There'd been nothing for two months, and he wondered. Had she gone too far on that mountain? Shot the wrong person? Had she paid with her life?

She had his private email address. He'd given it to her when he'd set her free months ago after she'd kidnapped Angie and Maddy and shot Colt and Jace. He'd set her free because he'd believed in her.

He still believed. Only now he feared that her masters had realized she was no longer theirs to command. That she was working for herself and not the Gemini Syndicate any longer.

He recalled her face when she'd told him they had something of hers. Stark, naked, raw. She'd been in pain and trying to hide it. What they had was something precious. He thought it must be a child. That was the only thing he could imagine they could hold over her. The only thing that would force her to do their bidding and return to them when he offered her freedom.

He closed the email and sat back in his chair, rubbing his eyes. Thinking.

To inquire after her would put her in danger if she wasn't already. If she was still out there, she would surface soon enough.

There was nothing he could do except wait.

———

WHEN ANGIE WOKE ALONE the next morning, she lay in bed and felt like her old self. It was almost as if she'd never been sick.

She knew Colt wasn't gone. She could hear him in the kitchen, fixing coffee and probably getting ready to make something delicious for breakfast. Her stomach growled in anticipation. She hopped in the shower and then dressed in jeans and boots with a sweater. She blow-dried her hair, which meant it was full and shiny as it hung down her back instead of sticking up everywhere. A bit of eyeliner and mascara, a swipe of lipgloss, and she was done.

She looked at herself in the mirror. Her eyes were bright and her complexion wasn't dull today. For the first time, she didn't look sick. She didn't feel it either.

For two days, Colt had taken care of her. He fixed her meals, washed her clothes, let her have his bed and bathroom, and gave her command of the remote.

Last night, she'd cuddled up to him while they watched television, and then she'd dropped off to sleep before the show ended and there was any awkwardness about bedtime.

It was wonderfully strange to sleep with a man, share body heat, but not be intimate with him. She and Colt had kissed only a couple of times, and yet they slept tangled together like an old married couple. It wasn't what she'd ever expected.

And yet she loved how easy it was with him. How comfortable. He never made her feel guilty for being sick, never suggested that he was tired of taking care of her. When she said she could go to the kitchen and heat up her own food if he was tired of doing it, he'd frowned and told her he wasn't. He'd pointed out that she couldn't cook.

She'd pointed out that microwaving soup wasn't cooking. He'd told her it didn't matter, it was his job. She felt like a princess because he took care of her so well. She was grateful and happy.

Thankfully, Colt didn't catch what she had. Angie headed for the kitchen where Colt was indeed doing something at the stove. She would have watched him work, the smooth muscles bunching and flexing beneath his shirt, but he was too aware of his surroundings for her to sneak up on him. He threw a glance over his shoulder, smiling at her, and her heart flipped and skipped.

"Hey," he said. "You're just in time."

"In time for what?" she asked brightly, trying to ignore the flutter of nerves in her belly. Why now? She'd been with him for days and this was the first she'd gotten an attack of nerves.

"Crepes."

She went to his side and looked into the pan. The man was making crepes. Homemade crepes. There was no more perfect man in this universe than Colton Duchaine. Holy cow.

"Oh my," she said. "How do you get them so thin?"

"It's the batter. And the technique. You have to swirl just right." He finished the crepe and then added fruit, ricotta cheese, and honey. "Here, try this."

He set the plate on the table and Angie picked up a fork and knife and sliced off a piece. It was heavenly, of course. Angie moaned. Colt laughed as he joined her. There was a stack of crepes on the plate he put between them, containing different fillings.

"I assume you're feeling better if you're eating the whole thing?"

She finished the first crepe and reached for a second, grinning. "Much. Thank you again for taking care of me."

His eyes were warm. "You don't have to thank me, Angie. It's what friends do for each other."

Friends. She liked hearing that word from his lips—but what if she wanted more? What if she wanted to feel his mouth against her skin, to laugh at his jokes, to eat with him every night, and to watch old movies curled up beside him? How had she gone so many months denying herself those things?

And what if she'd blown it? What if he no longer wanted any of that?

She ducked her head. "We are friends now, aren't we? I'm sorry I avoided you for so long. It was stupid."

He put his hand on top of hers. His palm was warm, his touch comforting. "It wasn't stupid. You had a lot to process."

"You're so forgiving. I'm not sure I'd be as understanding if I were you."

He arched an eyebrow as he picked up his fork again. "Do you want me to hold a grudge? Would that be better?"

Her stomach flipped. "Of course not. I just feel like an idiot about the whole thing. If I were you, I might hold my feet to the fire a bit more than you do."

"Not the way I operate, *minette.* I like you. I want to get to know you better."

Her nerves pinged and zinged through her body. Her nipples tightened. A hot, heavy ache formed between her legs. "I want that too."

"You do?"

She laughed to cover the butterflies swirling insanely in her belly. "Of course. You're a great guy, Colt, and I want to know you better. I like you."

"And if I'm talking about the kind of knowing where we spend time naked? Where I learn what makes you fly apart and gasp my name?"

Oh god, leave it to him to cut straight to the chase. She could pretend she'd misunderstood him the first time. Or she could just admit the truth.

"I know that's what you meant."

His smile was wolfish now. Masculine and hot. Her heart throbbed. She should be afraid. So afraid of what he could do to her poor heart. Oddly enough, she wasn't. He'd proven that he wasn't like Dan when he'd nursed her without complaint. That didn't mean they were destined for the altar, but she was pretty sure he wasn't the kind of guy who'd cheat behind her back. He was too honest for that.

He leaned toward her, captured her mouth in a kiss. He tasted like cream and bananas, and heat flashed through her at the press of mouth against mouth. But he didn't push his advantage. He didn't even linger. He sat back and smiled at her, and she thought she'd never seen a more handsome man in her life.

"Don't look at me like that, Ang. Did you think I was going to drag you to the bedroom and do it all right now?"

She nodded as a strange disappointment seized her when it was clear he wasn't.

"Oh, I want to. Believe me. But this is your first day feeling better, and I'm not the kind of guy who's going to jump on you the instant you're back to normal."

She couldn't help but smile. Of course he wasn't. Colt was the kind of man who cared about a woman's feelings. The kind who believed in taking his time and doing things right. How had she not realized these things about him before?

"You aren't like most men I've met then."

"No, I'm not."

"You're better." She turned her attention to the crepes to cover the awkwardness she felt at saying those words. "I mean look at these things. Perfection on a plate. No ordinary man can do this."

"I'm glad you approve."

"I definitely do. I think if you ever want to get out of the danger business, you could open a restaurant. Wouldn't that be fun?"

"I don't think that's my style. I like to cook for people I care about. But the public? Nah, not happening."

People he cared about? Oh my. "Then I guess I'm going to have to stay on your good side so I can pop over for crepes or omelets or whatever you're fixing."

His eyes glittered hot. "You can pop over anytime, baby. I'll always cook for you."

She thought about it. What she really wanted was to wake up with him and have him cook for her. That would be even better. Perfect, in fact.

But she didn't know how to say it.

———

ONCE THEY FINISHED EATING, Colt asked Angie if she'd like to get out of the house for a little while. Her eyes lit up at the suggestion.

"I'm feeling a bit stir crazy," she admitted. "Where are we going?"

"I need to get some groceries. Feel like walking around the store?"

"God, yes. Let me get my bag."

Colt set the alarm and led Angie outside and over to his Yukon. It was cold out and their breath frosted in the air, but at least it wasn't raining. "Are you warm enough in that?" he asked.

She glanced down at her red wool coat and houndstooth scarf. "Toasty."

"Good. Let me know if you get cold. I don't want you getting sick again."

"It was a stomach bug, not the flu."

"Still." He opened the door for her and she looked up with a smile that tugged at his heart.

She put her hands on his chest. "I love that you're concerned for me. Thank you."

She said it like she wasn't accustomed to people

caring, but he knew that wasn't true because she had Maddy and Jace. Still, he knew what it was like to feel alone in spite of the people surrounding you. He'd never felt fully French or fully American, and it made for lonely times as he tried to figure out where he belonged.

"Of course I'm concerned," he told her. Then he kissed her. No tongue, but a full press of his mouth against hers. It felt great to be able to do that. Right.

Her eyes widened as he pulled back. "Are you sure you don't want to go back inside?" she asked.

He laughed. "Hell, no, I'm not sure. But we need food, Ang. And you need to get out before cabin fever makes you do something crazy."

"Such as?"

"I don't know—ask me to teach you to cook?"

She snorted. "As if." Then she hopped up in the Yukon and he shut the door and walked around to the driver's side.

Colt backed out of the drive and started down the road.

"I don't care that it's gray out and looks like it might snow," Angie said. "I love being outside again."

"I thought you might."

She sighed. "I love hanging with you Colt, though I would have preferred not to be sick. Please don't think I'm ungrateful when I ask this—when can I go home again?"

"I'm not sure yet. A couple of days probably."

He didn't really know, but the only new development since yesterday was that Steve Gorky had left town with his wife, flying to Miami and the winter home they kept there. He'd golfed all afternoon and drank at the yacht club last night. His young wife shopped and lounged around the pool with her socialite friends, working on her tan. Basically, business as usual for the Gorkys.

Gorky's grown sons were scattered from New York to Georgia, running Gorky Construction offices—and engaging in mafia-related activities, naturally. None had been seen in town recently.

Shaw and Sobol were still around, and Charles Martinelli hadn't surfaced. Colt didn't think he would.

Then there was Jenny Clark. Her death wasn't suspicious enough for the police to think it was anything other than suicide. Whoever she'd been having sex with, he hadn't come forward. Nobody'd expected he would.

Ian had gotten her phone records because of course he had. She'd had several calls from a number that turned out to be a burner phone. That was suspect, but really only pointed to the idea she might have been having an affair with a married man. Someone who wouldn't want to use his own phone— and definitely wouldn't come forward once she'd been found dead.

It was also a possible motive for suicide. Except she'd still been the one to erase files from the server—

or her login had been compromised so someone else could do so—which made her sudden death very convenient for Gorky. She'd sent Angie a text message about wanting to talk.

Or had she? Someone else could have sent it using her phone. They might never know, but it hadn't been the last time the phone was used. There'd been one call to a burner afterward, and then nothing.

Angie turned in her seat. "Everyone at Triple B is still shocked about Jenny. Do you know anything more about her death yet? Did she really commit suicide?"

Colt hesitated. "It looks that way, *minette.*"

"But why? That's what I don't understand."

"Does anyone ever really know why someone kills themself?"

"No." She sighed. "There was a girl in high school —Maddy knew her too. She was popular and everything, not the kind of person you'd think would want to kill herself. But she did. She stepped in front of a train. It was shocking. They had counselors come and talk to everyone in her class. That wasn't us, but Maddy and I talked about it a lot. We both agreed that we'd never do something like that without telling the other one we were feeling that way."

"And did you? Ever feel like that, I mean."

She hugged herself. "No. And neither did Maddy. We had each other. I think that girl must not have had anyone, even though we thought she did. Her name was Christie Nelson. I'll never forget it." She let out a breath. "I wish Jenny had talked to someone. I still can't believe she'd do that though. Her kids meant everything to her. She fought so hard to keep them."

"You never know what someone's breaking point is." He made a decision. "She was having sex with someone, Ang. She took calls from someone we can't identify, we're assuming male based on the sexual activity, but it was a burner phone—untraceable. Which might suggest she was having an affair with a married man. She could have reached the end of her rope."

"Okay. Wow. She never mentioned a man, but then we weren't anything to each other except coworkers. She barely talked about Dwight and the divorce at work, though she sometimes did when it got bad. Even then she didn't say much, just that he was pond scum and the judge had been insane the day he'd given Dwight shared custody."

"Maybe she was trying to move on with this new guy. If he was married, it might have pushed her to the breaking point. Or someone could have forced her to take the pills that killed her. We don't really know."

Angie looked sad and a little shocked. "Is that possible?"

"It's a theory. But we don't know."

"Poor Jen." She touched his arm. "Thank you for telling me. I know you didn't want to, not really, but I appreciate it."

"I don't want to tell you things when I don't know

what's true. But it's something we talked about, so yeah, I'm telling you. You asked me not to keep the hard things from you."

"I did ask. Thank you."

They reached the grocery store a few minutes later and Colt parked the Yukon. Angie was slumped in her seat, thinking, and he decided he needed to make her laugh. "You ready for some fun?"

"I don't think the grocery store is all that fun. Is it?"

He wiggled his eyebrows. "Hell yeah, it is. We can fondle the produce and try samples from the deli. You've never had such a great time as you're about to have with me."

She laughed. He was glad because he'd wanted to get her mind off the sad things for a while.

"Let's go then. I'm dying to fondle produce," she said as she opened her door.

"Me too, baby. Me too."

Chapter Fifteen

He was right. Angie'd never had such fun at a grocery store in her life. Maybe it was because she was purposely shoving the horror of Jenny's death from her head, or maybe it was just being with him.

She and Colt went up and down the aisles together, discussing the kinds of things they wanted to eat and what other things they might need. They picked up staples like bread and milk and coffee, and he showed her how to select ripe produce as well as the best cuts of meat. He bought cheese and deli meat, and then they went to the wine aisle. There was a lot of wine.

"How do you know what to get?" she asked as they strolled down the aisle. She pushed the cart because she'd insisted since he was choosing every-thing. She leaned on it as he moved slowly along.

"You can select by grape. A Cabernet Sauvignon

is heavier than a Pinot Noir, for instance. You think of wines you've liked, what kind of grape it was, and then you narrow it down. If you're looking at a California wine, you look at how narrow the appellation."

"Huh?"

He pointed to a bottle. "See that one? It says Napa Valley. The grapes are only from Napa Valley. But a California wine has grapes from all of California."

"And that matters because?"

He laughed. "It might not matter at all, but a wine produced from grapes that come from a specific region will have a different flavor than grapes from everywhere."

"So don't just pick up the bargain box and head for the checkout."

"You can if you like it. I'm not judging."

"Oh please. You'd be horrified."

He grinned. "I might." He picked up a couple of bottles of California wine. They rolled past the French section. He stopped suddenly and picked up a bottle. He almost seemed surprised. The label read *Chateau d'Duchesne.*

"Is that a good one?" she asked.

"It used to be."

"Not anymore?"

He put the bottle down. "I don't know."

"Let's try it then. I'll buy it."

"Angie—"

She tilted her head when he didn't finish. "What? It's not that expensive. And you promised to let me contribute to the grocery bill. After all you've done for me, I should buy all of it."

He shook his head as he put the bottle in the cart. "Okay, let's try it. But you aren't paying for everything. I'll let you give me some cash if you insist."

"I insist. How do you say that name anyway?" she asked as she looked at the label.

He met her gaze evenly. "It's said like this." He pronounced it the same as his last name.

"It's your family winery?"

"It is."

She sensed she'd bungled something. He'd told her he hadn't joined the family wine business. He'd never said why. "We can put it back. I didn't know."

He put a hand out to stop her as she reached for it. "It's okay, Angie. I was surprised to see it in this store. They must have gotten a distribution deal, which is great for them."

"I don't want to get it if it bothers you."

"It's fine. Come on."

After they checked out and loaded everything into the Yukon, they swung by Maddy and Jace's. Angie had to convince him, but he finally relented when she pointed out it was cold enough that the groceries would be fine for a short while. She would be with him the whole time, and they'd just gone to a public store where anybody could see them, so why not?

Jace was out but Maddy was waiting with hot tea and freshly baked cookies. She hugged Angie, hard. "I'm so glad you're doing better."

"Me too. It was pretty awful for a while."

Maddy's gaze strayed to Colt. "But you had Colt, and he took good care of you."

Angie felt herself turning red. "He did. He's been terrific. And so was your soup."

"I'm glad."

There was a banging sound from the addition and Maddy turned as a man with a shock of gray hair poked his head into the kitchen. "Miss Cole, we need to test the breakers. You might lose power for a few minutes."

"No problem. We're set in here."

The man's gaze slid over the three of them and then he nodded. He ducked back out again. Angie picked up her tea. It was hot and sweet, just like she liked it.

"We're getting so close," Maddy said. "I hope we'll be in the new master by March first."

"That's really exciting," Angie replied. "I can't believe all the work you've done in a few short months. Hey, where's Kitty?"

"I had to shut her in the bedroom. She doesn't like all the noise and then she tries to dart into the addition when they open the door. I'm afraid she'll get out if that happens." Maddy lowered her voice. "The workmen aren't exactly cautious about the doors."

"Got it."

"I went to see Mimi this morning," Maddy said. "I've been telling her all about the renovations, but she doesn't understand. It's just something to talk about."

Maddy's grandmother was in a memory care facility. She had good days and bad days, but she was well-cared for. Maddy seemed to breathe easier now that she had Jace in her life to share the burden, and Angie was glad. She'd watched her friend spiral into worry and quiet desperation in some of her darker days. She hadn't known how to fix it.

But Jace had. Maddy was whole with his love and support, and that was the best thing that could have happened. Even if the way they'd met had been unorthodox. Angie didn't know everything—more of that sensitive information stuff—but Jace had apparently mistook Maddy for a criminal and apprehended her.

Which is how Angie's life ended up containing muscled men who carried weapons and exuded an air of danger and confidence that was intoxicating under the right circumstances.

Mostly, the right circumstances were when the man was Colt and he was doing his utmost to take care of her.

The power flickered and the lights died. Angie felt Colt tense but then the lights snapped on again a few seconds later. Maddy kept chatting about her visit to

The Oaks to see Mimi, the renovations, and how happy she was that Angie was feeling better. They talked about Barton, Barnes and Blake and the effort to reopen. They briefly discussed Jenny, but Maddy hadn't known Jenny.

Angie felt Colt's gaze on her, as if he was urging her not to say too much. She took the hint and didn't discuss anything that Maddy didn't bring up.

"We should get going," Colt said when they'd been there for half an hour. He gave Maddy a kiss on the cheek. "I need to put the groceries away and start dinner."

Maddy smiled up at him. "Listen to you, sounding so domestic. Fine, run home and put dinner on."

She winked at Angie, and Angie felt the beginnings of another blush.

"Thanks for taking such good care of my bestie," Maddy said.

"It's been my honor," Colt replied. Angie's heart squeezed at how serious he sounded. Like she was important. Special.

His gaze met hers, and butterflies swirled like they'd been caught in a tornado.

Good lord, she was a goner.

———

ANGIE WAS silent on the ride home. Other than a quiet "Thank you, Colt. I needed that," she didn't say anything more. The ride wasn't far, only a couple of blocks, so he probably shouldn't be surprised. He checked the house before he let her inside, then returned to get the rest of the groceries. Angie waited in the kitchen. When he set the bags down she started to pull items out and place them on the counter.

"Do you have a particular way you want the cold stuff put away or does it matter?"

"It doesn't matter," he said. Even if it did, he wouldn't tell her. He'd let her be helpful because she wanted to, and then he'd shift it all later if it mattered to him. Which it really didn't.

Angie opened the fridge and put things inside while he put the dry goods in the pantry. It was more than he usually bought since he never knew when he'd be out of the country, but he'd enjoyed shopping with Angie. He'd kept thinking of things he wanted to cook for her.

She picked up a box of pancake mix and frowned.

"Everything okay?" he asked.

She handed it to him and he put it in the pantry.

"The last time I saw Jenny, we had pancakes. I never imagined it would be the last time."

"I know. I'm sorry."

She sighed. "Like I said, we weren't close or anything. It's just so awful that she's gone. And even more awful if someone killed her. I hope you find out if they did, and then I hope you make them pay for it."

"If she was murdered, we'll make them pay for it."

"I know you will," she said with a soft smile. She shook herself. "I don't want to think about it anymore. I'd rather think about happier things. Like dinner. What's the plan?"

He put his hands on her shoulders, skimmed them down her arms, and held her lightly. She didn't pull away, and he felt a hot wave of possessiveness flood him. So much progress in such a short time. He wondered how much farther they could go, but he wasn't going to push. He dropped a kiss on her forehead, inhaled the scent of her shampoo, and straightened.

"How about that *coq au vin* you wanted before? I can get started on it and it'll simmer until dinner."

"Mmm, sounds good. Can I help?"

"You can chop vegetables."

She put her palms on his chest, stared at the backs of her hands. He held her lightly so she could break away if she wanted. But she didn't. Finally, she looked up at him, their gazes locking. He saw trust in her gaze. And heat.

The heat sent a signal to his brain that nearly short-circuited it. *Easy, boy.*

"You've been so good to me," she said. "Even when I didn't deserve it. And I... I like being here with you."

"I like being with you too, Angie."

She smiled. His dick grew harder. He wanted to kiss her, but he knew if he did it would be almost impossible to stop. And he wasn't making the first move. It was up to her. He hadn't realized that's what he'd decided until this moment, but he had. It felt right.

He skimmed his fingers over her cheek and took a step back. She seemed puzzled for a second, but she turned toward the fridge and pulled it open. "What am I chopping, chef?"

"Carrots, onion, garlic, and mushrooms."

"Already sounds delicious."

They worked together like a seasoned team. Colt browned the chicken, then removed it from the pan and cooked the vegetables. Angie watched everything he did, handed him seasonings as he needed them, and opened the oven when it was time to put the pot with the chicken, wine, and vegetables inside to bake.

"How long do you leave it in there?" Angie asked.

"A couple of hours."

She grinned at him. "I'm completely impressed with you right now. The omelet and crepes were delicious, and you make a mean piece of toast, but everything you just did? Wow."

He shrugged. "My *grand-mère* believed everyone should know how to cook. Boys and girls equally. It's a skill I'm glad I have."

"You'll never have to subsist on microwave meals and bags of popcorn."

"No, thank God."

He started the water in the sink. Angie hip-checked him. "I'll wash the dishes."

He grabbed a towel. "I'll dry."

They worked together, cleaning up the mess. When the sink was empty, Angie turned to him. "You like cooking, don't you?"

He wasn't sure where this was leading, but he answered honestly. "When I have time. It's relaxing. Makes the world go away for a while."

She fiddled with the paper towel she'd grabbed to wipe water off the counter. "Dan knew how to cook, but he resented that I didn't. He used to get mad that I couldn't fix dinner unless it was microwavable. Like I was doing it on purpose. He tried to teach me to cook, but like I said, I'm a disaster in the kitchen."

Colt's senses went on high alert. She was telling him something personal. He knew Dan was her ex, the one she'd planned to marry. All she'd said before was that he'd cheated on her and she'd dumped him.

"Or maybe he wasn't patient enough with you."

She frowned. "That too. He'd tell me it was so easy, all I had to do was pay attention. When I'd burn something, he'd get mad. And you know what, I think I could have learned. I think part of me stubbornly didn't want to. I was working long hours, teaching school and going back to get my accounting degree. I was burning the candle at both ends to build a better life for us, and he was pissed because I didn't fix dinner more often. I should have realized sooner what a jerk he was."

"We don't all have the same talents or interests. You probably could learn to cook, no matter what you think about your ability. But if it was a skill of his and you cleaned up everything like you just did for me, I don't know why he'd have a problem with it."

She tossed the paper towel in the trash and crossed her arms over her breasts. "Because he came from the kind of background where his mother did everything while his father lounged on the couch after work, even though she worked too. Dan just wanted somebody to cater to him, like his mom did for his dad. Only he didn't put it that way. He tried to pretend he was all about sharing the burdens, but he really wasn't."

"I know you already know this, Ang, but he was a fucking idiot."

She blushed. "Well, I certainly think so. Thanks for agreeing with me."

He stalked over to where she leaned against the counter. Put a hand on either side of her, trapping her there. "Do you know why I think he was a fucking idiot?"

She blinked up at him. Shook her head.

He focused his gaze on her plump lower lip. He wanted to nibble that lip, suck it between his own like a ripe cherry. "He was a fucking idiot because he'd convinced you to marry him and then he did everything he could to ruin it. He had no idea how lucky he was to have you. I hope he's miserable as hell right now."

Angie's color was still high. She smiled as she sort of melted against the counter. She put a hand on his abdomen, trailed it up his chest and palmed his cheek. "I hope so too. He got married a few months after we split. Last I heard, they had a kid and then he left her for another woman. So he's paying child support to the first and planning a wedding to the second. I had a lucky escape."

She straightened herself against him, put her other palm on his cheek and cupped his face. He had to force himself not to move. Not to press his dick against her and show her how she affected him.

Let her make the moves, dude.

"You know, I don't really want to talk about Dan," she said. "I'm not still hung up on him and I don't miss him at all. I just wanted you to know that I think you're pretty incredible—and maybe I've spent too much time in my head comparing you to Dan and thinking you'd turn out to be the same way because that's how guys are. But I think I was wrong. I've had enough time to watch Jace and Maddy, and he's nothing like that. Neither are you."

He didn't want to fuck this up, but he also had to know. "Why did you want to marry him, Ang?"

She let out a breath. Shook her head. Then her liquid green eyes met his. "I'm not sure anymore. He was the first guy to ask me. Which is crazy, I know—but I didn't have a lot of confidence back then. I still don't sometimes. I just hide it well."

He put his hands on her hips, pulled her in close enough to feel how she affected him. Her eyes widened a little, but she didn't pull away.

"I think you're the sexiest woman I've ever met. Don't you have any idea how gorgeous you are?"

She smiled up at him. "You're sweet. I know I'm attractive, but I'm not special or anything. My hips are too big, and my chest isn't quite big enough. And then there's all this crazy blushing I do because I'm so pale."

"I like the blushing. It's how I know you're attracted to me."

"See? I couldn't deny it even if I wanted to."

"Why would you want to?"

She rolled her lips inward. "To protect myself?"

"You don't have to protect yourself with me, Angie. I won't hurt you. It's the last thing I'd ever do."

"I know. I didn't always know, but I do now." She spread her palms over his pecs. "If you decide you're done and want to move on, I'd appreciate knowing it up front, okay? No pretending or trying to figure out how to let me down easy. Just tell me and let me deal with it."

She was talking crazy. Once she was his, he had no intention of letting her go. Oh, he'd thought at one time he'd walk away because she deserved a normal guy. But that's not what was going to happen. He knew that now. Angie was his. He just had to prove that he'd be there for her no matter what. There were things he still needed to tell her, but he'd get to that. Soon.

"I'm not ever going to be done with you."

She frowned at him. "Colt, be serious."

"I am being serious, *minette*."

"You can't be serious. We barely know each other. I might snore. Or nag. Or any number of crazy things you'll hate."

"You don't snore, except when you're sick, and even that's barely on the Richter scale. You might nag, I don't know, but I can handle that. As for knowing each other—isn't that what we're doing? Getting to know each other better?"

She nodded. "Yes."

"So let's go watch a movie while we wait for dinner to cook. We can watch one of your old favorites and you can tell me what your grandfather liked about it."

She nibbled her lip. "What if I have a better idea?"

"What's that, *minette?*"

"I-I want you to kiss me."

Chapter Sixteen

"THAT ACCOUNTANT BROAD IS STAYING WITH THE GUY she was with the night Tommy tried to break into her condo. Big, tough looking dude. Military or former military. One of Ian Black's people."

"Do you know where they are?" Paul Sobol sat at his desk and frowned at the computer screen in front of him, listening to the voice on the phone. This whole fucking thing was a disaster. It'd gone sideways in more ways than one. First Charles, then Jenny Clark, and now this Angie Turner chick.

Steve was pissed as hell. Calling him from Miami, telling him to take care of things. He fucking hated Steve. Asshole married his sister and thought he owned Paul too. Well, he fucking didn't.

Paul had been skimming money right from under the asshole's nose and he had no clue. The plan was to take enough to disappear one day. But then Charles had to go and get a conscience. He'd had no problem lining his own pockets until he found some transactions he didn't like. What did Paul care if Steve wanted to funnel weapons to a bunch of terrorist jerk-offs in Afghanistan? Let them kill each other. Who the fuck cared? And if a few U.S. military troops got in the way, well, that's just the way war worked.

Paul hadn't sent them to a war zone. Neither had Steve. But Charles—shit, you'd have thought the dude was personally being sent over there to join them the way he'd reacted. Yeah, his little sister had been in the military, but she'd died in a car accident in Germany. So what the fuck was his problem? His sister couldn't get killed again.

Charles had threatened to blow the whole operation wide open. He'd sworn they wouldn't get caught if they exposed Steve, but Paul knew it wasn't possible. The blowback would get them all killed because Steve wouldn't go down without taking as many people with him as he could. That's what Charles refused to understand.

While Paul didn't have any problems stealing from his brother-in-law, he had huge problems with dying. Hence the current mess.

"Yeah, I know where they are," Marco said. "It's not far from her friend's house. They were there for tea and fucking cookies today when our boys were working on the electrical. We tagged his vehicle while they were inside playing tea party."

Paul could almost breathe again. Almost. "Don't do anything until I call you again. I'll be in touch."

"I'll be waiting."

———

HER HEART RACED. Little beads of sweat popped up on her skin. Had she really asked him to kiss her?

Colt stood near, his big form towering over her. Today he wore a gray T-shirt that clung to his muscles like a second skin and a blue plaid button down with long sleeves, open and untucked. His gaze grew hot.

He slid a hand around her back and tugged her closer, tipping her chin up with the other.

"Nothing would give me more pleasure, Angelica. Just so we're clear—a kiss and then a movie? Or a kiss and let's see where it goes?"

Angie swallowed. On the one hand, she was mortified that she had to say what she wanted. On the other, she loved that he wanted to make sure. How many guys would do that?

None that she'd gone out with, that's for sure. She hadn't had sex with any of them in recent years, but that didn't mean they hadn't tried to push her into it.

"The second one," she said on a whisper.

One corner of his mouth lifted in a feral grin. "That's what I was hoping you'd say. But Ang—nothing happens without your permission, okay? If you don't like something, tell me. You're calling all the shots here."

Oh, she loved that he'd said that. Loved that he meant it. Because she knew he did. Colt Duchaine was masculine enough and badass enough to be utterly confident. He wasn't going to take it personally if she put the brakes on. It wouldn't be a blow to his fragile ego or an insult to his manhood. He was bigger than that. Better than that.

He was a protector, and he was determined to protect her. Even from himself.

Angie shivered. She didn't want to stop anything, but she knew it was a possibility. What if she panicked? It'd been over two years since she'd had sex with a man. A vibrator wasn't the same at all, even though she'd worked hers out pretty regularly. Mr. Dick was big and glittery pink—and very satisfactory —but he wasn't attached to two-hundred and twenty pounds of prime male flesh.

Hard, beautiful, delicious male flesh.

Colt stepped in closer, though she'd have said it wasn't possible. His mouth dropped onto hers. Angie moaned as firm lips pressed down. Her mouth fell open and his tongue slipped inside. It was only the second time she'd kissed him this way.

It. Was. Glorious.

Tongue against tongue, sliding, dancing, thrusting, retreating. Her heart was a reckless wild thing, leaping and racing and rushing blindly through the forest of her fears. Fears that seemed smaller and less important than they had not that long ago.

Angie melded her body to his, wrapped her arms around his neck, and kissed him back with all the passion she possessed. His hands on her tightened, but he didn't lose control. She could feel his cock pressing into her abdomen, and it didn't scare her.

No, it turned her on. For the first time in a long time, she wasn't afraid of the idea of more.

Colt broke the kiss gently. "Baby, you need to know that I can't do much more of this."

"Why?" she asked, confused. She was holding off on hurt until she understood. But it was there, under the surface. Waiting to break free. "Is—is something wrong?"

His brows lifted. "Wrong?" He flexed his hips and she felt his cock against her. "Believe me, there's nothing wrong. I want you, baby. I want to take you to my bedroom, strip you naked, and lick you into a screaming orgasm before I slide inside you and take us both the heaven. I can't keep kissing you like this if it's not going to happen. I've wanted you for a long time, and the more I kiss you, the harder I get. But I'm not pushing you, so I have to stop."

Angie slid her hand down and over the bulge in his jeans. He hissed in a breath. "Angie. Jesus."

"I want you too, Colt." He leaned toward her again and she put a finger against his lips to stop him. "I have to tell you something first."

"Okay."

She gathered her courage. "It's been a long time for me. I haven't, um, had sex with a man since Dan left. So I want you to know that, because it worries me it might, um, be uncomfortable."

Colt hugged her to him without hesitation. Her eyes blurred and she pressed her cheek to his chest, breathing in the warm, masculine scent of him.

"*Minette*, I promise you I will do everything in my power to make it great for you. If you're not having fun, neither am I."

God, he was nothing like Dan. Or any other man she'd ever dated. He actually cared about her pleasure and not just his own. How had she been so stupid before? Why had she ever put up with any man who'd made her feel bad about herself? Why did any woman?

Angie tilted her head back. "Thank you for saying that."

"I mean it."

"I know you do."

He toyed with a lock of her hair. "I want to see you wearing nothing but this hair in my bed. I've dreamed of it for months."

"I'm ready," she said. "I want that too."

She really did. So much.

He hooked an arm behind her knees and picked her up. She squeaked in surprise, clinging to him as he strode through the house and into the master. He

229

set her down on the bed, then stepped back and slid the plaid shirt from his shoulders. Angie lay back on her elbows to enjoy the show.

When he reached behind him and tugged the gray shirt up and off with one hand, Angie sighed. "That is the sexiest move ever."

He laughed. "I've got more."

He unbuckled his belt, unbuttoned his jeans and unzipped them, and then produced a pistol. Angie blinked. She hadn't known it was there. He set it on the nightstand and advanced on her without pushing his jeans down his hips the way she wanted.

She lay back on the bed as he came down on top of her, hovering over her rather than pressing her into the mattress. She let her gaze slide over his bare chest. The scar from where he'd been shot was smooth and shiny, a round disk of flesh that was far too close to his heart. Her eyes filled with tears as she looked at it.

"Hey," he said.

She dragged her gaze to his.

"I didn't die. I was very, very lucky. Or Natasha was a great shot. Either way, the outcome was the same. I'm here, now. I'm with you and I don't want you to dwell on it or blame yourself or any of that crap, okay? It happened and it's done."

She reached up and traced it with a finger. "I know." The lump in her throat was huge. "I'm working on not blaming myself, okay? It's just that I've never seen the scar before."

He dropped his head and kissed her softly. "Want me to put a Band-Aid on it?" he whispered.

She pushed back enough to see his face. He was grinning at her.

"That's ridiculous."

"I know. But if it gets me laid, I'm all for it."

She caressed his cheek. "You're still getting laid, sweetie. It was a moment, not a roadblock."

"Thank god for that," he growled—and then he kissed her again, a full-on assault that obliterated any defenses she might have still had.

Angie smoothed her hands over his skin, exploring the dip and swell of strong muscles. He rolled to his back and took her with him. She straddled him, and though she was still fully dressed, the feel of his erection pressing into that space where she ached for him was intoxicating.

She rubbed herself against his hardness and sparks flew behind her eyes. Colt's hands slipped beneath her sweater, sliding against bare skin as they moved north. She expected him to go straight for her breasts, but he didn't. Instead he traced little circles against her skin, going higher each time. When he got to the swell of her breasts, he traced the undersides of them without trying to move beneath the fabric.

Angie was holding her breath by the time he slid a thumb over one of her nipples. A shot of pleasure vibrated through her, connecting to her pussy. She was wetter than she'd been in a long time, and she was tired of waiting for more.

She pushed herself upright, breaking their kiss, and dragged her sweater over her head. Then she dropped it and reached behind her to unhook her bra. Colt sat up, his fingers covering hers as he helped her unhook it. He slid it from her shoulders and down her arms. She almost folded her arms to cover herself, but she didn't.

Colt's gaze was rapt. "Baby, those are the prettiest breasts I've ever seen."

Angie snorted, though she was ridiculously pleased. "Stop it. They're just boobs. Like so many others."

"You aren't changing my mind," he told her.

He reached up and pinched her nipples gently between thumb and forefinger. That intense drip of pleasure in her veins intensified. When he leaned forward and licked the tip of a nipple, she shuddered, curling her fingers into his shoulders.

"Colt," she gasped.

He licked her again. "Yeah, *ma petite?*"

Oh god, he was planning to talk French while he fucked her. She was going to die.

"More of that. I want more," she moaned.

"My pleasure." Colt slid his hands around her back, arched her toward him, and began to lick and suck her nipples like they were the key to her orgasm.

Which they very well might be considering how

turned on she was. Every pull of his mouth on her breasts made lightning sizzle down into her deepest core.

"Colt," she called out when she didn't think she could take another moment of torture. "Please."

He didn't have to ask *please, what?* He rolled her to her back and lifted himself high enough to unzip her jeans and tug them down her hips.

"Shoes," she said, and he moved to take off her boots and socks before stripping her jeans and dropping them onto the bed with her sweater.

"Holy shit, Ang." His gaze swept her from head to toe. "You're fucking amazing."

She felt a blush happening. There was nothing she could do to stop it. "So are you," she breathed.

He grinned. He stood and stripped. Her mouth dropped open as his cock sprang free.

Oh my…

He was nothing less than stunning. Of course. His body was beautiful, packed with hard muscle that was lean and defined. He had a flat abdomen—naturally—and those gorgeous hip bone things that slanted into a vee and pointed to his cock.

He was long and thick and slightly curved. Angie reached out to touch him before she could think twice about it. He groaned, his head tipping back as she stroked the velvety skin.

"You have no idea how many times I've imagined you doing that," he told her.

"I've imagined it too." She scooted to the edge of the bed and bent toward him, intent on tasting him.

"Ang, you don't have to—"

She licked the tip of him and his breath hissed in. He tasted salty and she swiped her tongue over him again. She loved the way he jerked.

"I know I don't. I want to."

"This isn't supposed to be about me, *minette*. It's supposed to be about you. I promised to make *you* feel great."

She stroked him. "And when do you get to feel great too?"

"I already do." He swallowed. "Just being here with you. Touching you. Tasting you."

Angie slid her tongue along the underside of his cock and his head dropped back. "Fucking hell," he said.

Emboldened, she opened her mouth and took him in. Or as much of him as she could. Her jaw stretched wide as she moved lower, taking more of him. She cupped his balls with her other hand. They were tight. Firm.

"Angie, baby. You're killing me."

"Not trying to," she said before she sucked him in again. God, she was enjoying this. Enjoying having this kind of power over him. Colton Duchaine, French-American soldier of fortune. Hard-muscled badass. Amazing man who could cook like a dream and took care of her without complaint while she was sick. He was tender and sexy and serious.

She couldn't love him more if she tried.

Love?

Yes, love. She really did love him. She'd tried not to, tried so hard to keep her distance and not let him in. It was all for nothing.

They hadn't had sex yet and she loved him. *You've done it now, Angelica. You're doomed.*

She must have hesitated because he reached for her, tugged her up until she was standing on the bed. She wasn't much taller than he was from that vantage. He held her loosely, looking up at her with those soulful blue eyes. Her heart ached with everything she felt for this man.

She couldn't tell him. It was far too soon for that. And she was far too vulnerable.

"You okay?" he asked, searching her gaze.

"I'm fine, Colt. More than fine."

He smiled and pushed her hair from her face. "You looked a little emotional for a second."

"I am emotional." No sense lying. "I feel amazing with you."

"You are amazing, baby. Now lie back and let me lick you."

She sucked in a sharp, pained breath. Love hurt even when it felt good. "Do you think we could save that for the next time? I want to feel you inside me the first time I come with you."

Chapter Seventeen

SHE WAS GOING TO MAKE HIM COME UNGLUED BEFORE this was over. When she put her mouth on him, he thought he would lose it and embarrass himself before he ever made her come. By sheer force of will, he didn't explode all over her tongue.

Now she wanted him inside her instead of letting him taste her first. Not what he'd expected. But the way she said she wanted to come with him inside her the first time—hell, it made him want to pound his chest like a gorilla.

His girl wanted to ride his cock worse than she wanted his mouth on her clit. Amazing.

"Do you think you're ready?" he asked. Because she said it'd been a long time for her and she was afraid it might be uncomfortable. He didn't want to shove his way inside her and have her regret it.

"Honestly, Colt, I don't think I could get any wetter. Or more ready."

He took them both down to the bed, holding her tenderly, cushioning her fall. She wrapped her legs around him. He took a moment to appreciate the fact he was about to live out one of his wildest fantasies.

Getting balls deep inside Angie Turner, the sexy redhead who'd been haunting his dreams for months. The source of a thousand nights of jerking off onto his belly and wishing he was inside her.

He reached between them and slipped a finger into her folds. Holy hell, she was wet. She moaned a little as he circled her clit, flicking it softly.

"Shit," he said. "Condom."

She dropped her legs from around his waist and he sat up and reached for the condom he'd set on the nightstand earlier. Angie watched as he tore the package open and rolled the condom on. He knelt between her legs and met her gaze across the valley of her belly and the peaks of her breasts.

So pretty, his girl.

"You still good with this?" he asked.

Her eyebrows rose. "Are you kidding me? If you don't make me come, I will *die*. I'm so turned on right now it hurts."

He understood that kind of turned on. Felt it too. He dropped down on top of her and she wrapped her legs around him again. Then he kissed her, tongue against tongue, tasting and teasing while she arched her body up to his and tried to get his cock inside her.

He stopped teasing her and eased inside. Slowly, so she could adjust.

So he could adjust.

Her body opened to him and he slid home with ease. She was so fucking wet and he wanted to pump hard until he exploded.

He didn't though. He held himself still, just kissing her. He could feel her heartbeat, fast and sure, and he knew his own echoed it.

"Colt," she whispered between kisses. "It's fine. I'm fine. Please, *please*, move. Take me to heaven."

"Anything for you, *mon ange.*"

He started to move, slowly and surely, stoking the fires between them. Angie's eyes drifted closed and she caught her lower lip between her teeth. "Oh, yes," she moaned. "Like that."

Her pleasure was the most important thing in the world to him. He needed her to beg him, and he needed her to come. Only then would he let himself go.

He didn't have long to wait. Angie gripped him harder, her arms and legs tightening around him as his thrusts intensified.

"More," she gasped. "More."

He gave it to her, sliding a hand beneath her ass and lifting her to him, rocking into her body faster and harder. He could feel the tightening in her limbs, the quickening of her breathing. She was close.

"Look at me," he told her.

Her eyes popped open, their green depths hazy with pleasure.

"Come for me, Angie."

"I've never—" she choked out. "Oh, God."

He felt it happening. The rippling of internal muscles gripping him tightly, the stiffening of her limbs, the uncontrolled gasps and moans. She came apart around him. It was beautiful to watch. He said things to her in French, words tumbling over themselves to spill out and tell her how gorgeous she was, how perfect, and how much he cared for her. Really cared.

Hell, was this what love felt like? He hadn't had eyes for anyone else since the first moment he'd seen her on Maddy's couch. He'd been intrigued, attracted, mesmerized. He'd thought he'd seduce her, have some fun, and they'd part company.

It hadn't worked that way. Here they were, months later, and she was a fire in his blood that didn't feel like it was ever going to go out. He was buried deep inside her, she was splintering apart around him, and all he wanted to do was make it happen again.

"Colt," she whispered, and he ran a thumb across her bottom lip. "That was—I can't—" She closed her eyes. "I want to feel you come."

He captured her lips, thrust his tongue into her mouth, and rocked into her with new determination. He wanted to make her come again, and he wanted to go over the edge with her. He slipped a hand between them, found her clit and stroked it until she was panting.

When she soared over the edge this time, he was right behind her, groaning her name against her neck. He emptied himself into the condom, shuddering with the force of everything he felt.

This was home. She was home.

He was in love for the first and last time in his life.

———

AFTER COMING TWICE, Angie fell asleep. She didn't want to, but her body was still a little weak from being sick and she had no choice in the matter. She grew drowsy, and then she dropped off when Colt got up to dispose of the condom. She felt him climb into the bed and draw her close, but all she did was snuggle up to him and pass out.

When she woke, it was dark out—and she was alone. She lay there confused for a moment....

And then it all came back and heat rolled over her. She'd had sex with Colt.

He'd rocked her world. She'd been so excited that she came with nothing more than the pressure of his cock inside her the first time.

That had never happened before.

She pushed the covers back and searched for her clothes. She could hear Colt banging around in the kitchen, and she wanted to join him. She found her panties, but nothing else in the tangle of covers. She slipped those on. In the light coming through the open door, she saw Colt's plaid shirt draped on a chair. She put it on and buttoned it. It came to her knees. She padded into the hallway and toward the kitchen at the other end of the house.

The rooms were small and boxy, cut off from each other by walls. The house had potential though. For the first time, she thought of how it would look with the wall between the kitchen and living room knocked down. Get rid of the avocado appliances, put in some new cabinets and countertops—maybe an island too. Add some new flooring, and badda bing badda boom, a showpiece kitchen.

Angie shook her head with a small laugh. Damn Maddy and her decorating shows.

She hesitated when she was almost there. What would Colt say to her?

Would he look at her like he'd been there, done that, and now he was marking time until she could go home again? Had she made a mistake to sleep with him?

Her heart throbbed with fear and indecision. Her head told her she'd made a mess of the whole thing.

She'd fallen for him, had sex with him, and now he might be ready to move on.

You should have waited to fall for him, dummy. Or maybe you should have fucked him months ago, then kicked him to the curb.

"No," she muttered, shaking her head. Colt wasn't like that. She knew he wasn't.

Angie took a deep breath and walked into the kitchen. Colt looked up from where he sat at the table with his phone in his hand. He shot to his feet.

"Baby, what's wrong?" he asked, taking her into his arms.

She hugged him, burying her face against his gray T-shirt. "Nothing. I'm fine."

"Are you sure?"

She pushed back and gazed up at him. "Yes. I was being silly. I thought I'd walk in here and you'd be done with me. Like the look on your face would tell me you'd gotten what you wanted and now you were done."

He kissed her forehead, her cheeks, her lips. He murmured in French. She didn't know what he was saying. Maybe the same things he'd said when he'd been buried inside her, or maybe something different. She didn't know, but she loved it. Felt comforted by it this time, whereas before it'd been the sexiest thing she'd ever heard.

"I'm not done with you, *minette*. I'm addicted to you," he said, and she shuddered with quiet bliss.

"That's good because I think I'm addicted to you too." She could say it because her face was pressed to his chest, but she blushed just the same.

He tipped her chin up and kissed her, a soft slow sweet kiss that curled her toes and started the fires burning in her core again. So easy for him. She felt like she could come again and again if he wanted her to.

He broke the kiss and stepped back, but he still held her lightly. "Are you hungry?"

She started to tell him yes, she was hungry for him —but her belly growled and she had to laugh. He laughed too. "Imma take that as a yes," he said. His gaze dropped over her. "I love the way my shirt looks on you."

"I couldn't find my clothes, so I grabbed it. I hoped you wouldn't mind."

He smiled. "I don't mind." He slipped a hand beneath and squeezed her ass. "In fact, I prefer it."

She giggled. Like, seriously? Since when did she giggle?

Apparently when a big, strapping, hotter than hot man who spoke French in her ear and kissed like a dream grabbed her ass and told her he liked her in his shirts.

He let her go and pulled a chair out for her. *"Mademoiselle,"* he said.

Angie sat. It wasn't really odd to be at the table in his shirt, with only panties beneath, because it was a lot like wearing a dress. Except it was way better than a dress because the shirt smelled like him.

Colt served her *coq au vin* with crusty bread and a nice Pinot Noir. He played French music through the wireless speaker sitting on the counter. It was romantic and homey. She didn't care if the appliances were avocado and the floor was old vinyl tile, it was far better than sitting in a fussy restaurant with table-cloths and hovering waiters.

And more honest too. They were themselves. No pretense.

"What do you think?" he asked when she'd tasted the first bite of her chicken.

"I think it's a wonder you aren't married yet," she teased.

He laughed. "Yeah, well, I guess I never met the right woman."

"Ever come close?"

Because she was completely curious. Overwhelmingly so. Yet her heart tapped out a faster beat as she waited for his answer.

His blue gaze sparked. "Nope."

She thought he wouldn't say anything else, but then he did.

"I didn't think my life was the kind I could ask anyone to share. Plus I never met anyone who I wanted to ask before."

He held her gaze for a long minute, and her heart throbbed. She told herself not to read anything into it, but of course her crazy heart wanted desperately to do so.

He took a sip of his wine, and the spell broke. "What really made you want to marry Dan? There had to be more to it than he asked."

Angie's belly tightened. She'd started the topic, so she wasn't going to suddenly beg off it. He'd seen through her previous answer.

"I thought I was in love. I guess I was for a while, really. It's a lot easier to say in hindsight that you didn't love someone—but the truth is I thought I did while it was going on. I felt like getting married and having a family was one of those things I was supposed to do. Dan was handsome and educated, and he had a great career ahead of him. He was going to Georgetown Law. I thought he was the perfect man to build a future with. I was wrong."

"He was an idiot, Ang. I said that before. But I'm glad he was because we wouldn't be sitting here if you'd married him."

Her mouth curved in a smile. "You say the nicest things."

"It's not nice. It's true. His mistake was my gain. You're sitting there in my shirt, you aren't wearing a bra—which has been on my mind since you walked in —and I've got the rest of the night to explore every inch of you." He lifted his wine glass. "To Dan."

Angie giggled. She clinked her glass with his. "To Dan."

"I'm sorry he hurt you, Angie. I know I'm joking about him, but I also know it wasn't fun to go through what he did to you."

"No, it definitely wasn't." She studied the wine for a second. "I thought it was me. I thought I was the problem. I wasn't enough for him. If I couldn't be enough for him, how would I ever be enough for anyone else?"

Old hurts rose to the surface but she swallowed them down. She shrugged as if it was nothing. Colt reached over and put his hand on hers. She looked up at him.

"You know the problem was all his, right? It wasn't you at all."

Love, sharp and sweet, squeezed her lungs. "I know. But it's made me cautious."

He lifted her hand and kissed it, and the sweet ache of desire slid through her veins. Oh what he did to her.

"I get it, *minette*. When we were in bed and you said you'd never... what did you mean?"

Heat washed over her. She remembered that moment. Vividly.

She dropped her gaze from his. Took a moment to find her courage. "I've never come that way before. With a man inside me. No, um, direct stimulation."

She looked up again, her face on fire—and found him smiling broadly. Proudly. She relaxed.

"You're thrilled about it," she said with a laugh.

"Damn right. I mean yeah, I'm kinda pissed the other men in your life were too damned incompetent or impatient or whatever, but I'm ridiculously happy I'm the one it happened with. Maybe we can make it happen again. So long as you aren't too sore."

It was a little tender down there, but not in a bad way. More of an *I want to do that again as soon as possible* way.

"I think I can handle another round."

Colt winked. "Better eat up then. You might need the energy."

Chapter Eighteen

THEY ATE DINNER, CLEANED UP THE KITCHEN together, and then snuggled on the couch to watch *Doctor Zhivago*. Colt had never watched it before. He soon knew why.

It was long as fuck, but Angie was enthralled.

Though she dozed against him at one point. She dropped off, her head on his chest, her body curled against his. He sat there watching the beautiful and tragic Lara with her lover Yuri, feeling the impossibility of their situation, and wondering in spite of himself how it would turn out.

He thought about taking Angie to bed for the night, but it wasn't all that late yet and he knew she'd wake soon. It was probably the food that did it rather than any lingering tiredness.

Sure enough, she woke about twenty minutes later. He could feel the change in her body as she became more alert. She looked up at him and smiled. "Sorry. I didn't mean to nap."

"It's okay," he told her. "You must have needed it."

He loved having her beside him. Trusting him as she slept.

"I'm not typically a napper. I'll get back to normal soon."

She didn't push away from him. He liked that. She snuggled closer. He slipped a hand beneath the blanket she'd tugged over her body and cupped her ass cheek. She didn't say anything as he caressed her.

He tried to pay attention to Lara and Yuri, but the sensation of Angie's skin beneath his hand, and her soft body pressed beside his, made the blood start to flow south.

"Colt," she choked out a short while later.

"Yeah, *minette?*" He tipped his head down to meet her gaze.

She surged up, straddling his lap, and pressed her mouth to his. "This," she whispered against his lips. "You make me crazy."

She plunged her tongue into his mouth. Her hair fell around them, curtaining them. He speared his fingers into it and cupped her head. He knew what he wanted this time. They kissed, long deep kisses that made him harder than stone. And when he'd had enough of that, he pushed her onto her back and reached beneath his shirt to hook his fingers into her panties.

He stripped them off easily. Dropped them to the floor.

"Colt," she said as he unbuttoned the shirt and parted it. He didn't remove it though. He wanted to see her spread out before him, his shirt hugging her body.

"My turn," he told her before dropping to suck her nipples. She gasped and speared her fingers into his hair.

He dropped lower, over her belly, kissing her sweet pale skin. He made his way lower, his shoulders between her legs. He looked up at her. She bit her lip, her eyes heated and sexy.

"Do you know what I'm about to do?"

She nodded.

"Tell me you want it."

He knew she did, but he wanted to hear her say it.

"I want it. Your tongue on me. In me. Make me come, Colt."

That was all he needed to hear. He spread her apart with his thumbs. Then he licked her in one long swipe, from wet seam to clit. She moaned.

It made him bolder. He flicked his tongue against her clit, swirled around it, sucked it. She squirmed and moaned and it spurred him on. He wanted to make her scream. He wanted to taste her when she came and know it was because of him.

He added two fingers, fucking her slowly, hooking them into that area that contained her G-spot. Her hips gyrated and bucked, but he didn't let up.

When she came apart, it was something to behold. Her eyes popped open, widening as she stared at him. "Colt…."

She moaned his name. It was the most beautiful fucking thing he'd ever heard. Her hips bucked harder, riding his tongue until she collapsed onto the couch and tried to close her legs.

He thought about pushing her into another orgasm. He decided against it since she was still getting her strength back. He kissed his way up her body, taking her mouth in a hot, wet kiss that he knew would taste like her.

She didn't retreat. She kissed him, sighing.

When he lifted himself away, she caught at him. "I want you inside me."

His cock ached for her, but he didn't want to push her too far. "You sure? It might hurt a bit."

"After that? Hell yes I'm sure."

"Baby, you don't have to do it because I took care of you. I can wait."

She frowned. She almost looked hurt. "Really? You can wait?"

"I don't want to wait, Ang. I *can* wait. There's a difference."

She tugged at him. "I don't want to wait. I can't."

He laughed softly. "You just came. Do you really want more?"

"Of course I do. Are you crazy? I've been deprived for far too long."

"Condoms are in the bedroom. I have to get one."

She reached for his cock, squeezed. Lightning streaked through him.

"What if you don't? I'm on the pill. I've been tested for diseases. I don't have any."

His heart skipped. "I always wrap it up. I've never gone bare."

"Do you want to? With me?"

"Fuck yeah I want that. Are you sure?"

She smiled. "I'm sure. I don't feel like this is a one night stand. Is it?"

He stroked the skin of her belly. Dipped between her legs and into her pussy. She hissed in a breath. He loved the way it sounded. "Not for me. I care about you, Angie. I've cared for a long time."

Her eyes were luminous. "I care too."

"I want a lot more nights of this. Me and you, nothing but skin and heat and closeness."

"I want the same thing."

He lowered himself on top of her. "I feel like there's a lot more we need to discuss, but I'm not capable of it right now."

She wrapped her legs around him. "Me neither."

He slid inside her, bare skin to bare skin. The

rightness of it made him groan. "That's fucking amazing."

She was smiling. Laughing softly. "It's incredible."

He gripped her ass and started to move. "Hang on, babe. This is about to blow your mind."

———

THEY SLEPT NAKED. Angie loved being pressed up against Colt in the night, feeling the solid weight of him. The heat of his skin. The steady beat of his heart.

She woke a couple of times, confused about where she was in the fog of sleep. It came rushing back each time and she sighed in contentment. She was in bed with Colt, in love with Colt, and they had something between them that was new and beautiful.

They hadn't talked about the future. They hadn't talked much at all. Not with words anyway.

There was time for that.

She didn't know how he felt about her. He didn't talk like a man who planned to throw her out tomorrow, but she didn't really know what he was thinking. It worried her if she thought about it. She told herself not to think about it.

She'd thrown herself into this thing. It was too late to back out.

And she didn't want to back out.

When she woke again, something was chirping.

Angie pushed herself up. Colt wasn't in bed. It was still dark out. But really dark, like someone had flipped a switch on the world.

"Colt?"

"I'm here."

His voice came from the direction of the hall. She couldn't see him.

"What happened?"

"Power outage." A light flickered, illuminating his face as he looked at his phone. He stood near the door. He'd pulled on sweats that hung low on his hips and he held a pistol.

Angie swallowed. "What's that noise?"

"The battery backup for the alarm. It's an old system."

"I'm surprised you didn't replace it. Don't you guys have state of the art stuff over there at BDI?" She grappled for her panties and the shirt she'd been wearing. Tugged them on and stood.

Her phone was in her bag. She'd left it in the kitchen. At least he had his so they could see.

"We do. I didn't replace it because there wasn't any reason. I'm renting—and I can handle burglars."

Angie yawned. She wasn't going back to sleep with that chirp. It was loud. Annoying. "We could make coffee. Oh, wait." She sighed. "I guess not. I hope the power comes back soon."

"Me too. Maybe put on some warmer clothes in case it stays out for a while. The system's probably been overloaded in this cold. Too many people trying to make their houses a balmy seventy-five."

"I can't see to find my clothes."

"Hang on. I've got a battery-powered lantern in the kitchen. We're gonna need it anyway, so let me go get it."

She heard the solid weight of the pistol land on the dresser with the television, and he disappeared through the door.

Angie waited. The alarm kept chirping. She patted around the bed and over to the chair, hoping her clothes were there. Maybe she could find them before he got back.

She hated being immersed in darkness so complete she couldn't see her hand in front of her face. She'd never been particularly afraid of the dark. This was enough to make her rethink it.

"Yesssss," she said as her hand hit fabric she recognized. Her leggings. She tugged them on and patted some more. Her bra was there, but she didn't care about that. Her fuzzy socks.

Oh thank you Jesus because her feet were cold. She pulled on one and then the other. Her toes warmed immediately.

"Hurry, Colt," she called out. The darkness had weight to it as it pressed in on all sides. She hated it. He didn't answer and her belly took a slow tumble to the floor as the silence stretched. She told herself to stop being silly. He was looking for the lantern.

Maybe he'd had to step into the garage. He'd be back soon.

She heard something banging in the kitchen. She held her breath, trying to make out what he was doing. It stopped and a light flared in the hallway. Relief made her knees wobbly.

"I'm glad you found it. I can't see a damn thing, but I have my clothes. They're probably on backwards and inside out."

The light beamed into the room, shining in her face. Angie put her arm up to shield her eyes. It was too bright after so much blackness.

"Careful," she said.

Before she could acclimate to the light, rough hands grabbed her and jerked her toward the door. She knew instantly they didn't belong to Colt.

Fear surrounded her heart with icy fingers.

Angie screamed, lashing out at whoever had her in his grasp. She kicked, but it was useless because she wasn't wearing shoes. Her toes bent painfully as they connected.

"Shut up, bitch," someone growled. Not the person holding her. Someone else.

A hood fell over her head, blocking the light once more. The inside of the hood smelled sweet. Her attacker tightened it around her neck as she struggled. Angie sucked in a breath to scream again. Nothing came out. It was like her lungs weren't working.

"Did you bind him?" the man holding her asked.

"Yeah. He ain't coming to anytime soon. We should light this place up before we go."

"Against orders. Hey, there's a gun on that dresser. Grab it."

That was the last thing she remembered.

———

THE SIDE of Colt's head—his face, actually—ached like a son of a bitch. The floor beneath him was hard and cold. He came awake slowly, wondering how the fuck he'd gotten onto the floor.

His cheek pressed to the vinyl tile and his arms were behind him. He tried to move them, put his hands on the floor and lever up. But his arms were restrained, and that triggered a memory. Somebody had hit him from behind. He didn't remember falling, but his side hurt where he must have landed. He got his legs beneath him and shoved himself up to a sitting position.

Angie.

He knew better than to call out for her. She wasn't there. He knew it because he was still alive, and restrained. If someone had come to kill her, they'd have killed them both. If they'd only intended to kill her, they wouldn't have restrained him. They'd have incriminated him, which meant leaving him unrestrained and probably holding a smoking gun.

Fuck. His gun. He'd set it on the dresser when he'd

gone to get the light. Fucking stupid thing to do even if he'd already searched the house and found no breach. He'd also verified the power was out on the entire street. Everything had been dark, not just his house. He'd treated it like a routine outage when he should have been on his guard.

His carelessness had put Angie in danger. He had to get up and he had to find her. *Now.*

He got his legs beneath him. Got to his feet. Concentrated on the way his wrists were bound. They were behind his back and he could feel the bite of plastic in his skin.

Fucking amateurs. Though could he really call them amateurs when they'd gotten the jump on him?

Colt growled. Then he bent at the waist, lifted his arms as high as he could behind him, and brought them down fast and hard.

The zip ties broke free. His wrists stung, but it didn't matter. No amount of pain mattered right now. It was still dark outside but the room was no longer black. The clouds that'd been blocking the moon had drifted part and light shone into the kitchen.

Colt's eyes were acclimated to the dark so he didn't bother trying to find the lantern he'd been looking for. He only needed his phone.

If they hadn't taken it. He'd been holding it in his hand, shining the light as he'd walked. And then something heavy crashed down on him. He thought he'd been holding the phone when he fell, but he didn't know if they'd taken it from him.

Why was he thinking in terms of *they*? What made him think there was more than one?

Because he'd heard voices. He remembered it now. Two voices. In the seconds before he'd lost consciousness—or maybe he'd been drifting between being out cold and awake—he'd heard them talking in low voices about restraining him and taking the girl alive.

Alive. Thank God.

The glimmer of a light from the floor caught his eye. He fell to his knees and reached beneath the table. Tugged out a smooth rectangle and turned it over. The surface was cracked as if someone had stomped on it.

Fucking idiots. They'd have done better to take the phone with them. It might look like an ordinary iPhone, but there were modifications. There had to be for a man in his profession.

Colt tapped the surface. His contacts came up, and he conferenced Ian and Jace. They both answered immediately though it wasn't yet two a.m.

"What's happened?" Ian asked.

"Angie," Colt said, his throat tight. "Somebody took her."

Jace swore. "I'll be right there."

"I'm heading to the office to manage this," Ian said. "But I'll send Ty and Jared so they can help evaluate the scene and bring you in. I assume you're in no condition to drive."

He wasn't. Not yet anyway. "Thanks, boss. And Jace," he added. "Don't leave Maddy alone. I feel like that'd be a bad idea."

"Gotcha, brother. I'll take her to BDI and wait for you to get there. Don't worry. We'll find her."

"I know," Colt said. They *had* to find her.

Failure wasn't an option. He couldn't contemplate failing. Angie meant everything to him—and he hadn't told her. It'd seemed too soon to tell her something so important.

But it was never too soon when your heart was on the line. You had to tell people you loved them. Before they were gone forever.

Chapter Nineteen

WHEN ANGIE WOKE, SHE THOUGHT SHE WAS STILL wearing the hood. It was black as pitch. But as she moved her head, she realized the hood was gone. There wasn't any fabric impeding her air. She could breathe easily.

Angie bit the inside of her cheek to stifle the panic rising like bile in her throat. Had she been closed into a room with no windows?

Tentatively, she moved. She wasn't bound. She lay on a lumpy mattress with a blanket on top of her. Which she needed because the air she breathed in was cold. Not freezing, but definitely not warm.

The air was also dank, musty, like you'd find in a basement or a room that hadn't been used in a long time.

When she put her legs over the side, she discovered the mattress was on the floor. She put her hands in front of her, searching for walls.

There was nothing so she turned and tried behind. Nothing there either.

"Hello?" she said softly.

Her voice echoed back to her. An empty room. An empty something.

Except for her and a blanket and a mattress. Her legs trembled as she stood. Every bit of her wanted to stay on the mattress and not move away from it, but a small corner of her brain told her she had to search the space.

Carefully. *Slowly.*

She put her hands in front of her again. They trembled as she took a shuffling step. She strained to hear any sound. There was nothing, not even the muted shuffling of her feet. But she was only wearing socks so they wouldn't make noise, would they?

There were no cars driving by, no planes, nothing she could for certain make out. There might be something in the distance, but she couldn't tell what it was. Banging? The rumble of a diesel engine?

Her blood rushed in her ears, and that didn't help. She wanted to turn and collapse on the mattress again. Hide beneath the blanket. Close her eyes and pray.

But she'd been in this situation before and she'd been useless. They'd had light then, and she'd still been useless. Not this time.

She stood very still and thought for a minute. What would Colt do? He would try to find a wall and then he'd make his way around the room, searching for a door or a window. He'd get the lay of the room, then he'd make a plan.

She could do that much, even if she didn't have the first idea what to do about it. It was terrifying to move in a space with no light. She didn't know what was in front of her, what kind of obstacles might wait. What if the space was endless and she lost the mattress with its warm blanket?

"That won't happen," she said to herself. "You heard the echo when you said hello. It's not that big. Hello," she said again, louder this time.

The word echoed back to her and she did it again, moving slowly. The room wasn't too big. There were walls. Metal walls, maybe.

The floor beneath her was solid. She shuffled so she didn't accidentally step into a hole. What if there was an opening to a room below and she fell through?

"You don't even know if there's anything below you, fool."

It was stupid to talk to herself, and yet it might also keep her sane.

"Bend over and feel the floor. You haven't done that yet."

She dropped down and put a hand to the surface beneath her feet. It was concrete. She knew because it was rough like concrete. It was also cold. She was thankful she'd found her fluffy socks before the men grabbed her. They were thick, with a non-skid bottom. Almost like a boot, except for the lack of structure.

She stood again and shuffled. And her fingers connected with metal. A metal wall. She felt her way along it until she reached a corner, then she felt her way along that side until she reached another corner.

She felt for windows or doors, but there were none. When she encountered a chair, she almost wept for joy. It was something.

She left it where it was and continued on again. There was a crate against one wall. She decided it was a shipping crate based on the feel of the wood. Rough, not polished. No opening for legs so not a desk. Not a cabinet because, again, not polished. She felt around it, looking for a way to open it, but there wasn't one she could feel.

Angie continued like that until she came to a door. Excitement flared as her hand landed on a metal door knob. She turned it. It didn't give way. She grabbed it with both hands and shook it.

Nothing happened.

"Keep going," she said.

She moved around the room. She didn't find another door, but she reached the chair again. She knew it was the same chair because she'd been counting the corners. The crate was on the opposite wall from the chair and the room was a rectangle.

After she'd mentally mapped the exterior of the room, she felt her way into the center. There was a pole, probably for support, that she hadn't encountered before. It was metal, square. An I-beam.

If there was one, there was likely another. She thought about the length of the longest wall and decided there were two or three beams. A warehouse?

"With no windows?" she grumbled.

She felt around the beam, then moved forward. Her toe kicked something. It stung and she cussed a blue streak. She reached out again—and discovered a much narrower metal beam.

Except it wasn't a beam. It was the support to a step. Angie moved her hands around until she connected with the railing.

Stairs…

Angie started to climb, pulling herself along carefully.

Something rattled and she froze.

A door squealed open on creaky hinges and a light swept the room. Angie cowered on the steps, her head turning away from the light. She told herself to concentrate on whatever the light revealed. The mattress was in the middle of the room, close to a steel support beam. There was a bucket nearby as well.

The light swept from the bed, hooked around the walls, and then upward until it stopped on her. "Where do you think you're going, bitch?"

———

COLT RETRIEVED the lantern and made his way to the bedroom to pull on some clothes. His chest tightened at the sight of the bed. The sheets were rumpled and the covers thrown back where Angie'd been the last to leave it.

He swept the light through the room, methodically checking everything. Her leggings were gone. Her thick fuzzy socks. Her bra was still hanging over the chair, and her sweater was there too. She'd been wearing his shirt, he remembered. Whoever'd abducted her hadn't taken a blanket or a coat for her because her coat was still in the kitchen where she'd left it.

Colt swept the light around the bedroom, looking for anything that might help him figure out where they'd taken Angie. He didn't see anything so he retraced his steps to the kitchen, checking the rooms as he went.

They'd come in through the dining room window at the back of the house. One pane was neatly cut out, the sash raised. The crappy alarm system the homeowner installed only monitored doors for breaches, not windows.

Colt returned to the kitchen. Angie's handbag was gone. That meant they'd taken her phone and ID along with her computer. It was the first bit of hopeful news he'd had. If her phone was with her, BDI could track it. He wished her kidnappers had taken his computer because it had a tracking device inside, but they hadn't. It was tucked into the bookshelf in the living room where he kept it when not in use.

Fuck.

Headlights swept across the wall. Ty and Jared. Colt opened the front door and they rushed inside.

"What happened?" Jared asked, looking pissed and worried at the same time.

"The lights went out, as you can see. The power was out up and down the block. Looked legit. I checked the house for a breach anyway, but didn't see anything."

"Looks like they took out a transformer. The power's out for a few blocks. Didn't reach as far as Jace and Maddy's. It goes in the other direction."

Colt rubbed the side of his face gingerly. He was scraped up and swelling, but he'd live. He'd decided he must have broken his fall on one of the dining room chairs, which was on its side, before he landed. Still hurt like a motherfucker though.

"I'm going to need to check you for concussion," Jared said, taking in the state of his face. "But finish telling us what happened."

"After I checked the house, I returned to the bedroom. They must have entered when I was there. Angie couldn't see to find her clothes, so I went back to the kitchen to get a lantern so I could set it on the bedside table. Somebody hit me when I walked in.

They came through the dining room. Used a glass cutter to remove a pane, then slid the window up and climbed in. I didn't hear it happen, probably because of the chirping of the alarm battery and talking to Angie."

Disgust ate at him. He should have been paying better attention. He shouldn't have relaxed his guard for even a moment, no matter how legit the outage seemed. He shouldn't have left her side. He could have held his fucking phone so she could dress, then he would have had his gun and been in a defensive position when the attackers were forced to come after her.

"I left my gun in the bedroom. They took it. When I came to, I was on the floor with my arms zip-tied behind my back. Angie was gone and so was the gun. They took her bag. Her phone's in it, so we need to start tracing it."

Hot anger and cold fear rolled together in his belly as he thought of Angie. She was probably scared out of her mind, and there was nothing he could do about it. Yet.

"Agreed," Jared said. "Let me have a look at you, then we'll check the house, see if we find something you missed while you call Ian."

Colt nodded, holding onto his calm by a thread. "I didn't see anything, but I welcome you looking. I've got no pride in this, man. I want Angie back safe. I fucked up."

It nearly broke him to say those words. He *had* fucked up.

Ty put a hand on his shoulder. "Doesn't sound like it to me. You cleared the house. The outage didn't appear targeted. If anybody fucked up, we all did. We should have been watching. We were lulled because there'd been no movement from the other side."

Colt shook his head. "This is my fault."

Jared clapped him on the other shoulder. "Not buying it, dude. Now sit down and let me check you out. We've got work to do."

————

TWO HOURS HAD PASSED. Colt paced inside the war room at BDI. He had ice on his face and on the bump on his head, but Jared had pronounced him concussion free.

"It's a miracle you're so hard-headed," Jared had said back at his place when he'd finished Colt's examination.

Hard-headed he might be, but he was about to lose his mind. Dax Freed tapped on his computer and chased whatever leads he could find but so far he'd found nothing. Angie's phone was either dead or somebody'd been smart enough to block the signal. They couldn't get a position on it yet.

Ian had been on the phone, yelling in Russian at one point, cajoling in Italian at another. Slamming the receiver down and tugging his hair while cursing in Chinese. Or at least Colt thought it was cursing.

Jace walked back into the room from his trip down to the fourth floor where Maddy presumably fumed in one of the conference rooms. Colt met his gaze.

"Can you please go see her?" Jace asked. "She wants to talk to you."

Colt's gut twisted. He'd avoided Maddy so far because he didn't want to see the accusation in her eyes. This time he nodded and strode from the room.

If anything happened, he knew they'd call him back. He exited the secure area and went down the stairs to the fourth floor. Maddy paced the hallway, spinning at the end and marching back toward Colt. When she saw him, she stopped. Her eyes were red-rimmed and his heart damn near broke.

"Oh Colt," she said, rushing up to him and throwing her arms around him. He stood in her embrace, stunned. Then he hugged her back.

"I'm sorry, Maddy. It's my fault."

Her gaze was fierce as it snapped to his. "No. You're not taking that on, Colt. You wouldn't let Angie take the blame for you getting shot. Wouldn't let me take it either. So hell no, you do *not* take the blame for this one."

She'd shocked him into silence. "I should have protected her," he finally managed. "It's my job."

She squeezed his arms. Shook him. "Listen to me, you stupid, adorable man. You did protect her. You got her out of danger in the first place. You took care of her when she was sick. And you'll continue to take care of her. I know you will. You just have to find her —which you *will*. It's what you guys do."

His head was reeling. He almost laughed, but he couldn't. "Is this why you wanted to see me? A pep talk?"

She looked militant. "I knew you'd be up there blaming yourself. I knew you'd take on the weight of the world if nobody stopped you—and none of them will because you *all* do it. Every single one of you thinks this world can't turn without you spinning it."

"You're insane, Maddy. In a good way, but still insane. And don't tell Jace, but I think I love you for it."

She grinned. There was pain in it, but it was still a grin. "I won't tell. But do you love Angie? That's what I really want to know."

He hesitated. "I haven't said those words to her yet."

Maddy squeezed his arms and stepped back. Her smile was watery. "But you want to." She swiped a tear that spilled down her cheek. "I'm so glad, Colt. You're perfect for each other. I knew how you felt when I saw you looking at her yesterday."

He didn't argue with her. "And how was that?"

"When the electricians turned off the power, you had a moment where you were ready to throw your-self in front of her to protect her from harm. Then you remembered it was just the contractors and not an attack."

"Electricians," he said stupidly. The work on the addition. The man who'd peered into the living room while they sat and talked. *Holy shit.* Steve Gorky owned a construction company. Could it be as simple as that? "Maddy, where did you find those guys?"

She blinked up at him. "Johnson Electric? The general contractor recommended them when their usual guy couldn't come this week. Why?"

He kissed her on the forehead. "Tell you later."

Then he turned and ran for the fifth floor. It took precious minutes to get through the security checks, but then he was inside and racing down the hall.

"Jace," he called as he skidded into the war room. "The electricians working on your place. One of them saw Angie and me at your house yesterday."

None of them moved as they stared at him. Processed what he was saying. Someone had targeted a transformer, not a single house. For that kind of work, they'd needed to know what they were doing or they'd get barbecued trying. Whoever did it used an electrician. Or *was* an electrician.

"Gorky Construction," Dax said, looking up from the computer. "Johnson Electric does a lot of work for them. They have the contract to wire all their new construction."

"Fucking hell," Jace said. "They've been inside my

house. Wiring my damned bedroom. Is every contractor around here connected to Gorky?"

"Find their office," Ian ordered. "Who owns the place? Where does he live? We're going to go and wake his ass up."

Finally. Now Colt felt like they might be getting somewhere. He'd been telling himself if all someone wanted was to kill Angie, they'd have already done it. There was no need to abduct her first. Which meant they wanted something else.

But what?

"Got it," Dax said. "Twenty minutes from here."

"Let's roll," Ian said. "Dax, stay here and keep us informed."

"You got it, boss."

The rest of them rushed to the armory and grabbed their assault gear. Then they piled into a black SUV with blackout windows and generic tags. Moments later, they were rocketing down the highway toward Harvey Johnson's suburban home. He might not be the one who'd orchestrated the attack, but Colt didn't much care right now.

Johnson was connected to Gorky. And Johnson was about to find out what a cattle prod to the nuts felt like.

Chapter Twenty

ANGIE THOUGHT SHE RECOGNIZED THE VOICES. THERE were three men who'd spoken thus far. She couldn't see them because they'd hooded her but the voices were familiar. Two of them she'd heard in Colt's house. But the other? She didn't know, though she'd heard him somewhere.

When they'd entered the room a few moments ago, one of them flipped a breaker just outside—she'd heard it flip—and the lights sprang to life. Though she'd wanted to look at everything, it'd hurt too much and she'd kept her eyes slitted until they could adjust.

In that brief time, she'd tried to see her surroundings. All she'd had was an impression of space and emptiness. There were some wooden crates in the center of the room, not far from the mattress, but she'd been too blind to make out any markings.

One of the men had put a hood over her head

before she could see anything else. There was a small bit of light coming through the fabric so it wasn't nearly as dark as it had been with no lights. But she still couldn't make out shapes.

"Who did you give the spreadsheet to?"

The voice was to her left. It was the one she thought she'd heard before but not at Colt's house. Angie swallowed. "Spreadsheet?"

She didn't see the blow coming. Her head snapped to the side as someone slapped her hard on the right cheek. Pain blossomed in her jaw. Tears sprang to her eyes. Somehow, she didn't make any sound. She sucked in oxygen, trying not to cry.

Inside, the hood was stuffy with heat and the moisture from her breath. She needed to calm down or it would only get stuffier.

"Don't lie to me," the man growled. "Charles Martinelli had a spreadsheet with incorrect data. Isn't that what your emails said?"

Oh shit. She'd never said Charles had a spreadsheet of incorrect data, but she wasn't arguing with this man.

"Um, yes, of course. I, um. Confidential information. I wasn't sure you were authorized."

What a crock of bullshit, Angelica.

She braced herself for another blow. But he laughed. "Spunky. I like that. Who did you give that information to? Ian Black?"

A shiver ran through her. She was cold now and

the blanket was out of reach. They'd shoved her into a chair. Presumably the one she'd encountered earlier.

"Um…."

"Don't bother lying. It won't help. If you tell me the truth, there's a possibility you'll make it out of here alive."

"Yes," she whispered. "I gave it to him."

The man swore. "Why would you do that? It was none of your fucking business."

He sounded angry. And maybe a little desperate?

Angie knew she needed to be careful what she said. She couldn't know too much—or could she? If she bluffed her way through this, they might let her go. But there was danger in pretending to know more than she did, especially if they caught her in a lie.

She decided to only tell him as much as he asked for and hope it was enough. "I gave it to him because the office where I worked burned down. And then somebody tried to break into my apartment. I needed help. I thought he could help me."

"Stupid fucking bitch," the man growled.

Angie tried not to flinch from the implied violence in his tone. She wasn't quite successful. Where had she heard him before? He had to be someone she'd talked to. Or, and the moment this thought occurred to her it excited her a little, he was someone who'd been to Barton, Barnes and Blake in the past.

Was he one of the Cardinal Group people? Had to be. But who'd gone to the office to see Charles in the past? The owners of the Cardinal Group were Shaw and Sobol. She remembered that from the tax information. They had employees though. Each man had a secretary, there were a couple of associates with secretaries, and a receptionist. With the exception of the receptionist and two secretaries, everyone else was male.

Which meant this man could be any one of six people.

"Did you get her phone and computer?" the man asked.

"Yeah, it's here," someone said. She'd heard that voice at Colt's. He was the one who'd thrown her over his shoulder. Number Two, then. She'd number them to keep them straight.

"Give me the computer," Number One said, snapping his fingers.

She heard rustling and the sound of the laptop powering up.

"Code," One said.

Angie told herself to breathe. Just breathe. Don't react. Let them do whatever they were going to do.

"Bitch, listen up," One said again, sharper this time. "Give me the code to open the computer."

Angie jerked. "Sorry. It's just zeroes."

"Where did you save the spreadsheet?"

"Under 'My Documents'."

He swore under his breath and she knew he must have found it. Whatever was in it, he didn't like it.

"Now your phone code," he demanded.

"169105."

"Good girl." She heard the laptop snap closed. "Come on, let's go."

"I want to have some fun," the third man said. He was the one who'd talked about lighting up Colt's place. Number Two had told him it was against orders. "Make her scream."

"Not now," One said. "Later."

Angie didn't move. She strained her ears to hear movement. Number Three's voice sounded in her ear, making her jump. "I heard redheads feel more pain than other people. Is it true?"

"Come on," One said, sounding impatient. "We have work to do."

There were footsteps moving across the floor. Angie sat very still until they were gone. The door clanged shut and she reached up to rip the hood from her head.

Crates, concrete floor, metal walls, steps that led up to a gallery that ran along one side of the room. A door? Was that a door up there—

The lights snapped out and Angie plunged into darkness.

———

THEY WERE ALMOST to Harvey Johnson's house when Colt got a text.

Angie: *I have something you want.*

"Fuck," Colt said as adrenaline shot through his veins. "I just got a text from Angie's phone. We need to get a lock on it."

"I hear you," Dex said through the speaker. They'd kept the line open to him so he could give them point by point directions while watching for traffic and other obstacles. "Initiating trace."

It wasn't the kind of thing most people could do, not without going through the phone company and getting permission, etcetera. But BDI wasn't most people.

Colt met Jace's grim gaze. "We'll get her," Jace said.

"I know." He tapped a reply, reading it off as he did so. *What do you suggest?*

Angie: *There's a park across the street from the former BB&B building. Be there at 6am. I want to make a trade.*

Colt read the text to them. "What the fuck does that mean?"

"Sounds like he's desperate," Ian said.

Colt: *What kind of trade?*

Three dots appeared. Finally, the text came across and he read it aloud. *I'll give you actionable info against Gorky. And I'll give you the girl, but first you have to give me something I want. If you don't, I have no incentive to keep her alive.*

Ian's brows rose. "Interesting. Actionable info against Gorky? Could be a bluff. Then again, he must

279

think he has something good because the second he gives us some bullshit, we could expose the information in the spreadsheet. Dax, is Gorky's account still there?"

"It's there. If he transfers the money, we'll trace it. We're still working through the transactions. It's dirty money, of course. But nothing that's going to stick if we try to nail him now."

"Good work. Keep searching. Confirm the meeting, Colt."

Colt pressed send. "Gotta be Sobol we're dealing with, right?"

Ian nodded. "I think so. Shaw could be involved, but if he is, he's an idiot for failing to get more money out of Gorky's account. I'd say Sobol's the one with the most to lose at this point. He doesn't want Martinelli's information getting back to Gorky."

"Got a location," Dax interrupted. "It's coming from a block of warehouses off 301. Belongs to... Gorky Shipping. Surprise, surprise."

"It's four-thirty," Ian said. "We need to get over there asap. If Angie's not there, then we've got to get to the meeting by six and find out what Sobol wants."

It was more than a matter of driving up to the warehouse and knocking on the door. They had to infiltrate a shipping company's operations, which ran around the clock, and pinpoint the precise warehouse Angie was in. Then they had to breach it, disarm and disable any guards, and rescue her before the clock ran out.

If she wasn't there, they had to make it across town to the meeting before her kidnapper decided they weren't coming and killed her out of spite.

"Make a left turn at the next street," Dax said.

Jared was driving and he did exactly what Dax told him to do for the next twelve minutes. Colt checked his weapons. The rest of them did the same. When they reached a spot about a mile from the warehouses, they ditched the SUV and went on foot.

It added time, but it was necessary to stealth.

They had to scale a brick wall and cut through barbed wire, then they skirted the perimeter. There were trucks backed up to loading docks and a steady pace of activity as trailers were loaded and unloaded.

Colt and his teammates wore black assault suits, night vision goggles, and they had state of the art weaponry. Each one of them had been a military special operator at some point, whether in the military of the United States or a foreign military, and they knew what they were doing. They weren't cautious for their own sakes. They were cautious for Angie's.

If a direct assault was needed, they'd do it. Not one of them gave a shit about killing anyone who intended to harm Angie. For now, stealth was the correct action. Until someone gave them a reason to abandon it.

Ian held up a hand when they reached the far end

of the complex. One warehouse sat by itself, away from the rest. It was older and smaller than the others, a rusted hulk of a building with a crumbling loading dock. There was only one bank of windows with light spilling over the sills. A single entry door stood on the dock level near the windows. There were also two loading bays with their sliding doors all the way down.

A white van sat in front of the building along with a sleek McLaren.

Ian signaled Jared, Ty, and Brett to head around the right side of the building. It was understood they'd report if they found anything. Ty snapped shots of the license plates as they went, using the digital camera embedded in his goggles. He would send them to Dax, and they'd know who owned the vehicles in minutes.

Jace and Colt crept over and slapped trackers on the car frames, then took the left side of the building with Ian, moving through the overgrowth that swept up the side and onto the roof. It was probably kudzu, except it was too dark to know for sure. Halfway down the side of the building, the path cleared and a metal staircase appeared. It went up to the second floor of the warehouse. A door with a padlock stood at the top of the stairs.

Colt looked at Ian. Ian nodded and Colt started up the rickety structure, being careful to move slowly so he didn't make too much noise. If anyone saw him, he'd be a sitting duck up there. When he got to the top, he tried the lock. It was newer than the door. He dug into the gear at his belt and produced a set of picks. Then he went to work on the padlock.

"Red team, report," Ian said in his ear. "Black team's found a door. We're breaching."

"Nothing to report," Jared said.

"Watch for movement in front," Ian told him.

"Roger that."

"Let's get inside and see if she's there," Ian said. "We have approximately fifteen minutes before we need to hit the road if not."

Colt buckled down and worked harder on popping the lock. It was supposed to be pick proof, but they hadn't planned for the likes of him.

Colt could pick anything.

———

PAUL KNEW what he had to do. It was too late to salvage the situation so he was going to do what Charles had wanted in the first place. Fucking Charles and his goddamn conscience. The dude had stolen plenty of dirty money from Steve and hadn't cared where it came from.

Get some Afghani terrorists involved and suddenly he was the Virgin fucking Mary.

Now, the only way out Paul could see involved selling Steve and his sons down the river. His sister would get over it eventually. Maybe.

Before Paul did it, however, he was going to use Angie Turner to get himself a new identity. A new face, a new name, new everything. Ian Black hated the mafia, but he was a man of his word. Paul had heard that often enough whenever Black's name came up. Steve hated him, but he also kind of perversely admired him.

Paul stood. Tommy looked up at him. Tommy was a sociopath who never shrank from dirty deeds. Tommy liked killing. Marco, though... Marco was calmer, cooler. He did what needed doing, but Paul didn't think he particularly got any pleasure from it. Further, Paul suspected Marco was there to report back to Steve more than he was there to do Paul's bidding.

"Time to head to the meeting," Paul said.

Tommy was spinning the gun he'd taken from Colt Duchaine's place around his finger like a toy. If he shot himself, Paul wouldn't waste any time calling an ambulance.

"Want me to stay here with the girl?" he asked. There was a strange light in his eyes that told Paul that'd be a terrible idea.

"No, I need you with me. Marco can stay."

"I got it," Marco said. He didn't look up from his phone. He was playing a game. Bejeweled, it looked like.

"Man, I want to fuck her. She looks like an uptight bitch that'll scream good for me," Tommy said.

"There's no time. You can fuck her when we come back."

It was a lie and Paul felt no remorse saying it. If Black agreed to his conditions, they would have to release her. No damage or the deal would fall apart.

Tommy shoved to his feet. His eyes gleamed. He rolled the gun around his finger like Clint Eastwood—then pointed it at Paul.

"Put that damned thing down," Paul ordered.

Tommy grinned. It was a stupid grin, filled with malice and maybe a touch of insanity. Then he flipped the weapon and shoved it into his pants.

Paul thought if there was any justice in this world, the damned thing would go off and Tommy would lose a nut.

It didn't though.

"If you're ready?" Paul asked coolly.

"Yeah, man. Ready when you are. Let's go meet these assholes."

Marco looked up with an arched eyebrow. There was wisdom in that gaze. And a touch of meanness. Had to be to work for Steve.

"Guard the girl," Paul said. "I don't want anything happening to her."

"Got it, boss," Marco replied with a smile. "She's safe with me."

Chapter Twenty-One

ANGIE MOVED IN THE DIRECTION OF THE STAIRS AS soon as the men were gone. It took her a little bit of time, reaching blindly in front of her, to find the metal railing. She didn't really think the door at the top was a way out, but she had to try.

It was better than sitting on her ass and waiting for them to come back. Especially the creepy one who'd asked if redheads felt more pain than other people. She didn't want to be alone with that one, ever.

Angie moved cautiously. She hadn't had enough time to assess the condition of the stairs before the lights went out. She'd had a vague impression of metal stairs and railings leading up to a gallery. But were they safe?

She didn't know, hence the caution. She knew she had to be careful once she reached the top. The door wasn't directly in front of the stairs. She remembered that. She would have to turn to the right and make her way along the wall. If the door didn't open, she'd need to get down on hands and knees to make her way back. She'd be less likely to lose her balance that way.

Angie was about halfway up when she heard a scratching sound. It was soft, deliberate. Rats?

"Shit. Not rats. Please no rats."

Rodents hadn't occurred to her before, but that didn't mean they weren't there. Didn't mean they hadn't crawled over her while she'd been passed out on the mattress, or hadn't scurried out of her way as she'd made her circuit of the room.

The thought gave her the heebie jeebies. The scratching continued and she pictured rats, everywhere, with their long yellow teeth and red eyes. Waiting to jump on her. Angie's heart beat harder, making it difficult to hear the scratching over the pounding in her ears.

She had to keep moving. Had to get to the door and find out if it opened. If it didn't—well, she'd worry about rats afterward.

———

MARCO STOOD up as soon as he heard the van drive away. That little prick Tommy thought he was going to fuck the redhead. Maybe he was, but Marco was going first. Paul and Tommy would be gone for an hour, maybe more. Plenty of time for Marco to make her strip naked for him.

He'd keep the flashlight in her eyes so she couldn't see him. Then he'd put the hood on her if she'd taken it off again, and make her get down on her hands and knees so he could fuck her doggy style.

His dick was already hard thinking about it. He'd been thinking about it since he'd tossed her over his shoulder and held her by the ass. She wasn't wearing a bra, and her nipples were so sharp they could cut glass. He couldn't wait to get his hands on them.

Marco grabbed the keys as he passed from the office to the interior hallway. Then he walked down a set of stairs to the door which led into the warehouse. There was a flashlight on a table beside the door. He grabbed it and inserted the key into the lock.

When he had the flashlight ready, he opened the door and shined it into the room. The girl wasn't on the chair or the mattress. He shined the light up—and found her on the stairs. She'd lifted an arm over her eyes to shield them from the light.

She was almost to the top. Marco walked inside and shut the door behind him. He pocketed the keys and took out his pistol. Gun in one hand, flashlight in the other.

"What're you doing up there, girlie? Better get down here before you hurt yourself."

He talked nice because that's how you coaxed a

skittish woman to do your bidding. You were nice to her. If that didn't work, then you shoved the barrel of the gun into her mouth and threatened to blow her away.

"What do you want?" she asked. She wasn't moving, though. She gripped the railing tight and looked off to the side, away from the light.

"I want to help you. The others are gone. It's just you and me."

He saw her hesitation. Then her jaw firmed. "You aren't going to let me go, so what do you really want?"

"No, I can't let you go. But if you come down here and play nice with me, I won't let them hurt you. I'll make sure you get to go home when this is over."

"I don't believe you."

Marco was a patient man. He was also a horny one. "You can do this easy or you can do it hard, princess. When they get back, he's gonna let the young one have at you. I can stop it, but only if you're nice to me."

She didn't speak. And then she did.

"Define nice."

Marco smiled. He had her now. Whether she knew it or not.

———

HE MADE HER SKIN CRAWL. She couldn't see him because he kept the light shining in her face, but she didn't need to see him. He was scum, just like the other two.

And she knew what he meant by nice. Her skin crawled even more. What was she supposed to do? Stay up here and stay away from him, or go down and do as he said? If she pretended to go along with it, maybe she could get the gun away from him.

She'd have to touch him. Or let him touch her. She'd have to take a risk that she could win, all while letting him feel her up. And if she failed, he'd shove himself inside her and make her afraid again. She'd have to endure being raped—and then, if she lived beyond today, she'd have to fight violent memories while trying to have a relationship with Colt.

It would be almost impossible. She could lose the man she loved and all because some asshole wanted to ruin everything she and Colt had begun by taking what he didn't have a right to.

She hated him. If she could take his gun and blow his brains out, she'd do it without hesitation.

"Come on down here and we'll discuss it," he said. "It doesn't have to be unpleasant."

Bile flooded her throat. She turned her head, breathing deep, trying to think of what to do. On the next to last stair at the top, not too far away, lay a metal pipe. It looked like it wasn't attached, but maybe it was. If she could get to it, she'd have a weapon of her own.

Against a gun? Are you crazy?

"You have to move that light. I can't see," she said, her heart pounding a crazy rhythm.

"I think I'd better keep it on you," he replied.

"Shine it at the bottom of the stairs. It's blinding me and I don't want to fall. It's not like I can run away, is it?"

He snickered. It was an evil sound. "Nope. Nowhere to go, little mouse."

"Please then. I'll come down if you move the light."

It was several seconds before the pool of light dropped to the floor beneath her. She didn't know if he could still see her or if she was completely shadowed, but she made a decision to take a chance anyway. Angie grabbed the pipe and held it tightly to her left side, which was the side that faced away from him. Her heart raced as she took the steps down. When she stood in the pool of light, she didn't turn. She just stared down at the floor and didn't move.

"Good girl," the man said.

The light bobbed and she knew he was moving toward her. She kept her head down, like she was defeated, and prayed he wouldn't ask her to turn toward him. The pipe in her hand was solid, rusty beneath her fingers, and about three feet long.

Angie didn't look at him. He kept the light on the side of her face to prevent her from looking. She knew when he stopped to pick the hood off the floor. He planned to make her put it on again, of course. So she couldn't see his face.

Angie shivered with the cold, or maybe it was adrenaline racing through her veins. She watched the way the light bobbed out of the corner of her eye, watched as it got closer. Her grip tightened on the pipe.

He had a gun. She knew he did, but she couldn't see it. If she hit him hard enough, maybe she'd knock the gun away. Or maybe he'd shoot her dead and that'd be the end of it.

"Turn around," he told her. "Face away from me."

Angie shifted the pipe as she did what he told her to do. It was a stroke of luck she hadn't been counting on. She gripped the pipe in both hands, muscles coiling. She couldn't move too soon.

You shouldn't move at all. You'll get your fool self killed.

His footsteps were closer now. Almost there. Angie sucked in a breath—and then she whirled with the pipe, holding it like a baseball bat and lashing out with all her strength.

She caught him by surprise. The gun and flashlight went flying. The light rolled over to the wall, illuminating everything between her and the door he'd entered through.

It did not show her, though. Yet another piece of luck.

He came up raging, lunging toward her, and

Angie swung the pipe again. This time he grabbed the end of it and started to tug her toward him.

Angie fought, but he was stronger than she was. Instead of continuing to pull on the pipe, she aimed a kick at his kidney. It'd be a lot better if she had shoes on, but maybe she'd connect in the right place.

The man yelped in pain—and let go of the pipe. "Fucking bitch," he screamed. "I'm going to kill you."

Angie dashed around behind him and took a swing at his head. She connected with something that cracked sickeningly. The man dropped—and the door above her head burst open.

———

COLT HEARD voices in the room. He hesitated, trying to make them out, but all he could make out was a male voice and a female one. It might be Angie, or it might not be. He applied torque on the wrench and scrubbed the pick in the lock until all the pins were set. The instant the last one fell into place, the male voice inside roared in fury.

"Fucking bitch, I'm going to kill you!"

Colt freed the lock and kicked open the door. Ian and Jace rushed up the stairs behind him. He didn't know how many men were in the room, but he knew that two had exited the building. Brett reported them leaving in the white van eight minutes ago.

Dax was tracking them as they drove across town, so no fears they'd get away.

The room Colt burst into was black but he could see everything with the NVGs. A man lay immobile on the floor. Angie stood above him, holding a long cylindrical pipe. She raised it as Colt, Ian, and Jace hurtled down the stairs.

"Don't come near me," she growled. "Stay away."

"Angie, it's me."

The pipe dropped to her side. "Colt?"

"Yeah, baby. It's me."

Angie rushed toward him. He opened his arms and she barreled into them, throwing her arms around him.

"Colt, oh thank god. I fought back this time. I knew you'd come and I fought back."

He pressed her head to his chest, held her hard to him. His heart pounded and his eyes stung. She was *safe*. They'd gotten to her in time.

Jace checked the man's pulse. "He's alive," Jace said before flipping him over and cuffing him.

A door at the front of the warehouse opened. Jared, Ty, and Brett sauntered in, weapons at the ready. "All secure," Jared said. "Nobody else here."

Colt rubbed Angie's back. She hadn't eased her grip on him. "Are you okay, Angie? Did they hurt you?"

She sniffed as she tipped her head to gaze up at him. "One of them hit me. They left me in the dark. I couldn't see anything, Colt. I was so scared. But I didn't stop trying to get out."

Ice flooded Colt's veins. He wanted to kill these men for hurting her. For scaring her. He wouldn't, but he damned sure wanted to.

He slung his assault rifle around to the back and picked Angie up. She protested, but he shushed her with a quick kiss.

"You don't have shoes on, Ang. Or a coat. We're parked a mile away, so let me carry you."

They made their way through the warehouse complex, carrying Angie and the man she'd cracked over the head with her pipe. They dumped him into the back of the SUV and Colt got into the middle row with Angie. He held her tightly against his side and didn't let go for the entire ride back to BDI.

Once there, Colt carried her to the elevator while she lay her head against him and closed her eyes. He could see the purpling of a bruise on her right cheek and rage swelled inside him.

He took her to the fourth floor. Jared went with him. Brett had the man over his shoulder and he took him to a secure interrogation room and locked him in. Ian, Jace, and Ty headed into Annapolis to keep the meeting with Paul Sobol. Dax had traced the McLaren to him. They'd already known he was their man, but now they had confirmation.

Ian and crew would sweep him up with the other man and bring them back here.

Maddy walked out of the suite she'd been waiting in when she heard them coming. When she saw Angie, she closed her eyes and smiled as she lifted her face heavenward. "Thank you, Jesus."

"Jace will be back soon," Colt told her. "He's fine. Just mopping up."

"Thank you." She shifted her attention to Angie, grabbing her hand and squeezing it. "How are you, honey?"

"Cold," Angie said.

Maddy opened the door to the suite so they could pass inside. Then she hurried to the refrigerator and got a bottle of water, retrieved a stack of blankets from a closet, and rushed back to the couch where Colt set Angie down.

Her hair was a mess and her face was bruised, her shirt—his shirt—was torn, and the leggings and socks were streaked with dust and grime.

"What else do you need?" Maddy asked as she shook out a blanket and laid it over Angie. Angie opened her eyes and smiled up at her friend as Maddy shook out another blanket and tucked it around her legs and feet.

"I fought back, Mads. I didn't cower in the corner."

Maddy smoothed her hair from her forehead. "Oh honey, of course you fought back. You're fierce."

Angie smiled wearily. Colt thought his heart was going to break but he didn't do anything other than hold her hand while Jared checked her over for broken bones or abrasions. When he'd examined her, Jared exchanged a look with Colt.

Colt swallowed. He knew what Jared was getting at with that look. "Baby," he said to her.

"Yes, Colt?"

"Did they... they didn't abuse you, did they?" His throat was tight. Rage hovered beneath the surface. If they'd assaulted her, he would kill them all. He didn't care how hard a time Ian would have cleaning up the metaphorical mess, nothing would stop him.

Angie smiled, and he knew it was real. Relief rushed through him before she ever spoke a word. "No. That man was trying, but I hit him with the pipe. He never touched me."

Colt kissed her forehead. "You're amazing, Ang. I love you so damned much. You have no idea."

He heard Maddy gasp. Angie's eyes widened.

Jared stood. "On that note, I think I have some paperwork to fill out. Maddy?"

"Oh, yes. Absolutely. Me too. Let's go."

Colt didn't take his eyes from Angie's as Jared and Maddy disappeared through the door. He heard the quiet snick as it closed.

"You love me?" Angie asked, her voice filled with wonder.

He tucked her hair behind her ear, skimmed the side of her face that was uninjured. "Yes, I love you. I know it's fast, and I know you might not feel the same way, but——"

He didn't get a chance to finish the sentence because she surged up and pressed her mouth to his. Their tongues met, tangled, and hot emotion flared in his soul. Angie was *his*.

"I love you," she whispered against his mouth. "Love you so much."

"Je t'aime mon ange. Je t'aime."

Chapter Twenty-Two

ANGIE WAS STILL IN A DAZE WHEN TALLIE ARRIVED half an hour later. The daze wasn't because she'd been kidnapped and held in a pitch black room, or because she'd knocked a man out with a pipe. No, it had everything to do with the tall, blond, beautiful man who'd told her he loved her. In French and English.

"Angie," Tallie cried as she rushed into the room carrying a shopping bag that she dropped as she came over and gave Angie a gentle hug.

"Hi, Tallie. Thanks for coming," Angie said as she squeezed Tallie in return.

Angie huddled in a comfy chair, wrapped in a blanket, her legs curled beneath her, drinking hot tea with Maddy. Maddy and Tallie hugged, then Tallie picked up the bag again.

"I stopped and grabbed some clean things for you

from Walmart on the way in. Underwear, socks, leggings, a sweater, and some flats."

"You didn't have to do that," Angie said, feeling touched.

Tallie shrugged. "It was no problem. I figured you might be here for a while and you'd want to shower and change."

Angie loved these two women. She'd loved Maddy for a long time, but Tallie was turning out to be wonderful in her own special way. Tallie had the most remarkable eyes. One was blue and one was hazel. She was tiny and absolutely adorable in every way. There was also Sharon, Tallie's bestie who came up to visit sometimes. She wasn't around much, but she was every bit as great as Tallie. It was like having a group of sisters, which is something she'd never had.

"I would love a shower," Angie said. There was a bathroom attached to the suite they were sitting in, and it had everything she needed to take a shower. She'd already looked when she'd gone to pee earlier. She'd thought about it but she hadn't wanted to sit around in nothing but a robe.

Colt had to go up to the fifth floor with the guys, and she knew that might take some time. He'd apologized to her for it, but she'd caressed his puffy cheek lightly, feeling overwhelmed that she got to do that now, and told him she understood.

She really did. She was safe, he was safe, and she loved him. Even better, he loved her. She still couldn't believe it. It made shivers of happiness slide through her from head to toe. Amazing how life could change in a single instant.

She left Maddy and Tallie and went to clean up. The shower felt heavenly and soon she was dressed and feeling better than she would have expected considering what she'd been through since those men burst into Colt's house and took her.

When she emerged from the bathroom, Colt was waiting for her. Maddy and Tallie were still there, but they were quiet. Waiting and watching her and Colt.

Colt took her hand. "How are you feeling, *minette?*"

Angie smiled. She could feel Maddy and Tallie's eyes on her as they took in the pet name. Tallie lifted a brow. She spoke French, Angie remembered. She blushed in response, naturally.

"I'm much better now that I'm here at BDI."

"Good." His eyes searched hers. There was so much she wanted to say to him. So many things she still wanted to know. "If you'd like to come up to the fifth floor with me, Ian wants to tell you some things."

Angie blinked. Maddy said, "Whoa. I have *never* been to the fifth floor. How about you, Tal?"

"Nope, not me."

"Um, are you sure, Colt?" Angie asked, glancing at her friends.

He grinned that gorgeous white grin of his. "Oh yeah, absolutely sure. You ready?"

"Well, sure." She looked at Maddy and Tallie again. "Is this an episode of *The Twilight Zone?*"

Maddy laughed. "Could be. If we're eaten by aliens while you're gone, then you'll know."

"Stop it, Mads," Angie said with a laugh.

Colt laughed too. "You aren't going to be eaten by aliens. But I hear Ian ordered some breakfast to be delivered, so hang tight."

Maddy looked at Tallie. "It's a trap. Don't eat anything they bring," she whispered loudly. "That's how they get you."

Colt shook his head as he took Angie's hand firmly in his. "Come on, Ang. These two are off their meds."

Angie walked out of the room with him and down the hall to the elevator. She glanced over her shoulder before they stepped inside—and there were Maddy and Tallie, peeking out of the suite, grinning like fools the whole time.

The elevator doors closed and Colt put his arms around her, pulling her close. He bent his forehead to hers. "There are so many things I want to say to you, so many things I want to do. Soon, I promise."

Angie tipped her face up and kissed him gently. "I can't wait."

———

COLT ESCORTED Angie through the security proto-

cols, enjoying how her eyes widened at every new
thing. He couldn't quite believe Ian had decided to
bring her behind the most secure doors of any facility
Colt had ever been inside, anywhere in the world, but
he had. "Clear her," was what he'd said to Dax. And
Dax had done it.

There was nothing in Angie's background to
prevent her access. She was a native born American,
she had no questionable ties or affiliations, and no
criminal record. Not a single arrest or speeding ticket.
Besides, she'd already been investigated because of
her closeness to Maddy, who was engaged to marry
Jace. There'd been nothing in that investigation to
raise any alarms.

When Ian wanted something done, it got done
with amazing speed and efficiency. Far beyond what
it would have taken in any other facility, that's for
sure.

"Whoa," she said when they stepped through the
last locked door. The operations center was state of
the art, with all the latest in technology meant to
impress. And not just impress, but do the best job
possible.

"Come on," Colt said as he led her to the war
room where his team gathered. "I'll give you the tour
later."

Everyone stood as she walked inside. Ian was grinning broadly.

"Welcome, Angie."

"I… Thanks." She tilted her head. "Why am I here?"

"Because there are things you need to know, and they can't be said outside these walls. I told you I'd tell you what I could. Remember?"

"I do."

"I've decided I can tell you a lot. But what we say here doesn't go beyond this room. Understand?"

"Yes."

"Then have a seat."

Colt let go of her hand and pulled out a chair for her. He took the one beside her. He already knew what Ian was going to say. The things they'd discovered, thanks to Angie and Charles Martinelli. Angie listened attentively while Ian told her about Steve Gorky and the various accounts detailed in Martinelli's spreadsheet. They'd found other, hidden account numbers when they'd analyzed everything.

"It took a computer to do that analysis, Angie. You didn't miss it," he added. Colt was grateful he said it because he knew Angie would be upset she'd missed something that important.

Ian explained that Paul Sobol had clarified some things as well. He was the one who'd been having sex with Jenny. They'd met during one of his many visits to Charles at BB&B, but they'd only been going at it for about a month. He'd targeted her initially because she was easy to manipulate, and he'd wanted eyes on Charles because he'd been growing suspicious of his old friend and co-conspirator.

Sobol erased the files from the server, but Jenny logged in. He was trying to clean up the evidence, but not doing a great job at it.

"That's why she was nervous when I asked if she'd found any wonky accounting in Charles's files," Angie said.

"Probably so."

"Did he kill her?"

"He says he didn't. He says that Gorky ordered it because she was a liability, and Tommy Baskin carried it out. He's one of the men who grabbed you."

"The one who asked if redheads feel more pain than other people," she said.

Colt stiffened. She shot him a smile. "It's fine. I'm okay."

"They made it look like a suicide because that's the way these kinds of people operate. Jenny was known to be depressed about her situation, and Sobol knew she had a prescription for Xanax. The rest was easy enough to do. Gorky has always had strong ties to certain people in high places. Not that they're aware of his criminal activity, but they don't make it easy to investigate either. It's possible someone leaned on law enforcement to close the case when they had an obvious cause of death."

"She texted me that night. Was it really her?"

Ian shook his head. "I'm sorry, no. They were

trying to draw you out. When you didn't answer, they moved on."

"And Charles? Is he alive?"

"No, he's not. Tommy and Marco—that's the guy you clocked with the pipe—good work, by the way; he has a concussion, and one hell of a headache that he richly deserves. Anyway, Sobol talked Charles into meeting on the night of the fire. Charles had been lying low, but Paul sent him messages saying he was coming around to Charles's view. Charles eventually agreed to a meeting. They met in public, but Tommy and Marco grabbed Charles when he left the meeting and took him to the office. They were supposed to drug him and knock him out, then start the fire so he'd burn to death in the building. But Tommy shot him and they had to move him. They started the fire to erase the blood spatter evidence and disposed of the body elsewhere."

Angie had a hand over her mouth.

"You okay?" Ian asked.

"Yep. Just disgusted at how evil people can be."

"It's a lot to process, I know. I won't tell you how they disposed of him, but we've sent a tip to the police about where to look for remains."

Angie's nostrils flared. "Who tried to break into my condo?"

"Tommy. He was supposed to get your computer and take it to Sobol."

"And if I'd been home?"

Ian's dark eyes flashed. "Tommy Baskin kills indiscriminately. I think it would have been very bad if you'd been there alone."

Angie nodded. Colt was watching her closely for signs that it was too much, but she was taking it all in stride. His kitten wasn't helpless. She was fierce as fuck. God, he loved her.

"I appreciate you telling me everything. I honestly didn't think you would."

Ian smiled. "I know. But I was serious about you working with us, Angie. I know BB&B is moving into another location soon, and you already have a job there. I'd like you to consider working here, though. We need good analysts, and I've seen your SAT scores as well as your grades. I think you'd do great here." Ian shot her one of his trademark grins. "Plus you're already cleared for the fifth floor. Think about it."

She didn't comment on what he'd said about her SAT and grades. She was learning. "I will. What happens now? Can I go home again or what?"

"You need to stick with Colt for a few days, until we wrap up some loose ends, but you should be able to go home then."

"Would that be Steve Gorky?" she asked.

"That's right."

As predicted, Gorky had moved the money from his offshore account to another one he thought they didn't know about. But they had evidence Gorky was funneling money and arms to terror groups in

Afghanistan in an effort to destabilize the region. Sobol had added a little information of his own to their knowledge, which was basically that Gorky also sent arms to neo-Nazi organizations in the states because he liked the idea of white supremacists pushing back against black arrogance, as he put it. The fucker was a straight up white pride kind of asshole who pretended to hide it while posing for photo ops with black councilmen and bucking for deals to build houses for low-income families, many of whom were black.

Ian wanted to make sure they could nail Gorky to the wall this time before sending Angie back home. Tommy, Marco, and Sobol were locked up and unlikely to bother her. Christopher Shaw was still out there but his only crime was laundering money and taking kickbacks. He wasn't involved in skimming from a mob boss or murdering his associates. He'd get rounded up too, of course.

It was nearly 9:30 a.m. by the time they left BDI. After the fifth floor meeting, everyone adjourned to the fourth to eat a big catered breakfast together. Sobol, Tommy, and Marco cooled their heels in the detention facility, and the Feds prepared to raid Steve Gorky's Star Island retreat in Miami.

Jace and Maddy took Colt and Angie back to his place. He hadn't driven and his SUV was still in the driveway. A team from BDI had removed a tracking device from the bottom of the vehicle. The electrician at Jace and Maddy's was on Gorky's payroll. He'd called Marco, who'd swung by with Tommy to attach the tracker yesterday.

Colt hated that he hadn't looked for a device, but Ian had taken him aside and told him that everything —absolutely everything—was working out the way it should. If not for the device, if not for Angie being kidnapped, if not for the frantic search and a million other things, they'd have less on Steve Gorky than they did. They wouldn't have Sobol or Tommy or Marco either.

Perspective. It was all about perspective.

Colt tried to remember that as he and Angie walked into the house. Ian had sent a team to clean it, naturally. They'd swept for bugs, found none, and cleared up anything broken or upended. Angie had her bag with her laptop and phone. Colt had his gun. It was like none of it happened.

Except the part where Angie smiled at him and his world melted into a million bright shards of color.

"Come here," he said, opening his arms. She walked into them and put hers around him. He pressed her head to his chest, stroked her hair. "I love you, Angelica Turner."

"I love you too, Colton Duchaine."

"I want to take you to bed right now—" She gazed up at him. He grinned. "And catch up on our sleep."

She laughed. "Honestly, so do I. But if you wanted to make love first, I'd have agreed to that too."

"I always want to make love to you. But I'll do a better job when I get some sleep first."

They fell asleep tangled together, and everything was right.

Chapter Twenty-Three

PARIS, FRANCE
  1 week later

COLT HELD Angie's hand as they exited passport control at Charles De Gaulle Airport. His heart rate was a little faster than normal, but he knew what he was doing was right. He'd spent the past week with Angie, loving her, being loved by her, knowing without a doubt that she was the one and only woman for him.

Yet he still experienced mild anxiety about the one thing he hadn't told her yet. His family. What had happened.

He knew she wasn't going to care. He knew it, and yet he had to give her the chance to refuse.

She'd been so patient. She was still patient as he

flagged a taxi and gave the driver the address. They drove through the streets of Paris, and Angie marveled at the sights. Colt's gut tightened the closer they got to his apartment.

The car pulled up to the building, a marvelous eighteenth century structure in the heart of the city. It had somehow escaped much of the ruin that befell other buildings of the period. It had passed through various hands before become part of the Duchesne estate.

"This is a hotel," Angie said as Colt paid the driver and they exited the car. "I thought you said you had an apartment."

"It's on the top floor," he said, ushering her toward the doors.

The doorman in his livery straightened and snapped a salute. *"Monsieur le Comte. Bonjour."*

"Bonjour, Michel." Colt asked after the man's family, and Michel replied they were well.

Angie was watching them carefully. "This is Michel," Colt said. "He's worked for my family for twenty-five years. Michel, this is Angelica Turner."

"Mademoiselle," Michel said, bowing.

Colt led her inside. The reception was much the same, with several people coming out of the woodwork to greet him. The foyer was rich with antiques. Paintings, rugs, statuary. There was a front desk, and there were guests. Thank God. Colt was beginning to believe he should have told her another way.

By the time they exited the elevator—operated by a liveried attendant—into the top floor apartment, which was accessible only by a special elevator, Angie looked shell-shocked. She turned to him when the elevator closed. The apartment was filled with more antiques, more paintings and rugs. It was lush, rich, nothing like the rental house in Maryland.

"Um, Colt. What is this?"

He took her by the shoulders, turned her toward a painting that hung in the foyer of the apartment.

"That's you," she said.

"No, it's my grandfather."

She walked over to the painting. Peered at the plate attached to the frame. "Maxence d'Duchesne, the ninth Comte de Duchesne." She turned. "What is a comte?"

Colt spread his hands. "It's a title, Angie."

Her eyebrows rose. "First of all, I got that. Second of all—what kind of title? Translate, please."

"It means *count*. The Count of Duchesne."

"The Count of Duchesne," she repeated.

"It's like an earl. A British earl?" He said it as a question because she looked so dumfounded.

"I know what an earl is. I read plenty of historical romances growing up." She folded her arms. "What you're telling me, Colton Duchesne, is that you're a count. A French count, which is like an earl."

He nodded. "That's right."

She went over to a chair—an original Louis VI

chair—and sank down on it. "Well, I'll be damned. Why didn't you tell me? Why did we have to fly all the way to Paris for this?"

He shrugged, feeling a little embarrassed. A lot uncomfortable. "Because it's impossible to explain. I'm the tenth Comte de Duchesne. My real name is Maxence Colton Francois Duchesne. Colt Duchaine is an alias I use, but not my legal name. My mother insisted on the Colton part, in case you couldn't tell. But I'm a fraud, Angie. I don't own anything except this building. I have no fortune, I'm not involved in the family business, and I have no rights to any of it. When my father died, my uncle took control of the estate. He cut me out of it. All I got was this building because it falls to the man who holds the title. I get a stipend to take care of it—and yes, it's a hotel. It's been a hotel for decades because it's expensive as fuck."

Angie rose. Walked over to him with purpose and gripped his arms. "You thought this would matter to me? You thought I'd love you any less—because why? You're the same man I fell in love with, but now you have a sexy title and a really cool place in Paris—and that was supposed to make me not love you or something?" She shook her head. "Honestly, Colt, I fail to see the problem."

He lowered his forehead to hers. Sighed. His heart was beginning to beat normally again. "I had to show you. You deserved to know."

"I already know everything I need to know about you." She reached up and touched his face. "But I'm so honored you wanted to show me this."

Something inside him broke free. For the first time in his life, he felt like a weight had been lifted. Because she loved him. No matter what, she loved him.

He kissed her almost desperately. Then he stripped her and carried her to the bed—the ridiculous, antique tester bed with all the gilding—and made love to her in it until they were both so emotionally wrung out they fell into a deep sleep for the next several hours.

When he woke, Angie wasn't in bed. He rose. It was dark out, and he found her sitting by the windows —the glorious picture windows—that looked out on the city of Paris and the Eiffel Tower. It was an amazing view. One of the reasons he stayed here when he was in town.

Angie looked up, smiling. She was wearing a robe and she had a glass of wine. *Chateau d'Duchesne* of course. She poured him one when he sat beside her. He took a drink, appreciating the bouquet as the flavors burst on his tongue.

"You probably wonder why I joined the Marine Corp when I had this," he said.

"No, I don't. You're a man of action, Colt. You can't sit in a place like this—a glorious, wondrous place—and not do anything about the world's injustices."

He was almost stunned into silence. She knew him so well. Already. He couldn't sit idly in this gilded palace and do nothing while his uncle ran the company and he lived on a stipend given to him because of an accident of birth. "Parisians have a long history of fighting injustice."

"Yes, but that's not why you do it. You can't do anything else." She smiled. "I'm beginning to think I can't either."

It took him a moment. "You plan to join BDI?"

She held her glass out to clink. He met her. "Yes, I think I do," she said, and then she sipped.

He sipped too. "The Marine Corp wasn't quite right either," he said, because he wanted to tell her everything. "I loved being a Marine, the structure and camaraderie, but when I shipped out to Iraq, I learned how random fate can be. My squad was killed on a patrol when a terrorist detonated a bomb. I escaped. I still don't know how. Or why." He sucked in a breath. "Ian recruited me. Somehow, he knew I'd fit. I went to work for him and I haven't looked back. It's been a wild ride."

"You're amazing, *Monsieur le Comte*. And I love you, whether you're a count or an earl or just a plain old dude."

He put an arm around her, pulled her close. "What do you think about becoming *Madame le Comtesse?*"

She reared back. "Wait—are you asking me to marry you?"

"Yes. You'll be a countess, but in name only. We'll still have to work for a living." He said it lightly, but it meant everything to him.

She pressed her mouth to his, kissing him, and sighed. "Yes, Colt. I'll marry you. I'll be a countess if I have to—but being your wife is all I need."

———

MARCH 1ST

"I CAN'T BELIEVE you're leaving us," Liam said. "It won't be the same."

Angie smiled at him. They'd gone to lunch at a café near Barton, Barnes and Blake's new temporary location and they were waiting for their food to arrive. Angie had gone in to sign some paperwork, but she was officially done. Her clients had all been turned over to other accountants and tomorrow was her first official day at Black Defense International.

"We can still meet for lunch sometimes. And we can text," she told him.

He raised an eyebrow. "Are you sure your fiancé isn't going to beat me up if we keep meeting?"

Angie laughed. "Positive. Colt trusts me to make

my own decisions. He also knows how crazy I am about him."

Their food arrived and the waiter poured more water. Then he was gone.

"Old Mr. Barton is setting up a scholarship fund for Jenny's kids," Liam said. "We're all contributing to it. I know you're leaving but I thought you'd want to know."

"Absolutely. I'd love to contribute."

Jenny's death was still officially a suicide, and her involvement with Paul Sobol and the illegal activity he'd been part of would never be known. Ian said that her kids had enough to deal with, having lost their mother, and there was no need to add to that burden with information that served no purpose other than to show her in a bad light. Angie hadn't been sure how much she'd liked Ian until that moment, but now she knew she'd always adore him for that decision alone.

In the past couple of weeks since returning from Paris, Angie had put her condo on the market and moved in with Colt. The house was stuck in the sixties, but it had good bones and they'd been talking to Maddy about making an offer and doing some renovations. Maddy had promised to talk to the owners and see if she could persuade them Colt and Angie would be perfect for the place.

The only fly in that particular ointment came a couple of days ago when Angie waved at the old lady across the street as she was retrieving her paper. The woman had been wearing a fluffy purple robe and her hair was in curlers. When Angie waved, the woman flipped her off. Angie went back inside, a little stunned, and told Colt. He'd started laughing.

"Welcome to the neighborhood," he'd said. Then he told her everything. When he was done, Angie threw her arms around him and kissed him.

"You're the sweetest man in the world. Okay, now I have to do something nice for her. But anonymously, of course."

Colt laughed. "We'll kill her with kindness. She won't know what hit her."

After a nice lunch with Liam, Angie planned to swing by the grocery store and pick up some things for dinner—for Colt to fix, of course. It was nice being able to drive herself places again without fear of being attacked by shadowy people. That threat was completely over. Steve Gorky had fled the country to escape charges, but it hadn't done him any good. He'd been found shot to death in his car in front of a Moscow hotel. Paul Sobol had died in custody under mysterious circumstances. Christopher Shaw had disappeared entirely. Tommy and Marco were still incarcerated, but she wondered if their days were numbered too.

Her phone rang as she started the car. It was Colt. He'd told everyone his real name at work—Ian already knew, of course—and they'd all pretty much shrugged and said *that's cool* and *whatever, bro* and one memorable *dude!* from Dax Freed.

Angie knew it'd been a source of worry for Colt, but basically nobody seemed to care. It didn't change how they felt about him.

"Hey, handsome," she answered as her heart beat a little harder and excitement began to blossom in her veins.

"Hi, baby. How was lunch with Liam?"

"Great. Triple B is getting back up to speed, and they have plans to build a new, bigger office in Annapolis. Liam and the others were afraid they'd be shuffled to the Virginia location, but the old boys are all about tradition, and Annapolis is where it began."

"That's great. How do you feel about leaving?"

She smiled. She loved that he was concerned. "Still happy about it. I'll miss some of my coworkers, but not the job. I'm excited to start at BDI."

"Speaking of that... think you could swing by here? We're kicking back with some beers in the basement—"

"The basement? What?"

He laughed. "Yeah, Ian decided we needed to build a rec room and bar down here. So we did. We've got pool tables, game consoles, a full bar, a kitchen. It's pretty sweet."

"Wait, is this new? I don't remember any mention of this before."

"Brand new. We're inaugurating it today. Which is

why you need to get over here. Maddy and Tallie are coming too."

"I'll be there."

"Good. Hurry, baby. But be safe."

She laughed. "I will."

It took about fifteen minutes to get to BDI, get parked, and head for the building. Colt was waiting near the stairwell door rather than the elevator. He tugged her inside and kissed her.

"Get a room," someone said over the speaker in the hall, and they both laughed.

"You're going to love this," he told her before pushing open the door to the new lounge.

"Surprise!" the guys yelled.

Angie blinked. She looked at Colt, who was grinning. Maddy and Tallie were there too, grinning like crazy.

"Surprise for what?" Angie asked. "It's not my birthday."

Colt kissed her. "Welcome to the BDI family. Officially."

She flushed with pleasure as the guys all came over and shook her hand. "Welcome to the family, Slugger," Jace said with a wink.

"Slugger?" Angie looked up at Colt. He just shrugged.

Ian Black was there too, holding a long wooden box. He turned it around and held it up. "For you, Slugger."

It was the lead pipe, polished up and no longer rusty, mounted in a shadow box. There was a plaque. Angie read it and burst out laughing.

"Angie with a lead pipe in the warehouse. Oh my god, you guys are too much."

Colt took it for her and sat it on a table. Somebody handed her a beer. The rest of the afternoon passed in a happy blur of laughter and friendship and excitement for her new job. When Colt finally gave her a look—*that look*—she knew it was time to go and share the rest of the evening together, just the two of them.

"Are you happy?" Colt asked her much later when they lay tangled together beneath the covers, naked and spent.

She lifted her face to his. "Yes. Are you?"

"More than you can ever know. I've loved you for a long time, *minette,* even when I didn't realize it. I didn't think you could ever love me."

"All that running I did. I'm not running now, Colt. I'm never running from you again. I'll stand and fight. Always."

He grinned at her. "That's my slugger."

She pushed him onto his back, straddling him. Soon, she was riding him, giving them both all the pleasure—all the love—they could handle.

She'd found her purpose. Her man. The life she wanted to live.

Always.

LONDON, England

IAN STRODE along the rain-washed Victoria Embankment near the Palace of Westminster. He'd had a meeting earlier and now he was heading back to the hotel, but he'd wanted to walk along the river because it was pretty and it reminded him of early in his career when he'd been posted to London and everything was still so new to him.

It wasn't new anymore, and he wasn't as innocent as he'd been then. As if he'd ever been innocent.

"Flowers for your lady, guv?" A woman stood nearby with a bucket of flowers at her feet. They weren't especially great flowers, and she looked like she'd seen better days. Her clothes were tattered, her face grimy. Her hair was gray, but she had plump jowls. At least she ate regularly, he thought.

Ian took some coins from his pocket and handed them to her. He didn't count, but he knew there were a few pounds there. She grinned a black-toothed grin and handed over a small spray.

"Thank you, guv. Blessings on ye."

Ian kept walking. The embankment wasn't too crowded this gray afternoon, but he still had to dodge tourists as they stopped and gawked at the sights.

When he'd gone about a quarter mile from the

flower seller, he went over to leave the flowers on the stone wall along the path. As he tossed them down, something caught his eye. On the underside of the plastic-wrapped bouquet was a white piece of paper curled around one of the stems.

"Fuck," he said as he whipped around to see the flower seller. She wasn't there. He jerked the paper free and unrolled it.

Bang. If this had been a hit, you'd be dead.

Watch yourself, Mr. Black.

N

Ian dropped the flowers, stuffed the note into his pocket, and ran back to where she'd been. The bucket was still there with its sad bouquets, but Natasha was gone.

Ian burst out laughing.

She was still alive. And she was still on his side.

Book 5: HOT SHOT - Jack & Gina

Book 6: HOT REBEL - Nick & Victoria

Book 7: HOT ICE - Garrett & Grace

Book 8: HOT & BOTHERED - Ryan & Emily

Book 9: HOT PROTECTOR - Chase & Sophie

Book 10: HOT ADDICTION - Dex & Annabelle

Book 11: HOT VALOR - Mendez & Kat

Book 12: HOT ANGEL - Cade & Brooke

Book 13: HOT SECRETS - Sky & Bliss

Book 14: HOT JUSTICE - Wolf & Haylee

Book 15: HOT STORM - Mal ~ Coming Soon!

————

The HOT SEAL Team Books

Book 1: HOT SEAL - Dane & Ivy

Book 2: HOT SEAL Lover - Remy & Christina

Book 3: HOT SEAL Rescue - Cody & Miranda

Book 4: HOT SEAL BRIDE - Cash & Ella

Book 5: HOT SEAL REDEMPTION - Alex & Bailey

Book 6: HOT SEAL TARGET - Blade & Quinn

Book 7: HOT SEAL HERO - Ryan & Chloe

Book 8: HOT SEAL DEVOTION - Zach & Kayla

The HOT Novella in Liliana Hart's MacKenzie Family Series

HOT WITNESS - Jake & Eva

———

7 Brides for 7 Brothers

MAX (Book 5) - Max & Ellie

7 Brides for 7 Soldiers

WYATT (Book 4) - Max & Ellie

7 Brides for 7 Blackthornes

ROSS (Book 3) - Ross & Holly

—

Who's HOT?

Alpha Squad

Matt "Richie Rich" Girard (Book 0 & 1)

Sam "Knight Rider" McKnight (Book 2)

Kev "Big Mac" MacDonald (Book 3)

Billy "the Kid" Blake (Book 4)

Jack "Hawk" Hunter (Book 5)

Nick "Brandy" Brandon (Book 6)

Garrett "Iceman" Spencer (Book 7)

Ryan "Flash" Gordon (Book 8)

Chase "Fiddler" Daniels (Book 9)

Dex "Double Dee" Davidson (Book 10)

Commander

John "Viper" Mendez (Book 11)

Deputy Commander

Alex "Ghost" Bishop

Echo Squad

Cade "Saint" Rodgers (Book 12)

Sky "Hacker" Kelley (Book 13)

Dean "Wolf" Garner (Book 14)

Malcom "Mal" McCoy (Book 15)

Jake "Harley" Ryan (HOT WITNESS)

Jax "Gem" Stone

Noah "Easy" Cross

Ryder "Muffin" Hanson

SEAL Team

Dane "Viking" Erikson (Book 1)

Remy "Cage" Marchand (Book 2)

Cody "Cowboy" McCormick (Book 3)

Cash "Money" McQuaid (Book 4)

Alexei "Camel" Kamarov (Book 5)

Adam "Blade" Garrison (Book 6)

Ryan "Dirty Harry" Callahan (Book 7)

Zach "Neo" Anderson (Book 8)

Corey "Shade" Vance

Black's Bandits

Jace Kaiser (Book 1)

Brett Wheeler (Book 2)

Colton Duchaine (Book 3)

Tyler Scott

Ian Black

Jared Fraser

Thomas "Rascal" Bradley

Dax Freed
Jamie Hayes
Mandy Parker (Airborne Ops)
Melanie (Reception)
? Unnamed Team Members

Freelance Contractors
Lucinda "Lucky" San Ramos, now MacDonald (Book 3)
Victoria "Vee" Royal, now Brandon (Book 6)
Emily Royal, now Gordon (Book 8)
Miranda Lockwood, now McCormick (SEAL Team Book 3)
Bliss Bennett, (Book 13)

About the Author

Lynn Raye Harris is the *New York Times* and *USA Today* bestselling author of the HOSTILE OPERATIONS TEAM ® SERIES of military romances as well as twenty books for Harlequin Presents. A former finalist for the Romance Writers of America's Golden Heart Award and the National Readers Choice Award, Lynn lives in Alabama with her handsome former-military husband, two crazy cats, and one spoiled American Saddlebred horse. Lynn's books have been called "exceptional and emotional," "intense," and "sizzling." Lynn's books have sold over 4.5 million copies worldwide.

To connect with Lynn online:
www.LynnRayeHarris.com
Lynn@LynnRayeHarris.com